DEATH OF A FALLEN

VOLUME 2 IN THE RILEY SERIES

KELLY HOLLINGSHEAD

BQB

North Carolina

Death of a Fallen: Volume 2 in The Riley Series
© 2022 Kelly Hollingshead. All rights reserved.

This is a work of fiction. All of the characters, names, incidents, organizations, and dialogue in this novel are either the products of the author's imagination or are used fictitiously.

Published in the United States by BQB Publishing Company
www.bqbpublishing.com

Printed in the United States of America

ISBN 978-1-952782-38-1 (p)
ISBN 978-1-952782-39-8 (e)

Library of Congress Control Number: 2021950091

Book design by Robin Krauss, www.bookformatters.com
Cover design by Rebecca Lown, www.rebeccalowndesign.com

First editor: Caleb Guard
Second editor: Andrea Vande Vorde

This book is dedicated to the memory of my dear friend, Geoffrey Burleson, and to the memories of the twenty-two military men and women who commit suicide each day. Geoff, thank you for standing by my side and helping me through some of the best and worst times of our teenage-adult life. I love and miss you, and to this day I still struggle with the thought that I could have done more for you.

What we have once enjoyed we can never lose;
all that we deeply love becomes a part of us.

— *Helen Keller*

CHAPTER 1

R iley had purposely sat the alarm clock on the other side of the room so that he would have to physically get out of bed to shut the damn thing off. Today, however, more than most mornings, he regretted this decision as he went through the ritual of untangling himself from underneath the sheets, then shuffling the eight feet that he had, in fact, counted to the other side of the room.

Still exhausted, Riley felt a bit of satisfaction as a new silence enveloped the room, now that the alarm clock lay broken at his feet. That was until he heard Jonathan call out from the kitchen.

"I'll make sure to put 'new alarm clock' on the grocery list. Now let's try not to have a repeat performance of yesterday."

A mental image of a glass of water pouring onto his face brought him fully awake. "No need for the water. I can assure you that I will remain vertical!"

Pulling on jeans, a t-shirt that sported his landscaping logo, and boots, Riley went to the bathroom adjacent his room to finish getting ready for what he hoped would be an easy day. Now with teeth brushed and deodorant applied, but hair still a mess, Riley walked into the kitchen to find Jonathan sitting at the table reading a newspaper, a plate of food resting next to him.

After all this time that they had been together, Riley still couldn't get over the size of Jonathan. His height was close to that of a professional basketball center, except that he had the physique of someone who pumped iron all day.

Jonathan only read two sections of the newspaper, the missing person ads and obituaries. Riley sat at the table and asked in a musing tone, "Anything exciting happening in the news today?"

Jonathan folded the newspaper in half, dropping it on the table. "Eat quick. The work day is calling." With that he slowly stood, placed his dishes in the sink, and went outside, leaving Riley alone.

After eating, Riley grabbed his ball cap off the counter and walked out into the welcoming hot and humid Texas morning. Finding Jonathan already in the passenger seat of the truck, Riley climbed into the driver's side and headed towards their first job.

Things had changed so drastically over the past year. Riley and Jonathan now permanently lived at the lake home. Seven months earlier, Riley had said goodbye to the house in Taupe City that he had built for Allison when they first married. It had sold well under market value. His real estate agent and friend, Alex, had cautioned Riley that he wouldn't break even. But it was time to let go of the past—hard as it was—little by little.

If the last year had taught Riley anything, it was to always prepare for the worst. He lived as if something was just waiting to pop up at any moment. Fortunately, he and Jonathan had yet to encounter anything more from the Devil and his tricks. Life had pretty much gone back to normal, if living with a fallen angel could be called normal. However, the strain of living with the unknown had worn not only on Riley, but on Jonathan as well.

The town was still the same with some minor changes. For one, Paul's store, where Riley had almost been killed in an ambush, had been torn down and turned into Jackson Brothers Super Store. These big-box stores put tremendous strain on the small mom-and-pop shops in the area. Riley felt guilty for shopping there, but he knew it was just another way life moved on. Paul had been murdered by what authorities called a crime of passion. However, Riley knew the true story and was forever sorry that he brought such trouble to this small, secluded lake town.

Three demons had taken over the bodies of unbelievers and ended not only Paul's life, but also that of local boxer, Luis, whose very house was where the demons had sat, waited, and watched Riley and Jonathan for days to learn their routines. Jonathan blamed himself for both of their deaths as well as Riley's late wife, Allison. He had been her guardian but had failed her in the most profound way, costing her very life. With the deaths of both Paul and Luis, Jonathan chided himself for letting his guard down with the monotony of the day-to-day routine he and Riley had settled into. It was another topic they didn't talk about. As for Allison, her tragic death was the beginning of an unbelievable series of events that nearly killed both Jonathan and Riley and changed their lives forever.

Jonathan thought back to that day—the day Allison died. It was Riley and Allison's wedding day. They had their whole lives ahead of them, with bright shared futures. But in a flash, a demonic force had caused the horrific car accident that injured Allison so badly that she passed a short time later. Limited to work behind the scenes as a guardian angel, Jonathan could do nothing to save her. Riley had escaped without serious injury. After that, Jonathan was given the choice to return to Heaven forever or to fall from grace and become a Fallen, which meant he could reside on Earth where he could be a friend, a companion, and an earthly guardian to Riley for the rest of his days, but would lose many of his powers. Still, he had chosen to remain with Riley. Now Jonathan was Riley's guardian angel too.

A kind nurse at the hospital, who went by the name Granny, had cared for Allison. She, too, was a Fallen and had warned

Jonathan of the trials that would come his way. She had been a comfort to Riley, who didn't know her true identity, after the accident and had showed him patience, kindness, and strength when the time had come to finally let Allison go.

The real problem was that these trials were far from over, as Jonathan had told Riley, more than once. Riley continued to press until, one day, Jonathan broke down and answered. "Lucifer will never stop sending his demons after us until we are both dead. That I know for certain." After hearing what he already had come to suspect, Riley dropped the topic. Instead, he busied himself with trying to create a new life for himself, a new normal. He always had to worry, wondering when something might show up to take his life. He was thankful for work. However, things had changed. Now instead of having three crews that worked for his small landscaping company back in Taupe City, it was just Riley and Jonathan, which actually had its perks—Riley teased him about being able to boss a fallen angel around. After selling the house and moving out to the lake house, Riley took over Luis's small landscaping business. It consisted of little more than a dozen residents around the lake. But it was something that he could draw a sense of purpose from.

It was a hot and humid summer, something that Texas was well known for. It had become such a scorcher that it felt as if the sun had been turned on high. "I never could get used to this heat!" Riley exclaimed. "We should just sell the lake house and move to the Arctic."

Out of the corner of his eye, Riley noticed that Jonathan gave a shake of his head as if to say, *here we go again.* However, Riley wasn't finished as he continued.

"It's eight in the morning, for crying out loud, and it's already a hundred degrees!" Riley complained as he pulled up to the first property. He took his phone off the charger and checked his email to make sure no one else, as of yet, had asked to be serviced that day. "Thank you, God." he blurted.

"I take it that it's a short day?" Jonathan inquired.

"Yes, it is. You know what that means?"

Jonathan knew very well what Riley was about to say. "Yup, looks like we will be doing our training earlier than I thought."

Riley leaned forward and let his head drop on the steering wheel. "I don't want to go to the hole today." He had begun calling their gym in the metal Quonset building a "black hole" since it sucked the life out of him. By the time they were finished with their workout, Riley often would only have the energy to shower and go straight to bed. Sometimes without dinner.

"Do you realize that today is the Fourth of July? Your American Independence Day?" Jonathan asked. "We should finish this property, go buy some steaks, grill out, and watch the fireworks—maybe even get in the lake and cool off." Jonathan stepped out of the truck and closed the door.

Watching Jonathan through the passenger-side window, Riley was sorry about how he limped now. Although he was as strong as ever, it was still hard to see his friend struggle. It always made Riley feel guilty, although there was nothing he could have done to prevent the injury. Jonathan had battled two demons that had nearly beaten him to death. The wounds had taken a very long time to heal, and his right leg would never be the same. With all that they did during the day, it seemed to exhaust Jonathan. Before the injury, it wouldn't even have registered on Jonathan's radar. Now though, at the end of the day, he would lean back in a recliner and wince once his weight was off the leg.

The single time Riley commented on it, Jonathan got a little short with him. "It's fine, Riley," he said, irritably. "There's nothing anyone can do. I doubt modern medicine or your country doctor can do anything about a demon-inflicted wound. Just leave it alone, Riley. I'll be fine." As soon as the words had escaped his mouth, Riley saw the remorse on his face. "I'm sorry, Riley. I shouldn't have said that. I know you're concerned. Please don't worry. I think I'm just going to turn in early." He lifted himself out of the chair with a little more effort than usual. Then he went to his room and quietly closed the door.

Josh Hardin was the local doctor in the area, an older gentleman who still made house calls. They had called the doc out to Riley's lake house after the episode when the demons had shot Riley and nearly killed him. The country doctor got a quick education on the matter. Jonathan had to persuade Josh not to report the incident. Riley and Jonathan later learned these three demons were the ones who killed Paul and Luis. Eventually, Jonathan had to reveal to Josh what he really was. Surprisingly, Josh took the news quite well.

Because Jonathan had included him, Josh had become another innocent bystander whose life was affected by the trials that Riley was being put through. It had happened the day Jonathan had almost died. Josh had tried to intervene to stop the Devil from touching Jonathan, with the end result being that one of Josh's hands was so severely burned that the basic functions of that hand were now extremely limited. Even holding silverware was too much. He needed to teach himself to eat with the other hand. Because of this handicap, the only kind of doctoring he could do was little more than prescribing medication for the common cold, flu, or other viruses. His surgical days were now long behind him.

"Don't give it another thought," he had told Riley when Josh told him of his decision to step down from performing surgeries. "It was time for me to give up that kind of practice anyway. My hands were already starting to shake, so it truly was a blessing in disguise."

Still, it pained Riley to see Josh have to walk away from a practice he was passionate about.

As for Jonathan, his injuries still impacted him and his frustrations grew. Once, when loading up after a long day of landscaping, he went to pick up a pallet of leftover sod, something that truly did require super-human strength. Months before, it would have been no problem. However, his bad leg gave out and the pallet toppled onto him. In a cry—more out of frustration than pain—Jonathan threw the pallet to the side, scattering sod everywhere.

Riley walked to the back of the trailer where Jonathan was unloading the remaining supplies. He quickly reached for the weed eater so that Jonathan could ride the mower. Jonathan's temper flared up again. "I'm fine, Riley. Quit trying to coddle me!"

Knowing that Jonathan could hear his thoughts, Riley just let the moment pass. Jonathan grabbed the weed eater and primed it, then gave the cord a pull only for it to sputter. He tried it several more times before losing his temper. Lifting the weed eater above his head, he threw it to the ground, smashing it into pieces as he muttered to himself. Riley wiped his brow and looked up at him. "Jonathan, calm down. It's not that big of a deal."

Jonathan at once turned on his heels and gave Riley a hard shove to the chest, which launched him ten feet backward, landing him in the bushes next to the property's driveway. He stared up at Jonathan in shock. Jonathan immediately ran over to him.

"Riley, I'm so sorry. I didn't mean to do that. I'm so sorry," he said, offering him a hand up.

Riley paused a moment, then accepted Jonathan's hand. After being helped to his feet and a little angry, Riley almost told Jonathan: "I now know why you refer to yourself as a fallen angel. Guardian angels must have a better understanding of the rules they should follow when it comes to protecting their human." Except to have voiced this would have been hateful and untruthful. Immediately, Riley pushed the thought away, hoping that Jonathan hadn't already heard it. Jonathan was going through changes that he didn't appear to have any control over. Much like teenagers who act out after tasting their first bite of freedom. Riley only wished he could pinpoint the problem so that he could try and help Jonathan.

"Tell you what. Let's push this property off until tomorrow. No sense in working on a national holiday. I think we both could use a break. We've been working nonstop and are due for some downtime."

Not arguing, Jonathan apologized once more, retrieved the broken pieces of the weed eater, and tossed them into a box in the back of the truck. After everything was loaded up, Jonathan limped to the passenger side of the truck and got in. Riley hopped behind the wheel and started the engine. He attached his phone to the output and put on the song "If You Say Go." He was introduced to the song at a youth camp he had attended every summer when he was in high school. It remained one of his favorites. He thought it might help Jonathan's spirits. Instead, Jonathan asked Riley if they could ride in silence. Reluctantly, Riley turned the music off as they made the trip around the lake back to the house in deafening silence.

Arriving home, Riley parked the trailer in the expanded steel building that served as the "hole." The building had been Riley's idea. Together they had created a personal gym that rivaled what any Olympic team might use. Riley had made it large enough to store his truck and trailer and landscaping equipment. He had invested all his savings into it.

Riley now followed Jonathan to the house. Once inside,

Jonathan walked down the hallway that led to his room, then softly closed the door behind him without saying a word. Although it wasn't even noon, Riley grabbed a beer from the refrigerator and went to the back patio that overlooked the lake. Collapsing into one of patio chairs, he kicked off his shoes and toasted in the hot sun. Looking out across the lake, he watched as several boats raced across the blue water. *I guess this could be called some kind of paradise*, he thought. He drank a few swallows of his ice-cold beer. It wasn't long before he felt his head becoming heavy. He pulled his cap down low and settled into his chair. His head began to nod until, eventually, sleep overtook him.

He awakened a couple of hours later, his skin itching. He knew this was the first sign of a nasty sunburn. He stood up and stretched, lifting his arms as far as he could above his head and letting out a loud yawn. Then he trudged back inside, feeling the heat rising from his skin.

There was no sign of Jonathan. Riley decided to make a sandwich and watch some TV. After a while, he glanced at the clock. It was already late afternoon. He shut off the TV. A knock came at the door, breaking the dullness. *Perfect timing*, Riley thought. He walked over to the front door and opened it to see Josh. "Happy Fourth of July!"

"And the same to you," Josh said. His smile was from ear to ear. He was in his seventies with balding hair and a stomach that had seen one too many barbecue picnics. "Always a pleasure to see you," he said. He closed the door behind him and followed Riley into the kitchen. "Where is Jonathan?"

Riley had previously talked to Josh of the moodiness that Jonathan was starting to exhibit and how the lashing out had seemed to have gotten worse.

"Well, he's having a hard day, so we knocked off early and have just been relaxing." Riley said.

"Looks like you have gotten a little sun," Josh said, pointing to Riley's arm.

"I fell asleep on the back patio. And, of course, I was a little envious of everyone else's celebrations."

"Well, make sure you put some aloe vera on so you don't blister. It will help ease the pain and take some of the heat away."

"Always the doctor," he said. He opened the refrigerator, grabbed a couple of beers, and handed one to Josh. "Still up for grilling?"

"Sounds perfect," Josh said, setting his beer on the table. "But first, I think I'd like to check in on Jonathan. Why don't you go ahead and fire up the grill, and I'll be back in a jiff." With that, Josh turned and made his way to Jonathan's bedroom.

Riley bit his lip knowing that regardless of what he said, Josh would handle the situation as best as he saw fit. He pulled out the steaks from the refrigerator that had been marinating since that morning. Picking up his phone, Riley opened the grill app and set the temperature gauge on the outside grill, still amazed by what technology was capable of.

About an hour later, Riley had grilled the veggie packs and the steaks. Everything was just about ready. Neither Josh nor Jonathan had emerged yet. Should he go in and check on them or yell out that dinner was ready? He decided to wait a bit longer. He went to the refrigerator and grabbed himself another beer. As he closed the door, he turned to see Jonathan enter the kitchen with Josh behind him. Both men were smiling, which gave Riley hope that things were okay.

"Smells good," Jonathan said.

"Everything's ready. Go ahead and dig in," Riley replied.

They all sat down and filled their plates. They made easy

conversation and joked as they enjoyed their meal. The frustration and tension from earlier in the day seemed far behind them now. Afterward, they cleaned up and made their way to the two-story dock. They each grabbed a chair and settled in just as the fireworks show got underway. They continued to chat, drink their beers, and enjoy the evening, especially the cool breeze that started to make its way across the lake. As the night was winding down, Josh stood up, stretched, and announced he was heading home. He hugged each of them, whispering something to Jonathan before leaving.

Not wanting to pry, but curious just the same, Riley wondered how Josh had gotten Jonathan out of his slump. What could he have done differently? After a while, he couldn't stand it anymore.

"Okay, what can Josh say or do that I can't?" he said, trying to keep frustration out of his voice.

Jonathan chuckled. "Well, for one, he is a doctor."

"Yeah, well, the man is retired . . ." Riley trailed off, realizing that sounded a little foolish. "I mean, he's not a psychiatrist. He gives vaccines and treats broken bones." He felt himself getting flustered.

"Okay, okay. I'll tell you what he told me," Jonathan replied. "He's been doing medicine for over forty years and feels like he's seen just about everything. And no, he's not a therapist, but he does have a way of pulling things out of you and getting you to open up whether you want to or not."

"Well, that's just great!" Riley said with an edge to his voice. "I can't get you to talk to me even though we live, work, and spend every damn waking moment together!"

Jonathan sighed. "You're right. I should be able to talk to you about anything. It's just that—I don't know." He paused as if trying to find the right way to explain the logic behind his thinking.

As badly as Riley wanted Jonathan to talk to him, he thought maybe he should just drop it for now.

Jonathan sat quietly for a moment. "This injury to my leg," he started, "it's doing something to me. It's changing me. I can't really explain it, Riley." He paused again, and Riley watched as Jonathan massaged at his right leg as if it bothered him. "It, it takes hold of me and alters my mood and takes hold of my thoughts. I can't control the feelings it brings up. The moment it happened, I could feel the solidness of the blade against my bone, and then it somehow dissolved into me, and—it became a part of me." He stopped and shook his head. "And now I'm realizing that I'm no longer in control of my own powers." He stared directly into Riley's eyes. The once brilliant blue color of Jonathan's eyes now seemed faded to gray.

For the first time, Riley realized that he had not been honest with himself. Something was wrong with his friend. Jonathan was sick. How could he not have seen it?

"I try to keep my distance after I have an anger episode because honestly," Jonathan said, "I feel one day I could hurt you or—worse."

Riley was taken aback at this and had to look away. Despite all the questions that now overtook his thoughts, he couldn't believe their journey could be coming to an end. Staring off across the lake, he asked Jonathan one question.

"Do you really think that could happen?"

Jonathan looked up at the stars and gave the only answer he could. "I honestly don't know."

CHAPTER 2

Riley and Jonathan sat on the dock for what seemed like hours. Riley was wrapped inside his own thoughts about how to fix the problem. This was usually Jonathan's forte, but Jonathan was no longer himself. Riley was deep in thought when Jonathan stood to stretch his muscles. Riley saw, for a moment, the pained expression on Jonathan's face as he merely tried to stand. He hated to see him like this, but he had to quickly force the thought away, knowing Jonathan would sense it.

"I think I'll walk around the property for a bit," Jonathan said. "Need to stretch my leg out."

Riley was about to ask Jonathan if he would like some company, but then stopped himself since he already knew the answer. Truthfully, he couldn't blame Jonathan for not wanting his company when it was out of pity. Riley would be judging every step and resisting the urge to ask Jonathan over and over if he was okay and hoping he wouldn't say something to upset him.

"Would you like to come with me?" Jonathan's question caught him off guard.

Even though Jonathan's intention was good, Riley knew the response that his friend wanted to hear. "I think I'll sit here for a little bit and enjoy the stars a while longer."

"I don't mind if you want to come with me."

Riley looked at his friend for a long moment and wondered if this was the first time Jonathan had ever lied to him. Seeming to pick up on Riley's thoughts, Jonathan quietly turned and proceeded down the stairs. In that moment, Riley realized that Jonathan had just lied to him. Sure, it was a small one, but from the moment they had met, Jonathan had always told Riley that he could never lie and would always tell him the truth. However, instead of becoming upset, Riley felt pity for his friend and fear that Jonathan was, in fact, losing a part of himself.

Several minutes had passed since Jonathan offered the invitation to join him. Riley wanted to give him enough time so they wouldn't have to be in each other's awkward company. Riley went inside the house and collapsed onto his bed. He was asleep within a few minutes. Little by little, the nightmares that Riley had hoped were gone forever began to creep back in. They seemed to emerge from the corners of the darkness where they had once been laid to rest. One in particular, the worst, was the day Riley's life was forever changed.

Everything was the same as it had been that night—the rain, the words he and Allison had shared. Except now the dream opened up even further. Riley sat in the driver's seat looking out at the carnage that just occurred. Allison lay slumped and motionless in her seat. Blood was everywhere. A figure walked up to the passenger side of the car, leaned down, and spoke in a voice that sounded almost a whisper.

"*Memores sumus vestri in mortuis.*" Then the demon gave a horrendous scream and vanished. Riley shook his head and rubbed his eyes. When he looked again, the figure was Jonathan.

Riley bolted upright on the bed and looked around. He couldn't focus on anything in particular as he scanned the empty room. The morning sun creeped through the blinds, revealing dancing dust particles on its thin, outstretched beams. Riley wiped the back of his arm on his forehead. He got up and stumbled to the adjacent bathroom. He splashed cold water on his face to clear the cobwebs and dried his hands on a towel. He walked into the living room where he found Jonathan in his usual recliner.

In place of a "Good morning," Riley moved closer to Jonathan and said quietly, "*Memores sumus vestri in mortuis.*" In a blur of movement, Riley found himself now looking up at Jonathan, who had sprung to his feet and now towered over him. The grayness Riley had started to see in his eyes was now a dull blue. They sharpened into a piercing blue before turning into a purple so dark and unnatural that Riley tried to look away. However, Jonathan placed his hands on either side of Riley's face, forcing him to stare back into Jonathan's eyes. Riley tried to struggle away from him, but it was as if he had a refrigerator lying on top of him.

"Get the hell off me!" Riley cried out.

Jonathan then leaned closer and whispered, "Just focus on my eyes." His grip was so tight that Riley knew he could do nothing unless Jonathan allowed it. Giving in, Riley did as he was told. Staring back into Jonathan's eyes, Riley could see that the purple of the iris was slowly spinning. He felt the living room disappear around him. He could feel himself beginning to panic as the awful scene of the crash now appeared all around them. He clamped his eyes shut. After a few moments, bewildered and scared, he asked Jonathan to please stop. He opened his eyes only to see Jonathan standing nose to nose with him. Everything started to spin. He couldn't believe what was happening. Everything turned to black. Rain was falling all around them, the droplets splattering off Jonathan's shoulders.

All around them, people began yelling as hurried footsteps rushed to their aid. Riley heard someone cry out, "Oh my god! Call an ambulance!" Once again, he was reliving the most horrific day of his life. What was happening? He had tried so hard to push it to the farthest recesses of his mind and here it was, happening all over again.

Just as quickly as the dream appeared, it was gone, replaced by complete darkness and quiet. Was he awake or dreaming? Riley couldn't distinguish what was real and what was a dream. What was happening to him? Then he felt something shift to the right of him. A large hand gently touched his forehead. With some relief, Riley knew it could only be one person. He opened his eyes. He was lying on his bed. Jonathan sat beside him. He tried to speak, only to find that his mouth was as dry as a ball of cotton. He coughed from the strain of trying to use his vocal cords. As he sat up, a bottle of water was placed in his hand and Jonathan helped him raise it to his lips.

Jonathan spoke quietly. "Small sips, Riley. Take small sips."

Ignoring him, Riley downed several swallows as fast as he could, only to be rewarded with a coughing fit, which splattered water everywhere. Jonathan patted him on the back until the coughing ceased. Riley managed to get a couple of words out in a rough voice. "What happened?"

Staring at Riley, Jonathan wore a look of weariness and concern. He asked a question of his own. "What is the last thing you remember?"

Riley wanted to yell at Jonathan, but he relinquished and with some trepidation closed his eyes. Immediately, the quietness found him and just as he started to visualize his last thought, he shook off the remaining grogginess. He opened his eyes, staring hard at Jonathan. He said in an accusing tone, "Did you wipe my memory? Did you wipe my memory like you did the night *my* Allison was stolen from me? The night you failed to protect her!"

"No, Riley, I didn't," Jonathan replied softly. He felt the sting of Riley's accusation and his claim to Allison.

Riley found he was unable to look at Jonathan the way he once did. Jonathan tried to put a hand on his shoulder, but he shrugged it off. Feeling uncertainty and fear from the one person who was supposed to always protect him.

"I would never—" Jonathan began to say.

"I can't believe you anymore," Riley said angrily. "You aren't yourself, and I know you are lying to me. How do you expect me to be honest with you? I feel like I don't know you anymore. And then last night you tell me you're afraid you'll one day go over the edge. What does that even mean?"

Jonathan sat quietly for a moment. "Please, just tell me what you remember."

"Fine," Riley said irritably. "Last night after we called it a night, I had the dream that used to haunt me every night—the one that kept me in fear of falling asleep. This time I saw the demon that caused the accident. I still couldn't make out its face, but it spoke to me in a weird language."

"It was Latin," Jonathan replied. "Do you remember anything else? Think really hard."

No longer afraid to close his eyes, Riley concentrated. "There was a lot of shouting. The rain was coming down harder than I remember. I could see Allison and there were people running up to the car."

"Are you sure you couldn't make out the demon's face?" Jonathan questioned.

Opening his eyes and looking at Jonathan, Riley saw that his friend's eyes were once again their piercing blue. "No, I can't make it out. I can hear its voice, but that's it." Riley got up and did his best to steady himself. He wondered how long he'd been out for.

Jonathan read his mind. "Two days."

"What? How could that be!"

"I had to put you into a deep sleep for your own safety," Jonathan said calmly.

"Why?"

Jonathan's expression turned sad. "Because when you walked into the living room the other morning, you were speaking in Latin. You pulled a gun out and almost took your own life."

This time Riley's unstable legs did give out, but Jonathan quickly steadied him. "I did what?" But he didn't allow Jonathan to answer. "No. Why, why would I do that? I don't remember grabbing the gun out from underneath the bathroom counter."

"It gave me a shock as well. I'm just glad I still have the ability to move quickly when I need to. I managed to stop you just as the hammer started to fall."

Riley was shaken by the thought that somehow he could step that far out of bounds and attempt to kill himself. "My God, what the hell is happening to me? And I was speaking Latin? What did I say?"

This time Jonathan put both hands on Riley's shoulders, making him look at him. "It means: *Remember, you are a mortal.*"

Riley felt the goose flesh come up on his arms and shook his head. "So, what do we do now?"

"We need to leave and go back to Taupe City right away. I need to talk with Granny. I believe she will be able to help us."

Still in shock, Riley went through the motions of opening dresser drawers to retrieve things to pack.

"I've already packed a bag for you," Jonathan said. "I also emailed our clients to let them know that we had to leave due to a family situation."

At this moment, Riley couldn't care less about clients and lawns. He walked out of the bedroom and went into the living room where the nightmare had overtaken him. Quickly passing the spot, he went out the door and headed for his truck. Jonathan was close on his heels, carrying Riley's bag. He locked the door behind them and then followed Riley out to the truck. He watched as Riley climbed into the passenger side of the truck instead of the driver's seat. Sliding in with as much ease as his large frame could muster, Jonathan got behind the steering wheel. He flipped the visor down and the keys dropped into his hand. He started the truck, shifted into drive, and eased the truck down the long driveway.

Riley then reached over and grasped his arm. Jonathan turned to look at him. Meeting Riley's eyes, he could feel the plea running through his mind. *Please help me, I don't want to die.* Jonathan sent positive vibes of peace back to Riley and then spoke softly. "I won't let you. Trust me."

With that, Riley broke eye contact then went back to looking out the window. Jonathan maneuvered the truck onto the two-lane road, then headed for Taupe City. The sky, that just hours earlier had been blue and cloudless, was now covered in dark-gray, scattered clouds that stretched out before them. Every now and then the moon would peek through, offering some bit of light and hope, only to be covered again by darkness.

CHAPTER 3

Mary Allison Gregory, otherwise known as Maggie, sat in her home office on the thirteenth floor of the corporate office building she owned. It was where she had run her technology company, Gregory Portal Provider, for several years. She had long admired the beautiful building and dreamed of one day living in a penthouse at the very top. Years ago, she had persuaded the building's owners to sell the building to her and paid them a handsome premium to do so. Then she converted the entire thirteenth floor to a luxury condominium. She knew some people were superstitious about a thirteenth floor, but she secretly liked that it added to the mystique of her so-called celebrity status.

Maggie was like the Bill Gates of Internet streaming services. Her company, Gregory Portal Provider, had revolutionized the industry and was known for its superior customer service. In addition to being a hands-on leader, she had her finger on the pulse of the industry and what consumers wanted. She bought up most of the competition, but kept her holdings just this side of a monopoly. According to business and stock analysts, her stock had become so valuable that investors were eager to buy, buy, buy. What's more, she was a cultural icon. She was an attractive and successful young woman. The media loved her. Her photos had been splashed all over the tabloids, newspapers, and magazines.

Then, about a year ago, she was walking alone one night when she was accosted by two men and dragged into an alley to be raped, when a stranger stepped out of the darkness and rescued her. She was never able to get him out of her head. He had told her his name was Jonathan, but nothing else.

Now, nearly all of her time was occupied by trying to locate him. There was something about the memory of her rescuer that calmed her. At first she had been terrified of him. He looked like a giant to her and had nearly killed her two attackers. She didn't know whether she could trust him. But then he walked her to the hospital to get checked out. When she walked into the entrance, she turned around to thank him, but Jonathan had vanished. After being so terrified and in fear for her life, he'd rescued her and had seemed to cast an indescribable feeling of peace over her. She'd never felt anything like it. But it disappeared with him. She absolutely had to find him again.

Now, with all the contacts and connections that she had at her disposal, Maggie was hopeful she could track him down. At first, she attempted a search on her own for a few weeks. Calling in a favor from a friend at the DMV, she gained access to its database and worked day and night scanning thousands of files, but found nothing. She also used her connections to review the recordings of security cameras around the hospital. She had found the clip showing them walking up to the hospital, but afterward he disappeared from view and she wasn't able to pick him up again from any of the other area cameras. She played it several times a day and watched frame by frame, focusing on every detail about this strange man.

Maggie had eventually become so obsessed with uncovering Jonathan's identity that it consumed all of her time and energy and was interfering with her work. She decided she would step down as head of the company she and her father had built and turned everything over to her dearest friend, Stuart Branch. That had been six months ago. Now she was closing in on a year in her search for the mysterious Jonathan. The company continued to make a large profit despite her absence. Quite frankly, though, she didn't care. She was infatuated with the idea of finding this one man. Now she was a recluse working tirelessly in her search.

There was a time that she had consulted with high-level politicians and lobbied Congress and the FCC. She closed huge deals and bought out her competitors, basically monopolizing the streaming television market as far as she could, legally. According to one trade media article, Maggie was one of America's top female entrepreneurs. Around town, she was considered the number one bachelorette. Dozens of offers had come in, most of them ridiculous and laughable, from celebrities, senators, even a royal family member trying to court her. Yet all were met with a hard, resounding "not interested." She simply told her executive assistant not to return their calls or texts.

At twenty-nine years of age, the world was at her fingertips. She had taken the once small company that her father struggled with and turned it into a global empire. However, now she had secluded herself from the world. After the attention around her leaving the company subsided, she quietly began attending a small church—her only outlet for connection. Unfortunately, it wasn't long before the media found out about it and started hounding other attendees for any gossip they could share about Maggie. She pulled back and stopped attending, not wanting to force the spotlight on others. Now, she truly became a hermit, never leaving her penthouse suite.

Occasionally, she would see online tabloids that claimed Mary Allison Gregory, living in her mysterious thirteenth floor home, was part of a cult. She had not only laughed at this, but actually subscribed to several of the tabloids. It always gave her a laugh to read the outrageous headlines some poor misguided or misinformed lunatic had written.

Maggie sat at her desk for hours on end, simply staring at the four monitors staring back at her, mocking her as if they held the secret to Jonathan's identity and where he was but weren't going to tell her. When she tired of her search, she worked out to the point of exhaustion in her personal gym. Then she could sleep. She kept odd hours, never knowing exactly what time of day it was. She ate when she was hungry. Days could pass before she realized she hadn't eaten anything. Her search had overtaken her life so completely that eventually nothing else existed in her world. It was as if she was going crazy one day at a time and it was all because of one man—a total stranger named Jonathan.

Her phone rang, bringing her back to reality. It could only be one of two people these days: her assistant, or Stuart. No one else would dare disturb her. Looking at the caller ID and seeing that it was her assistant, she punched a button hard on the phone and barked, "Yes, what is it, Victoria?"

"Sorry to disturb you," the elderly woman's voice replied. "But you haven't put in your shopping order for the last couple of weeks."

Maggie was stunned. Had it really been that long? She used to absolutely love food, but now nothing really appealed to her. Come to think of it, she couldn't recall what she had last eaten. She looked around and noticed how tidy everything was. A cleaning service came every day, but always moved about very quietly, knowing they shouldn't engage with Maggie. She made it a point never to engage with anyone. Frustrated by the interruption, she spoke quickly to Victoria.

"I don't need to be bothered by this. Just place a simple order, understood?"

She heard Victoria sigh. "Very good, Ms. Gregory."

Maggie punched the "disconnect" button with a little too much force. After a long moment, she thought perhaps she should call back to apologize. Victoria had always been very loyal. But as her dad always said, never show weakness. Still, Victoria was an older lady and Maggie was aware of some of the details of her personal life. Her husband had Alzheimer's, and Victoria had needed to go back to work to help pay for his medical bills. She started working at the company two years ago. *No*, she shook her head. Victoria understood who she was and accepted her.

There was one idea that she had been kicking around for several weeks now, but it would mean venturing back into the world she had willingly closed herself off from. A world that terrified her but, she reasoned, what else was there at this point? All other avenues had been exhausted. There was just one thing left to do—speak with the men who had stolen so much from her and scared her so severely that it had forever changed her. As far as she knew, they could have been the last to see Jonathan, besides herself.

Maggie knew where the men were. They were locked up and serving time at the penitentiary, but actually tracking them down and then getting them to speak to her would not be easy. She knew of someone who could make all this happen, but she also knew it would cost her. He was as corrupt as they came, knew how to skirt the law, and had a lot of political ties. His name was Miles Jackson and he was the Commissioner of the Department of Corrections.

Blowing out a frustrated breath, Maggie pulled up her phone directory on the computer. Finding Jackson's number, she hesitated for a moment before dialing. Just as her luck would have it, he answered with a gruff voice after the first ring.

"Never thought I'd see the day when the great and powerful Mary Allison Gregory would show up on my caller ID. What in the world would make you want to talk with me?"

In the background, Maggie could hear people talking over one another. She immediately knew something must be brewing. She secretly hoped he was trying to conceal a cover-up or that he finally had been caught and was talking with lawyers to help keep his ass out of the very system he oversaw. Maggie smiled at the pleasant thought.

"Did I catch you at a bad time?" she said with an edge of sarcasm. She smiled again, anticipating his next words, but was disappointed to hear his husky laugh and reply.

"For you, Ms. Gregory, not at all!" He hit the *Ms.* part a little too hard, which maddened her. He had once propositioned her even though he was married and twenty years her senior. This made her question why she had even called. The search for one man had driven her to asking for favors from the lowest of slime.

"Well, I was hoping for a little privacy. I could call back when you are at home with your wife," she said, replying with a little sassiness of her own. That seemed to get all of his attention as she heard him cover the receiver, then mumble something. After a few moments, she heard a door close and then the old Miles Jackson came back on the line.

"Okay, what the hell do you want?" he said, clearly annoyed. "Calling me from that damned ivory tower of yours?"

"Aw, there's the Jackson that I know. Pity that this side of you only comes out when the cameras aren't on." She hit the mute button and laughed. She knew how to push his buttons.

"Kiss my ass! I'm hanging up now."

She didn't want to be on the phone with him any longer than she had to. She unmuted. "I need to find two inmates and I need to meet with them after visiting hours."

With that, now it was Jackson who laughed. Maggie could picture the man with his signature cigar in hand, just loving every minute of the call. This was going to cost her. He coughed hard several times. She wondered if he had emphysema, or perhaps lung cancer. The man smoked cigars all day long, so it wasn't hard to imagine him sucking on an oxygen machine in the near future. Pushing those thoughts out of her mind, Maggie let him have his fun. When he finished, his voice was rougher than before.

"You need a favor, huh?"

Knowing that he'd ask for a favor of his own, Maggie asked, "What is it going to cost?" Hoping to hurry the conversation along.

"Now, Ms. Gregory, do you think I would ask for something in return? I'm a hardworking and respected man here in our grand ole state."

"Just tell me a price so we can stop with the pleasantries."

"You really don't like me now, do you?"

Jackson was known for overseeing a prison system that mistreated inmates for his own sick pleasure, as if the crime they had been asked to pay to society wasn't enough. He had privileges removed, inmates beaten, and several transfers denied. Jackson always said he didn't want to send troubled prisoners to another penitentiary to simply become someone else's problem. Many inmates committed suicide, or tried to kill others, which in turn only lengthened their sentence. They would never see the light of day beyond the concrete walls and barbed wire fences.

"I don't like you and I don't respect you, and having to ask you for anything makes my stomach churn." Once more, she heard laughter from the man she loathed. *What am I doing?* she asked herself. *Why am I subjecting myself to this?*

"Now, let me see. You said two inmates, is that correct?"

Maggie knew where this was heading and it consisted of several zeros.

"How badly do you want to see these two? Because you know I am personally gonna have to jump through several hoops to make it happen, and there are expenses that go with it."

"How much!" Maggie blurted into the headset.

"Oh, I don't know. Let's say half a million an inmate. That should cover all the expenses."

The expenses bit was total garbage. Jackson could make the call, have it set up without a question asked, and in no time, she could be sitting in front of these two men. No one else would receive so much as a dime for jumping through these so-called hoops.

"Tell me where to wire the money. I want to meet the men tonight, after midnight."

"Now, Ms. Gregory, you think I can swing all that? Asking for tonight and it being secret and all? I mean, I have to make several calls—"

"Miles, make it happen tonight or I cut the payment in half. Or maybe I should place a call to someone I know in the media to plant a bug in his ear about all the illegal activity you're up to over there."

Jackson was smart enough to know she could cause trouble for him anytime she wanted. "Tell me the names of the men you want to see," he said, fury rising in his voice.

Maggie smiled, realizing how riled up she had gotten him with a threat of her own. "Well, do you have a pen handy?"

"Tell me their damn—"

"Joe Packton and Mike Mahoney. And like I said, it needs to happen tonight, Miles."

Jackson adjusted his tone. "Tonight will be just fine. Just as soon as I see the funds transferred. Then you can do whatever you want with them."

Her cell phone buzzed, alerting her to an incoming text. She looked and saw it was a bank account number. Jackson could work fast when he had the right motivation.

"I take it you got the text?" he seethed.

"Yes," Maggie replied. "It will be taken care of as soon as we are off the phone. Text me back when it's good on your end." With that, she quickly pressed the "end" button on her headset, disconnecting the call. A small part of her would rather have had the satisfaction of slamming the receiver down in the man's ear.

Maggie pulled up her bank account on the computer and then carried out her end of the arrangement. Once completed, she realized she was still in yoga pants and a sweater, not exactly the outfit of a business tycoon. People would take notice that for the first time the great and powerful Mary Allison Gregory had come out of hiding, looking as if she was going to the gym. The tabloid photos and rumors would be rampant. They'd likely chalk it up to a nervous breakdown or perhaps accuse her of an ongoing drug habit and that those closest to her should insist she seek professional help. She laughed at the thought as she walked into the bathroom. She turned the shower on and let her clothes fall to the floor. She could just see old Victoria and a couple of her board members sitting around planning an intervention. She hadn't laughed this much since Stuart's birthday party last year.

Stepping into the shower, Maggie thought maybe this could be her coming out party after being shut off from the world for so long. And why the hell had she become so scared of the outside world? Fear was never part of her life before that night when she was accosted in the alley. Now here she was, about to confront her fear and the two men that caused it instead of being afraid or worried about the what-ifs.

Wrapping a robe around her, Maggie sat down in front of the fogged mirror of her vanity. A steaming hot shower had been just what she needed. She noticed how small and fragile her fingers looked as she reached for her makeup. She examined one of her fingers, starting at the nail and then the first and second joint. Her fingers seemed to blur in and out of focus for a moment. She blinked several times, then concentrated harder. She positioned her right hand just a few inches from her face. The more she tried to focus, the more the fingers blurred.

An image took shape in the mirror, breaking her concentration. She already thought she was losing it, but now she was seeing shapes in mirrors. But for some odd reason, Maggie wasn't scared, or for that matter, worried. Instead she felt as if the image didn't come to harm her but to offer guidance. As she stared at the mirror, the image slowly took the shape of a man, a strikingly beautiful man. Then the image spoke and terror tore through Maggie, causing her to cry out. The voice didn't match the man's beauty—it sounded like death and pain.

"Take this as a warning, Ms. Gregory. Continue your search for the Fallen, and I will snap your tiny bones one at a time." As Maggie raised her right hand to her mouth, the man in the mirror reached out and grabbed hold of it. The once strikingly beautiful face turned sinister as the man's mouth stretched wider than it should, and the rest of his face was now outlined by shadow. "This will help you remember." Before Maggie could scream again, she blacked out with a cracking noise echoing in her head.

CHAPTER 4

Awakening on the bathroom floor, Maggie realized that she must have fallen out of the shower and bumped her head. She dismissed the craziness of the weird dream. *What is wrong with me?* she thought as she pushed herself up off the tile. As soon as the pressure of her body weight found her right hand, she emitted a long painful scream. Her pinky finger, at the second joint, was turned all the way to the side. Upon looking at the deformed finger, Maggie felt the room tilt as she passed out.

She wasn't sure for how long she was out when a beeping alert coming from her cell phone caused her to stir. Groggy, she reached out with her damaged right hand, wincing from the movement that sent pain shooting from her fingers up to her arm. She slowly rolled over, fumbling for the phone with her left hand. Unlocking the screen with her less dominant hand was tedious and awkward. She could feel the throbbing begin to intensify with each small movement.

She saw that there was a text from Miles Jackson. The message was simple enough:

"Both inmates are at Southwater Penitentiary. They will be ready for you at midnight. The warden will not ask questions. She knows that this is a personal favor for a very dear friend of mine."

Maggie's first instinct was to throw the phone at the wall, despite how much pain she was in. She couldn't believe that she had actually set this in motion. She cursed loudly, not just at Miles, but at her own stupidity. She ridiculed her shortsightedness. Then she wondered how many times this warden, or other officials for that matter, had turned a blind eye for this slimy worm. She cursed again and then dismissed the thought to focus on the task of finding her way upright. The process took four attempts, followed by more cursing.

Slumping into the vanity chair, Maggie was more afraid to look in the mirror than at her damaged hand. What if she saw the man in the mirror staring back at her, ready to cause her more harm? She looked down again at the broken finger. She started to feel sick about the next step she would make herself take. The last time she had looked at the clock on her phone it had been just after nine p.m. She wondered if she would miss her window of opportunity for talking with her two assailants. She'd had to stoop to a fool's level to make it happen.

Maggie grabbed a hand towel off the vanity and placed it between her teeth. She bit down as hard as she could. She blew several quick breaths out through her nose and held her right hand in her left. *Fast and quick,* Maggie told herself. *The pain will only last for a moment if I do it fast and quick.* However, after the popping sound, Maggie immediately knew she couldn't have been more wrong. What followed was coughing and dry heaving, from an empty stomach. Feeling the sweat drip from her forehead, she searched through the drawers of her vanity until she found some adhesive tape.

After wrapping the pinky and ring finger together for stability, Maggie let her forehead rest on top of the cold vanity. Trying to remain conscious, yet feeling the fatigue from the adrenaline dump, she wondered at how the night could go any more wrong. What just happened? Where did that thing come from? There was no way it was a man, or even human for that matter. Trying to reason it out, she remembered what the man in the mirror had told her: *You have been warned, Ms. Gregory. Keep searching for the Fallen and I will snap your tiny bones one at a time!*

What was a Fallen? Was something supernatural happening to her? Was this somehow connected to Jonathan? She had never really bought into stuff like that. But what had just happened made her start to doubt herself, or at least her sanity. This only deepened her drive to find him. For now, though, she would have to sort out her thoughts another time. She was probably just overly tired and her mind was playing tricks on her. She just had to focus on the task at hand. With that thought, she went to her closet and put on a dark, buttoned blouse and jeans. The buttoning was tedious, but trying to put on a pullover top would be the death of her. Maggie hoped that the darker colors would not draw attention.

Pulling a light jacket on as methodically as she could, she grabbed her bag and slipped out the door of her penthouse, only to stop and realize she had to call for transportation. She hadn't a clue where they even parked her vehicles. Besides, she didn't carry any of the keys with her. She always used the valet, and they did the rest for her. Realizing there was no other option, Maggie again cursed herself as she pulled her cell phone out and dialed the number for the garage. A moment later, a professional but polite voice was on the other end.

"Good evening, Ms. Gregory. My name is Spencer, how can I be of service?"

She responded with the air of authority she used to broker deals. "I am coming down shortly, have my car ready for me."

"Yes, Ms. Gregory. I don't have a driver right now but—"

"I'll be driving myself, thank you," she quickly interjected. "Please keep this off the books and I'll compensate you for whatever trouble this may cause."

She ended the call, gathered herself, and straightened her shoulders. Then she pressed the button for her private elevator. The door dinged at once. She stepped in with a slight sense of trepidation and then punched the button for the garage level. For the first time in a year, she was about to leave her sanctuary, and it frightened her.

When the door dinged again, she was in the parking garage. When she looked out, she saw a man, whom she assumed was Spencer, holding the door open to a white Cadillac Escalade. She didn't realize she owned one. Was it shameful not to remember all the vehicles you owned? She shook off the thought. "So much for being inconspicuous," she muttered to herself. Knowing there was no time to ask for something smaller, she simply said, "Thank you, Spencer."

As she got behind the wheel, Spencer closed the door and proceeded to walk away. Maggie rolled down the window and called after him. "I do mean it when I say I don't want this documented. Understood?" Spencer turned to face her and simply nodded. Then he turned again to walk away. "Do you like the job you do?" Maggie called after him, then realized how it sounded like a threat. "I mean, I'm just asking if you are treated well or if there is anything I should be aware of."

Spencer turned and looked directly into her eyes. "Yes, Ms. Gregory. I enjoy what I do. The pay is far better than other places. This job is helping me get through college. As far as you leaving this evening, it's no one's business but your own. I can assure you I will not tell anyone or log your departure. Just as you asked."

Feeling reassured, Maggie gave Spencer the nod this time, then watched as he turned and walked away. After pulling out of the parking garage, Maggie turned onto Brynn Street, which would take her directly to the highway. She spoke the destination to the GPS, and moments later, it pulled up the address to the

Southwater Penitentiary. Seeing that it was only thirty-four miles away and realizing that she had a bit of time to spare—and was hungry—she pulled into the fast-food place her parents used to take her to. More from nostalgia than anything else, she toyed with the idea of actually walking in and ordering. However, her so-called celebrity status kept her in the SUV. She had seen a newsfeed featuring a photo of her with the caption, "What is the billionaire princess hiding from?" The picture they used was godawful. She had been leaving a charity event when someone had yelled an obscenity at her and she looked their way.

Kent's diner didn't have a drive thru, but there was pullup service, so she parked at the very last spot. Even though the parking lot was nearly empty, she tried to be inconspicuous despite driving a $100,000 SUV. Not bothering to glance at the menu, Maggie pressed the button for the driver's window. If it was nostalgia she wanted, then nostalgia she got. As she placed the same order she always did when she was younger, a young female voice read her order back, then asked, "Would you like to add on a dessert? I recommend our chocolate cake shake."

Why the heck not, Maggie thought. "Sure," she replied.

Waiting for her order, Maggie closed her eyes and let herself drift into the thoughts of her childhood. She imagined her father sitting across the booth from her, browsing through the table-top jukebox's list of songs and telling her you had to find the perfect song when you eat. "It sets the mood and provides for better digestion," he said. She grinned up at him then looked over at her mother, who playfully rolled her eyes. Her dad caught the look then replied, "I'm serious, and I'll give you proof, Mags." That was his nickname for her. "The first time I took your mother to dinner this song was playing, and the rest is history. She was putty in my hands," he said, and then gave her a wink. The small jukebox started playing the song "At Last" by Etta James. Her mother chuckled. "I don't think this is the reason I became, as you said, putty in your hands."

"Of course, it was," he said. With that her dad stood and then leaned down and asked, "May I have this dance, Ms. Putty?"

"Oh, Charles," her mother replied, unable to hide her smile. "The food will be here any minute!"

"True, but I only need a moment of your time."

Her mother then allowed herself to be pulled up into his embrace. As they swayed back and forth with the music, Maggie couldn't stop smiling up at them.

"Excuse me, Miss?" A female voice interrupted Maggie's thoughts. "Hi, here's your order."

Looking out at the young female standing next to her vehicle, Maggie quickly snapped to attention and grabbed some bills from her bag and then thrust them over, trying to avoid eye contact. She took the bag of food and pressed the button to roll the window back up.

"Oh, Miss, this is far too much," the young woman said. "I can't make change for this amount." Maggie looked out to see her waving two fifties back at her.

"That's okay," she said. "Put it toward whatever teens buy these days." Maggie gave her a little wave and then put the SUV into reverse, wanting to make a quick exit.

"Could I get a picture with you really quick? I'd like to share it on my social media."

Damn, she thought. She had been recognized. Not wanting to be rude, but wanting to get out of this predicament as quickly as possible, Maggie looked at the employee name tag that read *Suzie*. "Would you like to do me a huge favor, Suzie?"

"Umm sure, but could we like get the picture first?"

"That's just it, I would really appreciate it if we don't do the picture. Could I give you an autograph instead?"

Disappointment immediately clouded the teenager's face. "What would I do with an autograph? It's just a picture. Please?"

Knowing there was no way out of the request, Maggie consented, trying to sound upbeat. "Well then, a picture it is, Suzie."

The young woman quickly pulled out her phone.

"Make sure you get my good side," Maggie said jokingly.

Suzie snapped a photo and then turned around and asked, "Could we get a couple more? I didn't like my smile."

This time Maggie found her voice. "I'm sorry sweetie, but I'm in a hurry."

Before the protest could come, Maggie put the Escalade in reverse and exited the parking lot. Looking in the rearview mirror, she could see Suzie holding her phone up, either snapping more photos or recording a video of her SUV.

"Teenagers," Maggie scoffed. "Why are they so obsessed with social media?" She pulled into an empty parking lot a few blocks away from Miss Suzie and her camera. She then dug into the food, ignoring the protests of her bandaged hand. After she finished off the food, she took her first sip of the chocolate cake shake. She felt like she now needed to thank Suzie for the recommendation.

Back on the highway, Maggie proceeded to the penitentiary where, hopefully, she would find some of the missing pieces of her search for the mysterious Jonathan.

CHAPTER 5

As Lucifer sat in the room bearing his torture chamber, he looked on with pleasure at a figure that appeared as a beast one moment and then a man the next. It was almost as if the two were fighting for control of one another. He was eerily delighted at the chaos taking place. He could honestly say he was the father—or perhaps "creator" was a better word—of this being. Not that so-called "god" who was supposed to love all despite judging and expecting daily repentance.

The thing was known as Legionaries, and Lucifer—the Devil himself—had possessed his soul for quite some time. Lucifer had allowed him to keep his human form. However, when Lucifer wished it, Legionaries took on the form of a beast, with the head of an eagle and the tongue of a serpent. His body was that of a lion's, except for a small strip of scales that ran from the base of the eagle's skull down to where the lion's tail began. Occasionally, the scales would ripple as bursts of electricity flowed over them like an eel.

Legionaries sat inside a cell, staring out at Lucifer, whom he had once called "Master." The cell Legionaries now occupied had been created for special circumstances. All Lucifer had to do was mentally transport a chosen victim from the pits of Hell and they'd instantly find themselves inside this cell within the torture chamber. All they could do was scream and beg for mercy.

Whoever was unfortunate enough to be trapped inside the cell experienced almost everything Hell had to offer.

When Legionaries appeared in his human form, his eyes darted around the room with panic. However, when he was morphed into a beast, he just sat there staring back at Lucifer with pure defiance. He knew that if he ever escaped the cell, he would take his revenge by attacking and then feeding on Lucifer.

Lucifer looked around the chamber at the dozen hounds around him. They never wavered in their constant watch of Legionaries. "Change, change, change!" Lucifer screamed at Legionaries. He then stood and walked with authority over to the cell in the middle of the room. Legionaries stood up and took on his human form, then approached the bars of his cell. Lucifer's hounds surrounded the cell and howled, begging Lucifer to open the cell so they could feed upon the flesh of Legionaries. Anything outside the cell could go in, but whatever was inside could not come out, unless Lucifer commanded it. With only two feet separating him from Legionaries, he leaned forward.

"Now, are you ready to speak civilly to me?"

"Yes, Master!" Legionaries cried out. Yet just as he spoke the beast suddenly appeared and let out a ferocious roar. Like a flash of lightning, the beast lurched toward the bars of the cell and swiped a massive paw at Lucifer, violating the sanction over leaving the cell's barrier. However, one of the hounds had moved even faster and jumped between the two, sinking its massive jaws into the beast's paw. Not bothered by the bite, Legionaries jerked the hound's body into the cell. Then the razor-sharp eagle's beak sunk into the hound's midsection, ripping its insides out and spilling them onto the floor.

Enraged, Lucifer screamed at the beast, "You dare defy me? What you're suffering now is nothing. I will fan the flames until you have no breath left to beg for mercy!"

The beast morphed once again into Legionaries's human form and began to beg. "Please, Master, I have no control of what's happening with …" but then morphed back into the beast once again, cackling as it did. "Lucifer, you barely have control of me now! What do you think will happen if *my* rage is turned up!" it hissed.

Lucifer was amused. *Damn, what a creation.* "Who, or I should say what, do you believe yourself to be?"

"You should know what I am, you overzealous ass," said Legionaries. "It was your nemesis, God, who created me thousands of years ago, when he performed an exorcism, then sent me into a herd of pigs that ran off a hill plunging to their death, taking me with them. Do you remember? How after God had cast me out that you kept me close by, constantly torturing me to make sure that this alter ego of mine, that I had forgotten all about, stayed suppressed. Only that one day you made a crucial mistake, by banishing me into the depths of Hell, where this beast that now stands before you finally came alive. Any of this dredging up a memory in that dim-witted—"

"Enough!" Lucifer commanded. He looked into the cell as if for the first time and saw the beast actually pawing at the ground.

"I knew you would remember me," the beast hissed. "It just took a little prodding on my part." The beast paused for a moment then, looking up, it glared back at Lucifer. "You look like the ass you truly are with that dumb expression. I know that look because I wore it myself for thousands of years. Remember? What was it you called me?" it hissed. "Oh yes—lackey—I was your lackey," the beast said in disgust.

Lucifer stared at the beast, then began to laugh, causing the beast to laugh as well. "My goodness, Legion, it is so great to see you again. Has it really been that long? You're just as ugly now as you were then!" More laughter. "I really had forgotten all about you. Besides, Legionaries was so much easier to manage than you were when you were merely known as Legion. That was until I grew tired of him, or should say both of you, since you are, in fact, one. But we had some fond memories. Don't you agree? Or has the proverbial cat got your serpent tongue?"

That damned eagle's head looked like it could be grinning, but it was always hard to tell with such creatures.

"Oh, come on," Lucifer said condescendingly. "It feels like yesterday when I sent you on that errand to claim that territory for me. But then that pathetic chosen one put a wrinkle in my plans, thinking he was getting rid of you with that exorcism." Lucifer's smile broadened as he thought about the pigs that Legionaries's soul had been forced into right before they took the death plunge. "Do you honestly think that if I were to let you out, that you would ever be able to pose a threat to me?"

The beast turned its back on Lucifer and sat down on its haunches. The eagle's head rotated around and replied. "Oh, you simple-minded, idiotic fool. It was God who cast me out! You are nothing more than a peasant believing one day you will ever be able to go up against Him," it hissed.

Despite how long it had been since he'd had to deal with this beast that called itself Legion, Lucifer was already growing tired of the insults. "Hounds!" he screamed. At once, the gathered hounds moved closer to the cell holding the beast and leapt at it, scratching at the bars. The scales on the beast's back rippled along a wave of electricity and flew out at the hounds, at once annihilating them with flames and turning them to ash that fell to the floor in small piles. Legionaries then assumed his human form once more. He laughed so loudly that the room actually shook, causing Lucifer to stumble back and fall.

"There is no more you can do to me," Legionaries said. "You

don't own me, and I know what I am capable of. You do not want to annoy me any further. So, are you ready to talk?"

Getting back to his feet, Lucifer mockingly dusted himself off. He then conjured up a chair and sat so close to the cell that his knees actually touched it. "You forget one thing, Legionaries—just one small little detail."

Legionaries grinned back at his nemesis. "Please enlighten me, O Dark One."

Lucifer leaned forward. "Come just a little closer and I will tell you."

"I am in no mood for games," Legionaries hissed. "Tell me, or perhaps I will reach through this cell and allow you a taste of Hell."

"Patience, my lackey, patience," Lucifer cooed.

With the hounds no longer there to provide Lucifer a shield, Legionaries thrust his arm through the bars of the cell, once more breaking the rule of its design, and grabbed hold of his neck. "Don't ever call me—"

Before he could finish, Legionaries screamed as he pulled back his arm. His hand was smoking and burnt the moment after making contact with Lucifer. Confused at how this could even happen, he looked up to find Lucifer's eyes had changed to black as night.

"Do not forget," Lucifer hissed, "Hell is my domain, and I alone control it. I am your god, you are the lackey. I can make you feel pain that will make you beg like a dog. While you may have the ability to overpower the simple-minded, there is one thing you will never do." He paused, then took a swipe at the bars of the cell, causing them to disintegrate. He then stood, took a step forward, and grabbed both sides of Legionaries's face, forcing him to stare up at him. "Your lousy existence will forever belong to me. I will never bow to you, never for a moment. I am your god. Do not forget." He squeezed Legionaries's face. "Do you hear me now, lackey?"

Legionaries burst into flames, screaming and begging once more before morphing back into the beast as he cried out, "Mercy!"

Legionaries watched as rage continued to build inside of Lucifer. The blackness of his eyes released a dark liquid that ran down his face—something that only happened when his rage was out of control and his own insanity poured out of him. As the hatred boiled out of him, the flames that ate at Legionaries turned white. The screaming ceased immediately as his body jerked and then curled into a ball on the floor. After a while, all that was left of Legionaries was his abandoned dark and tortured soul.

At last, Lucifer's rage subsided, now that he had put Legionaries back in his place. After spending two thousand years together, he had a sudden urge to check in on his former lackey. Instead of finding him beaten down and begging for mercy, he had found the defiant Legion who still was determined to replace him as the ruler of Hell.

Lucifer thought back to the day he had personally dragged Legionaries into the pits of Hell because he had struck his master. Moments prior, they had been in Lucifer's living room, everything perfectly normal, then Legionaries had done the unthinkable. For retaliation, Lucifer would have just let his hounds carry out the punishment, except that Legionaries had caused him to bleed in front of three other demons and there had to be retribution. To ensure that the three demons who had witnessed the whole ordeal couldn't spread rumors, Lucifer quickly disposed of them by hanging them in picture frames inside his home like trophies, silencing them to an eternity of having to relive their most terrible acts of their past lives.

Now the question was what to do with this new Legionaries? He couldn't simply throw him back into the pits of Hell with the rest of the simple minded. No, that could lead to far too many problems now that his former lackey had manifested into quite the formidable adversary. Which was odd to think about as he watched the black soul of Legionaries begin the slow, rejuvenating process of repairing itself back into a body.

"I'm not done with you yet, lackey. When I return, we will discuss how I can make further use of you." Walking towards the door to leave, Lucifer snapped his fingers, conjuring up six new hounds. "Watch that thing, and feed upon it after it has rejuvenated."

The hounds circled the dark soul, waiting with anticipation for a mortal body to appear.

CHAPTER 6

E xiting the torture room, Lucifer found his perfect and loyal servant, Esperanza, waiting for him. She was a little on the chubby side with short brown hair and dark complexion. Upon seeing him, she bowed her head and dropped to both knees.

"Permission to speak to you, Master?" she asked meekly.

"Rise, my child," replied Lucifer. "You are the song in the morning that causes me to smile."

Esperanza stood, keeping her head bowed. She would never meet his gaze, not out of fear, but out of pure obedience. He had given her a place in his home, which was such a rare commodity that not even the highest-ranking leaders of the regions were allowed. It was just the two of them residing in the Devil's massive house. She would do anything he asked if it meant she could stay.

"It is you, Master, who puts joy in my heart with just the thought of your presence. I am honored to worship you with every fiber of my being."

Lucifer found himself amused with her constant praise. She was just as perfect as one could be. Not as perfect as himself, of course, but still perfect in her own way.

"What can I do for you, child?"

With head still bowed, Esperanza spoke in a nervous, uneven tone. "Savior, I would very much like to announce your presence to the leaders of the regions at the trial today. That is, unless you think that I am overstepping."

Lucifer placed his hand under her chin and lifted it so she looked him in the eye. "Yes, if that is what you wish, then I will allow you to do it." He released her chin and she immediately cast her eyes downward.

"I would very much like to."

"Well then, let's not keep them waiting," he said. Taking her hand in his, Lucifer proceeded to a large auditorium that took up a whole wing of his house. The inside of the auditorium had gray rock walls, marble floor with gray streaks running throughout, with a black and shiny podium at the front shaped like an upside-down cross.

All the leaders of the regions, totaling 666—minus the two that were to be judged—were in place. This was one of the rare times they were allowed access to Lucifer's home. They would serve as the court, to pass judgment on Abel and Bryce, Lucifer's two sons who were now outcasts, not just for their failure to bring down a Fallen, but also because of their carelessness, and more importantly, the cavalier attitude they took in speaking about their father.

Arriving and standing in the back behind the stage, Lucifer could hear the leaders talking in the auditorium. He looked down at Esperanza. "You are absolutely the most stunning thing I have ever laid my eyes on. Please introduce me however you see fit."

"Yes, Master." Esperanza quickly bowed and then walked up the stairs and onto the stage. The room fell quiet. They all were aware that she had been personally chosen by Lucifer, and they would treat her with respect—or die a thousand deaths.

As she made her way to the stage, Esperanza stopped and glared at Abel and Bryce for a long moment before proceeding to the podium. Everyone grew silent as she spoke.

"We are here to oversee the judgment that this court is granted by our Savior. It is my honor and privilege to bring before you today my master. He found me when I was lost and spoke life into my soul. He has given me a second chance even though I didn't deserve it. He is truth and righteousness. To be near him makes me thankful for being cast into his world. I could speak of his mercy and what he brought into my life for eternity, yet it would only give you a glimpse of how special he is to me." She paused and looked out on the gathered crowd. "Everyone will now close your eyes and bow your heads."

Silence followed. Several minutes passed.

With the softest voice, Esperanza broke the silence of the room. "Do you hear that?" All heads remained bowed and not a soul answered, or moved. Esperanza then spoke a little louder and asked again. "Tell me, can you hear that? Not just hear, but do you feel it?"

Still, there was not a movement in the room as everyone knew they were about to be in the presence of greatness.

Speaking into the silence at full volume, Esperanza cried out: "That is not just love that you feel, that is not just silence you hear, that is the power of the one that I have pledged my life to, as you all have done."

The crowd erupted as each leader took to their feet. They all chanted in unison, "Savior, Savior, Savior!"

As Lucifer stood backstage, he was overtaken with supreme pride for his child and the cries of the crowd beckoning him. He walked on stage wearing his signature white suit. He smiled at the gathered crowd of regional leaders, waving one arm in the air. He turned to Esperanza, who had now prostrated herself before him. He smiled down at her and touched the top of her head.

"Well done, my child, well done. Now rise."

Esperanza obeyed, keeping her head bowed. Lucifer

whispered into her ear, "I am, and always will be, your Savior."
He took her hand and walked over to his throne, where he would
oversee the trial of his two wretched failed sons, Abel and Bryce.
Esperanza went to take her leave, but Lucifer called after her.
"Wait, you shall stand at my right." He motioned beside him.
Esperanza obeyed and took her spot standing to the right and
slightly behind Lucifer's throne.

The regional leaders were still on their feet applauding, with
several crying out, "Savior!" hoping that they, too, could receive
some form of acknowledgement. Lucifer leaned back in his chair,
smiling. Looking out at his chosen leaders of the regions, Lucifer
wondered which would try to overthrow him next.

"I relish in the next uprising, you simple-minded fools," he
muttered to himself. He raised a hand, motioning for them to
take their seats. Looking at Abel and Bryce kneeling several feet
away, he shook his head in disgust. "These proceedings will now
begin!"

On cue, the court stenographer, a small pudgy man, hurried
up to the podium. Barely able to see over the top, he stood on
his toes and reached up for the microphone, positioning it so he
could be heard more clearly. "Bryce and Abel, you are here to be
judged by a room of your peers. If found guilty, your sentencing
will be carried out immediately. I would ask how you plea, but we
already know. We will now watch the video of your last job and
see what transpired."

Bryce and Abel both had been fitted with mouth restraints
that were only used during court proceedings. The restraint had
microscopic teeth attached to it that roared to life after the head
harness was strapped into position and the restraint placed inside
the accused's mouth. Although quite small in size, it did the
job in keeping the unwilling participant absolutely silent. The
auditorium lights dimmed as a huge projector rose up from the

floor. Everyone watched the footage of Bryce and Abel in a car on their way to capture the Fallen. They were talking back and forth, Bryce being the more confrontational and boisterous, and carrying most of the conversation. All ears in the auditorium listened intently to every word said. Lucifer sat completely and utterly still, feeling the hate growing in him as he watched the video. He knew the first offense was coming soon. A moment later, Bryce started hurling insults about him. Just the sound of his voice made Lucifer want to scratch his eyes out.

"How many times do you think Father has taken pride in disciplining a buffoon like Legionaries? What satisfaction can be had with beating someone day in and out and declaring yourself a fearless leader when the fool can't even defend himself! If you ask me, that must be the smallest victory in a pitiful existence."

A small hand found Lucifer's shoulder as Esperanza began to cry softly. Lucifer reached back and patted her hand for a moment and then quickly slapped it off. He did not need her comfort. Furthermore, she should know that if she ever touched him again without permission, there would be a price to pay.

Meanwhile, the group of gathered leaders gasped at what they had just heard Bryce say. Some, out of a sense of loyalty to Lucifer, cried for justice. At the end of the video, when Abel and Bryce made the decision to leave the Fallen with the cat o' nine tails attached only to its leg, instead of finishing the job of ending him, more cries arose from the leaders. They knew how ignorant this decision had been.

When the video ended, the lights went back up. Lucifer looked out across the room, knowing what their decision would be, but it made no difference to him. He would be the one to enforce the judgment, not a room full of pathetic minions. The only reason Lucifer allowed for such proceedings to take place was to allow them to feel of some importance. It also allowed him to keep them in check.

The small, pudgy man still at the podium shook his head in disgust. "These supposed sons that our Great Master looked upon with favor spat in his face when he offered them nothing but support and compassion. There are no words for what we have just witnessed." He paused to let the crowd murmur among themselves and then cleared his throat. "Before I turn over my duties, I would like to ask for you leaders to let our Savior know that we support and adore him." The crowd cheered for Lucifer. After a few minutes, the room fell silent once more as the leaders discussed among themselves what fate should befall Abel and Bryce. They each had their own bloodlust to be satisfied.

CHAPTER 7

Any time Lucifer's regional leaders had witnessed a punishment being carried out, it reminded them of just how vulnerable they were. They knew one of Savior's favorite punishments was to seat the convicted offender in a chair to be fed upon by his hounds. The hounds always took their time circling the chair, occasionally howling at their soon-to-be meal. Once Lucifer snapped his fingers, the hounds lunged at their defenseless prey, mutilating it as they tore away at flesh and bone.

Lucifer finally stood and nodded at the pudgy man, dismissing him. Stepping up to the podium, Lucifer shook his head as if not knowing what to do with the twins, Abel and Bryce. He stood quietly for a moment. Then he addressed the crowd. "It's truly a sad day," he said. "These were my sons who not only mocked me, but also failed a job that I truly thought they were suited for. Surely, they would prove to not just me, but to you beautiful leaders, that they were capable of the task. For that I feel responsible." He dropped his head for further effect.

Cries immediately filled the auditorium, offering support.

"You will never let us down!"

"You are all wise."

"Praise our Savior!"

"We will follow you forever!"

The accolades went on and on until Lucifer, having heard enough, raised a hand for silence.

"Do you know what I want?" Lucifer said. "I want to hear these two speak and try to defend themselves."

"Their words aren't worthy of you, Savior!"

"Cast them out of your thoughts!"

"You are right!" Lucifer said. He gave a nod of his head, and the restraints fell from Bryce and Abel's mouths. The small teeth of the restraints continued to bite at the air, as if begging for more to eat. Bryce and Abel spat out clumps of blood and vomited pieces of their own tongues. Gasping from the release, they both fell prostrate on the floor at Lucifer's feet, hoping he would show mercy. However, they knew the pain they would endure was far from over. They had witnessed, firsthand, the many tortures Father could dredge up.

"I believe they may need a minute to learn to talk again," Lucifer said with a chuckle. "Perhaps we could listen to show tunes while we wait," he mused. The crowd laughed and applauded. Then he glared at Abel and Bryce. "You are only here for my amusement. I will make you dance."

Abel tried to call out to Bryce but could only produce a hideous gargling sound, no longer able to form words. Bryce's mouth was wide open. Inside where the tongue should be, there was now just a small flap of skin that appeared to be rebuilding itself. Despite the pain from his tongue regenerating, Bryce got to one knee, followed by the other, and stood on wobbly legs. He trudged over to Abel, then reached down and helped pull him to his feet. They looked up to see Father staring at them in disgust as an angry crowd called for their heads.

Abel struggled to whisper to Bryce. "Please, brother, let me do the talking for once."

Bryce looked at his brother's serious expression. "Well, we're doomed either way, but go ahead and try."

"Still a smart-ass till the end," Abel said, mustering a small smile. He then turned to face Lucifer. "Father, I—"

"Stop!" Lucifer interrupted. "You betray me, mock me, and now you stand to address me? Get on your knees!"

Abel did as he was told and fell to his knees, pulling Bryce down as well. Starting over, Abel bowed his head, not daring to look at Lucifer. "We are honored to be your sons, Father. We should never have said those things against you. And we failed in bringing you the Fallen." He paused for a moment. "But—" Abel raised his head and looked out upon the gathered crowd of leaders. "We did accomplish something that no one else here has been capable of in over two thousand years!" Now he looked at the crowd with defiance. "We bested a Fallen! We won, no matter what these idiots say to you behind closed doors. And yes, in a moment of stupidity, we let our egos get the better of us. And we are paying the price for our pride. Most here think they could do better than what we did. If so, then why have none of these idiots done it?" He could feel himself gathering steam and it felt good. "Are we young? Yes. Are we inexperienced? Yes. However, this is the question you should really consider." Abel paused and turned to face his Father, looking him in the eyes. "You are trying to pass judgment on your two sons, the best of all these supposed leaders!"

Immediate cries poured out from the auditorium. Some in the front row spat at Abel and Bryce.

Bryce leaned over to Abel. "Well, I didn't see that coming, but bravo! By the way, was it your intention to taunt the lion? Why not get in one last punch, eh? Would you care if I say something now?"

Abel shrugged.

Bryce looked first at Lucifer, then to the crowd and smiled

sardonically. He wanted them to know he didn't give a damn about what was to come. He spat a wad of blood on a leader in the first row, Titus, who leapt to his feet and lunged for the stage, but the leaders beside him restrained him.

Lucifer shook his head and raised his hand, calling for silence. Everyone quickly obeyed. He looked at the brothers. "I will now speak. Bryce, I have no interest in what you have to say, so be still!" Both knew what would be coming next. "You are the best. Hands down, the both of you are the best out of all these idiots calling for your heads. True, you are young, and it's also true that no one has been able to accomplish what you came so close to doing." He paused and looked around the room, fully knowing none of the regional leaders would have the nerve to protest. They knew better than to question him. Lucifer then looked back at Abel and Bryce. "As for what you both have done, I do applaud you." His eyes blackened as he leaned down to be face to face with them. "I could overlook your shortcomings in achieving the tasks set to you. But you crossed the line when you mocked me, and for that I hereby sentence you both to the Tower of Babel!"

Neither knew what Father spoke of, as they exchanged blank looks, then looked out at the leaders, finding that they, too, looked confused.

Rising again to look out at the crowd, Lucifer's voice deepened. "You all want to know what this punishment is, don't you? But I won't ruin the surprise for the condemned. No. Let me send them on their way and we will watch it unfold together." He pointed to the large screen on the stage. Leaning back down once more to look at Abel and Bryce, Lucifer placed the Judas kiss on both of their cheeks and whispered, "The son of God was betrayed with this exact kiss!"

Bryce and Abel were then dragged away by hands they couldn't see. Within moments, their images appeared on the giant screen.

Lucifer then turned once again to address the leaders. "What you are about to see, my ignorant 'fearless leaders,' is one of the oldest and most effective punishments in my arsenal. It is as old as time. I've been waiting for just the right time to employ it once again. I hope you will enjoy what is about to unfold before your eyes. I will be anxious to see the looks on your idiotic faces at the end."

The twins' new purpose in life was to carry a large boulder up to the top of a large tower called Babel. But whenever they made it a quarter of the way up, they were beaten until their bones were broken. Then the process would start again, the twins' bodies made new, and they would once more begin the treacherous, never-ending journey. Never realizing that they had already experienced the torture.

Watching the events occur on the screen, the leaders laughed and applauded as they watched the punishment of the twins play out.

"Tell me that isn't perfect atonement for what I have been put through?" Lucifer asked the crowd. "Now, get back to work! But before you leave, remember this day and know that if you ever cross me, I will introduce you to a punishment that you can't begin to imagine." He stood and walked off the stage, followed closely by Esperanza.

Once out of sight of the leaders, Lucifer abruptly turned and grabbed both of Esperanza's shoulders. "My dear child, let me explain something and hear me well. I will never need your sympathy, and if you *ever* touch me without permission in front of others I will torture you to the point that what you just witnessed will seem like child's play. Do you understand me?" he hissed into her face.

Esperanza, with her head lowered, replied, "Yes, my Savior."

"Good," Lucifer said and then turned to walk away. "Oh, one more thing. That was one hell of an introduction. I almost wept, it was so beautiful." Then he took her hand and they made their way back to the torture chamber where Lucifer had left Legionaries. They stopped at the door. "I need to see that beast I have locked inside," Lucifer said. "Please do as you want, but do not disturb me. Understood?"

"Yes, my Savior," Esperanza meekly responded. She waited in place as Lucifer entered the room and closed the door behind him. She didn't dare move an inch. No matter how long the wait, she wouldn't move, only hoping Lucifer would once again find favor in her.

CHAPTER 8

Before taking the highway into Taupe City, Jonathan, knowing what Riley wanted, made a detour. He turned into the neighborhood where Riley and Allison's first home sat. Held inside the walls were the promises and dreams for a future that would never come. Riley noticed all the new home builds and knew his real estate agent, Alex, was correct about how quickly the area would grow.

Jonathan parked across the street next to one of the new houses going up. Riley sat staring out the passenger window, at the house, wondering about the what-ifs and knowing that a beautiful part of him died here. Jonathan interrupted the silence. "Sure has changed a lot."

Riley didn't reply as he examined how much progress had been made during his short absence. Jonathan persisted. "Even though it has changed, she is not forgotten, Riley."

Riley forced a smile. "I know, Jonathan, but coming back here knowing that it will be my last time—on the one hand it feels good, about letting go of the past. I know it's not good for me to dwell there since no good can come of it. However, this is where my family was going to happen, and now . . ." He couldn't finish the thought and shook his head as if trying to clear out the pain that slipped in. He stepped out of the truck and began walking.

Riley let his feet take him where they wanted to go. The sense of direction was clear since he desperately wanted one more look inside his old house. Before he knew it, he had crossed the street, went up the porch stairs, and was now standing outside the front door. He looked at it and thought about him and Allison walking through it for the first time. He thought about all the plans they had made for their future. But now this house was a stranger to him. He shook his head at the lunacy of continuing any farther. As he turned to leave, the front door opened. A woman looked up at him, caught off guard by his presence, as a child suddenly ran in between them.

"We are going to be late for soccer practice. Come on, Mom!"

Riley could see the uneasiness on the woman's face as she spoke quickly to her daughter. "Lexie, stay right there and wait for your sister Lilly," she said, not once taking her eyes off Riley's.

"Hi, my name is Riley," he said. "I'm so sorry for the intrusion, but I used to live here about a year ago." Noticing she had a wedding ring on, Riley continued. "Forgive me for my rudeness, but I was wondering if your husband is home?"

He could see the woman's guard coming down a bit. "Frank, there's a man at the door asking for you," she called over her shoulder.

Riley heard his response. "Tell them we aren't interested in buying anything. Are you sure Lilly's shoes were in her closet?"

A smile broke across the woman's face as she tried to stifle a laugh. "As you might imagine with all the new builds in the neighborhood, we've had a lot of door-to-door salesmen trying to push something off on us."

Returning her smile, Riley actually chuckled. "Well, I can promise you I am not trying to sell you anything."

"Well, thank God for that small miracle. My name is Misty, and I'm assuming you would like to take a look around. I'm sure this house holds some good memories for you. Unfortunately, we're trying to make it to soccer practice on time for once. But if you want to come back later, we are going to have a cookout, for some family. Around five-ish?"

Almost sighing with relief, Riley now realized he didn't need to walk through the rooms of the house. Just coming back and standing here at the front door, talking to the new owner felt like enough. "Sounds like a great time, but I have to decline. I'm heading into the city next. I have a few things I need to get done today."

A small girl in pigtails darted past him and ran out to the minivan in the driveway where her older sister was waiting. "Mom, we're going to be late!" the younger of the two proclaimed.

"If we're late again, Coach is going to make us sit out the game this weekend," the older girl declared.

"Looks like you have your hands full," Riley said. "I'll let you get to the practice. Thank you for the offer though. I appreciate it." He turned and headed back down the driveway. As he passed by the girls, Riley couldn't help himself. "Score a goal for your parents this weekend!"

"I always do!" The little one replied, puffing out her chest to let him know she was that good.

"You do not," her sister said.

Leaving the girls arguing back and forth, Riley made his way back to the truck, finding that he wasn't nearly as depressed as he thought he might be. He opened the passenger door and hopped in where Jonathan still sat behind the wheel. "Let's go," Riley said. "I have my closure."

Jonathan put the truck in drive and they left the neighborhood. After they were back on the highway, Riley glanced over at Jonathan. He could see that his friend was smiling. Then he looked up at the sky, which was turning dark gray. "Can't believe those kids are going to actually practice in this," he said. "Any minute, those clouds are going to burst and from the looks of it, they're carrying more than just rain inside them."

Jonathan nodded in agreement. "I don't believe they're going to have practice for long. Unless the coach is a tyrant and only wants wins next to his name."

Riley laughed aloud. "I can see the coach now. 'Lexie, Lilly, you are late! Not only will you be sitting out the next game, but you will run laps until one of you pukes! Now drop and give me twenty on your knuckles!'"

Riley chuckled a little. When he looked over at Jonathan, he found his friend giving him a questionable look. This turned his chuckle into an uncontrollable fit of laughter. It felt good leaving the old neighborhood for what would be the final time without being depressed about it.

"If you don't like it, you can cry to your parents. They will also be doing laps," Jonathan said in a deep, gravelly voice. "I don't care if they are overweight or have joint issues. That is for losers and weak, simple-minded losers. This isn't rain, this is the fuel that drives excellence!"

Jonathan laughed at his own nonsense so hard he swerved a bit, causing the driver next to him to honk his horn. "Oops," Jonathan replied, chuckling as the other driver gave him a rude hand gesture.

"Well, would you look at that? According to that person I am number one!"

Riley snorted through his tears at Jonathan's unusual humor.

"Oh no, looks like this cop didn't approve of my rating from that driver."

Riley came to his senses when he heard the word *cop*. Jonathan didn't have a driver's license. Looking in his passenger-side mirror, Riley saw the lights and wondered what scenario they were about to be cast into. "Great way to welcome us back to the city," Riley said nervously. Jonathan maneuvered to the shoulder, stopping one exit away from a sign that read "Hospital".

"So close to our destination, and we're going to get hassled for a having a good time," Riley said.

"Said every drunk driver in the state," Jonathan answered back.

Riley laughed once more, despite his worry about what kind of trouble they might be in.

Jonathan could see that his friend was not going to be of any help. He decided to go with what he called a little relaxation therapy. Staring in the rearview mirror, he saw a young female police officer step out of the patrol car. He pressed the button for the driver's window as the officer approached with caution.

Arriving at the driver's side of the truck, she asked the same question that seemed to be on every officer's lips. "Do you know why I pulled you over?" She then looked past Jonathan at Riley, who was suddenly somber.

Jonathan answered with a little too much sarcasm. "Well, if I had to guess, I'd say it's because I swerved a minute ago and you're wondering if I have been drinking. But that's just a guess."

"License and registration please," the officer said.

Taking his eyes off the officer and placing them on Jonathan, Riley found him gripping the steering wheel so tightly that it was bending under the strain. The muscles in his arms and shoulders had tightened as he looked aimlessly out the windshield in search of something far off in the distance. A moment later, seeming to have found what he had been looking for, Jonathan closed his eyes, but right before he did, Riley saw them change from their normal blue to a dark purple. Unable to put a stop to the next chain of events, Riley was both relieved that he was still alive and saddened that he had played a part in hurting so many innocent bystanders.

"Oh God. Jonathan, what have you done!"

Jonathan, listening in on the officer's thoughts, pulsed for a second, sending out a supernatural energy field around them with the intention of turning the officer to his will. As other vehicles approached them, they swerved, nearly losing control, but then corrected before they caused an accident. Horns were blaring, but Jonathan didn't notice as his eyes were now locked on the officer who stood looking directly at him. There was a cloud preventing Jonathan from reading her thoughts, which unleashed a surge of frustration in him.

Jonathan pulsed again, but the energy caused several cars to collide with one another. The screeching of tires, the crashing of metal, and blaring horns.

From somewhere far off, Jonathan thought he heard Riley say, "Jonathan, what are you doing!"

Jonathan grew even more frustrated now that the officer showed no sign that the pulsing of energy had any effect on her, which made him pulse much harder. *This woman will submit to me*, he thought, as the frustration was now evident on his face.

The effects of the last pulse now affected traffic on the other side of the highway as metal crunched and crashed, followed by more blaring horns.

"Stop it," Jonathan thought he heard someone say. Then felt something push at his side.   However, he would not move under any circumstance.

"You will submit to me!" Jonathan demanded.

Riley flashed back to the scene on the dock when, for the first time, he felt a sense of fear for his own safety and wondered if

Jonathan could hurt him. Could this be the day that Jonathan would end him? The cries of a woman in pain from the other side of the truck snapped Riley back to the present.

It was the police officer. "Please, someone help me!" she cried. "Please, God, help!"

Riley couldn't believe it, especially after all their grueling training sessions where he was left drenched in sweat and Jonathan looked as if he had just woken up. But now Jonathan had sweat pouring off him, the veins in his arms and neck looking as if they may rupture. The highway median crumbled as the ground shook. The pavement on both sides of the highway cracked and erupted, forcing chunks out onto the road.

The officer had fallen to her knees next to the truck and let out another scream before going silent. Riley began punching Jonathan as hard as he could. The pain shot through his arms with every blow. It felt like he was punching a concrete statue. Although his knuckles were now bleeding, Riley continued to throw shots at Jonathan's shoulder, chest, and the side of his head. He screamed over the mayhem of the traffic. "Stop it, stop it, *stop it!*"

Even though Jonathan appeared to have been released from the grip of the anger that had overtaken him, Riley continued to throw strike after strike at him. That was until Jonathan turned to look at him, catching his fist before it landed another punch. "What do you think you're doing?" he barked.

Sweat and worry poured off Riley. He fell back against his seat, exhausted. He saw the look of confusion mixed with anger in Jonathan's face. Gasping to catch his breath, he pleaded with him. "Please don't go back to wherever you just were. Please don't allow your mind to take you to that place ever again." Riley then jumped out of the truck and ran around to the driver's side where he found the officer sprawled out on the ground.

Placing his fingers on the officer's throat and finding a pulse, Riley positioned her head on his lap. "Help is on the way," he assured her, not quite sure that she could even hear him. The name on her bloodied badge read PATTERSON. Blood poured from her nose as her eyes slowly opened, looked out into nothing, and then fell closed once more. Pulling out his cell phone, Riley dialed 911 only to be placed on hold. *What's going on?* As he turned and looked out across the carnage that Jonathan had caused, he found his answer.

Numerous people on both sides of the highway had a phone pressed to their ear, probably attempting to make the same call he was. He noticed that everyone seemed to be suffering from nosebleeds—except for him. He rubbed the back of his hand across his face only to come away with sweat. Cracks spider-webbed the pavement around him with the truck being the point of origin. The concrete median laid in rubble as far as he could see in either direction. Soon news helicopters would begin to circle overhead, like buzzards, waiting to feast on the horrific destruction that had just taken place. The highway was in total ruin.

Riley grabbed a blanket from the truck and carefully positioned it underneath the officer's head. That's when he saw Jonathan just standing there on the other side of the truck. Riley looked at him with confusion and anger and a bit of fear written all over his face. But then he could see that his friend looked dazed as well.

"I—I have no idea what just happened," Jonathan managed to say.

Riley had to look away from his friend because he could see that he was scared by what he had just caused. Riley shivered. Jonathan had been unable to control himself in such a minor instance, and there was no telling what else he was capable of.

CHAPTER 9

Maggie maneuvered her vehicle up to a small enclosed structure, assuming it was the visitor check-in. Looking around, she could vaguely make out outlines of large buildings just down the road. The place had a haunting look, like something out of a horror movie. She was startled by a knock on her window. She turned to see an older gentleman dressed in a dark rain slicker. She rolled down her window and held out her license.

"My name is Rolfe," the man said, pointing at his nametag as if to clear up any confusion Maggie may have. "I don't need to see your license since visiting hours are over. Please turn around and come back tomorrow. You can check our website for visiting hours."

Not being put off by him, Maggie quickly responded. "I think you should call one of your superiors or check the log sheet, and you will see that I am to be permitted on the grounds," she said, once again handing her license to him. The man looked at her for a long moment, clearly irritated, and then at her license. Shaking his head, he turned and went back into the visitor check-in booth the size of a closet.

Immediately, Maggie began cussing Miles Jackson for not holding up his end of the deal. Clumsily grabbing her phone, she was about to call him and tell him she was about to ruin him, but then the gates opened, allowing her access. Rolfe stepped out, handed her license back to her without saying a word, and motioned for her to drive through. She tucked the license back in her bag and proceeded through the gate. As she drove slowly down the road, she noticed a run-down building to her left that didn't fit her idea of prison security. As she drove farther, she saw an actual gas station that appeared to be open.

Thinking of how bizarre this all seemed, Maggie came to another set of gates that already stood ajar. She passed through them and onto a driveway that sported large trees. Their branches scraped the top of her SUV as she passed through. As she reached the end of the driveway, she found a small parking area next to a large building. Since official visiting hours were over, she decided to park close to the door, ignoring the handicapped parking signs. Maggie hopped out, grabbing her purse in the process as the rain pelted her, and then hurried up the sidewalk to double-glass doors. She looked for an intercom button or buzzer of some kind to let someone know she was there. Not locating either, she grabbed one of the door handles with her good hand and pulled. Surprisingly it gave way, allowing her into the lobby where she was greeted by a stern-faced woman.

"I'm Tasha Smart, the warden here at Southwater."

Maggie, not thinking, immediately extended her right hand. "My name is—" but the warden cut her off, not yet taking Maggie's hand.

"I know who you are, Ms. Gregory, and it appears you have powerful friends in high places. I don't believe that special circumstances should be granted to anyone despite their social standings. Then again, we live in different times now, don't we, Ms. Gregory?" She accepted Maggie's extended hand and shook it with a firm squeeze that sent blinding pain up Maggie's arm, causing her legs to buckle as she cried out. The warden released

Maggie's hand and quickly caught her before Maggie could fall. "I am so sorry," she said. "I didn't see the bandage on your hand." The warden showed brute strength for her size, as she basically carried Maggie to a nearby bench and sat her down, as if she were a small child. "Would you like me to take a look at it?"

Maggie gave a quick look at her hand, then tried to conceal it by crossing her arms. The pain from the movement sent another jolt back through her body, causing her to wince and her eyes to water. Warden Smart placed a hand on her shoulder and spoke reassuringly. "Please, let me take a look," she said as she gently took Maggie's hand and examined it. "From what I can see, from the swelling, it appears you broke the pinky. I would guess the middle phalanx, but would need to unwrap it to further assess. You shouldn't have taped it so tightly," she scolded. "It would have been better to apply ice and elevate it until you could make it to the emergency room."

Maggie, still wincing, replied a little sarcastically, "Are you a doctor on the side?"

The warden was not amused by the comment. She carefully placed Maggie's hand next to her chest and spoke with authority. "Hold it here and follow me. I want to apply some ice and get a better look and get rid of that makeshift bandage." She got up and walked with a fast, confident pace through the lobby as Maggie hurried to keep up.

"I'm really fine. I just need to see the two inmates that I assume you are already aware of, and then I'll head straight to the hospital."

The warden didn't seem to care about Maggie's agenda as she led her around a corner and arrived at an elevator. They stepped in, and the warden inserted a key and pressed the third-floor button. The doors closed at once and they ascended at a methodically slow pace. The warden stood like a statue, staring straight ahead, not once glancing at Maggie. Feeling awkward, as the elevator seemed to take forever getting to their destination, Maggie thought she'd take the time to make amends.

"I agree with what you said earlier. A so-called elevated status in today's society does not deserve any kind of special treatment. I am truly sorry for putting you in this situation."

As the doors finally opened, Warden Smart didn't bother replying, as if she hadn't even heard Maggie. With the same confident pace as before, she stepped off, leaving Maggie to once again hurry after her. They walked down a long hallway and arrived at a door with a sign on it that in gold block letters read, WARDEN. Unlocking the door, Warden Smart stood off to the side, allowing Maggie to enter first.

There was a large desk with two leather chairs facing it and old bookshelves along the back wall that stretched from floor to ceiling. The shelves held mostly law books, but in the middle there was a large photo. It was the warden and a child in a wheelchair. She had both arms wrapped around the child. Their smiles were genuine and the camera had captured the happiness of the moment.

From the corner of her eye, Maggie could see that the warden was looking at her. However, she offered nothing about the photo. "Please sit, Ms. Gregory," was all she said.

As Maggie sat down, she wanted to ask if the girl in the photo was her daughter but pushed the thought aside, knowing she probably wouldn't receive an answer. The warden opened a drawer behind the desk and pulled out a small bag. Reaching inside, she pulled out an instant cold pack and ace bandage. She smacked the bag to activate the cooling effect. She then came around the desk and knelt down in front of Maggie. Gently taking her hand, she unwrapped the self-made bandage that had been so ineptly applied. Maggie winced as the last of the bandage was delicately pulled loose.

"Hold your hand up," the warden instructed her. She placed a gutter splint around the broken finger to immobilize it and closed the splint by applying adhesive tape at the end of her finger and another piece near the base of the finger, making sure not to apply any pressure on the actual break.

"That is far better than I could ever do," Maggie commented, hoping the compliment didn't come off as patronizing. Saying nothing, the warden worked quickly to wrap the whole hand with the ace bandage. After one time around, she placed the cold pack on the fingers, then finished wrapping it with the rest of the bandage.

"This will do until you get to the hospital," she said. "Continue to hold the hand next to your body for elevation."

Maggie's curiosity erupted to the surface. "Were you a nurse or doctor before stepping into this line of work?"

"No, Ms. Gregory," the warden responded. "90 percent of the breaks that we see in our infirmary have to deal with the hand. Prison is a violent place. The only thing for inmates to really reflect on is how they ended up here. Eventually, those thoughts cause them to lash out, not just at one another, but anything that presents a target. After seeing so many of these cases, I had my staff learn how to administer help until the doctor could see the inmate. The doctor isn't always here, and when night comes, the loneliness of the cell breaks a person down and they harm themselves."

"That shows great forethought, to put that into action," Maggie said.

The warden, once again ignoring the pleasantries, walked to the other side of her desk and sat down. She pulled out two files

and got to the business at hand. "You are here to see two inmates,
Joe Packton and Mike Mahoney. There isn't a problem seeing
Mr. Packton, but Mr. Mahoney is a level-six inmate and is not
allowed any kind of visitation unless it's from his lawyer, which
you are not."

Maggie spoke up quickly. "No, I need to see them both. I was
assured that I would be able to see them both."

"Ms. Gregory, I don't care what you were assured of. My job
is to keep people safe from doing harm to anyone they feel they
can prey upon. You are not permitted to see Mr. Mahoney. That
is my call and it is final, understood?"

Never one to back down easily, Maggie came back with a
threat that she wished she didn't have to use. "If I need to call
Miles Jackson, I will. But I will be seeing them both. Now. Do
you understand?"

At this, the warden leaned back in her chair, crossing her
arms over her narrow frame, then placed a sympathetic gaze
on her face. Maggie immediately felt uncomfortable and could
understand why this woman was a warden. She never raised her
voice and seemed to only speak when it was of importance. She
was the definition of control, reminding Maggie of her former
self. That was until she went out on this crazy search to find
Jonathan.

Finally, Warden Smart spoke. "There are six levels of security
in most penitentiaries. Levels one and two are allowed visitation
because they are short-term sentences for petty crimes. Therefore,
they do not pose a risk. Levels three and four are long-term stays,
however, they are allowed visitation. Levels five and six are for
life sentences and death-row inmates. They are not allowed any
visitation because of the stress they are under, which creates risk.
Mr. Mahoney falls under this category. Levels one through four
will eventually get out, but five and six will never see the light

outside these walls unless a miracle happens. They may learn to accept the path their choices in life have taken them down, but it is a horrible and difficult way to exist. As such, most go on suicide watch." The warden leaned forward in her chair and paused a moment. "So now I pose a question to you. Would you, Ms. Gregory, be able to accept the fact that for the rest of your life you are granted only privileges that others in authority say you are allowed? If you were in their shoes, would you want to satisfy someone else's curiosity simply because of that person's social status? If you can truly say yes, then I'll bend the rules just so you can be satisfied."

Stunned by the scenario being turned around on her, Maggie could not with a clear conscience say yes. She had become so obsessed that she didn't realize just how low she had stooped simply to get information that she felt she was entitled to—that is, if either man even had any information that would help her in her search. Unable to make eye contact with the warden, Maggie looked at the floor, wanting to leave. Perhaps Jonathan would just have to live on in her memory.

The warden came around from behind the desk and sat in the chair opposite Maggie. "I have spoken with Mr. Packton, and he has agreed to see you. I don't have a problem with this. It would have been better if you would have come during normal visiting hours. However, seeing as how you've already made the trip, I will allow you to see him, but only for the normal allotted amount of time, which is an hour." The warden then leaned back in her chair, still looking at Maggie. "Look, Ms. Gregory, I have been doing this job for fifteen years, and in all this time I've never granted this type of request. So don't treat me like an idiot and I will show you the same respect."

Maggie didn't think she could be belittled any further, but the warden wasn't finished.

"I honestly don't care what is so important to a woman such as yourself. But I would like to offer you some advice—whether you take it or not is up to you."

Maggie was dumbfounded, but she had a new respect for the woman and now actually valued her opinion.

Seeing that she had gotten Maggie to actually look up, the warden continued. "Miles Jackson is not a man to be trusted, and you are now in bed with him. So tread with caution, Ms. Gregory, and tread very lightly." To further the point, she reached over and touched Maggie's shoulder. "He will sell you out if it will benefit him," she said, this time speaking with more urgency and leaning forward in her chair to drive the point home. "Be wary and know that this visit you paid for may very well come back to haunt you in the end. Do you understand?"

Maggie sat stunned and now realized what she had done, but knew it was too late to go back. "I understand," she said.

The warden stood and grabbed a radio and keys off her desk. Without asking if Maggie was ready, she opened the office door and resumed the same stride as before, heading down the hallway with Maggie hurrying once again after her. Heavy thoughts now filled Maggie's mind.

Once back in the lobby area, Warden Smart spoke over her shoulder, "This is just the administration building. We will have to go outside to get to the actual housing of the inmates and visitation area. The jail consists of three buildings behind the administration building and is closed off by a double set of gates with guard towers around the perimeter."

Walking out into the night, the warden turned to Maggie. "I hope a little rain doesn't bother you. We do not cover this section due to radio frequency interference, and I do not permit umbrellas that hide our faces. I want the towers and all the cameras to see who is coming and going."

As they reached the first set of gates, the warden spoke into the radio. A moment later, the gates slid open. Once inside, they waited for the first gate to close before the second gate slid open. They proceeded to the first large building in front of them. The warden scanned her key card at the entrance and the door released. A uniformed officer stood waiting for them.

"Good evening, Warden."

"To you as well, Mr. Sterling. Is Packton ready for us?"

"Yes, he is waiting in the visiting room." The officer stepped into a small, glass-enclosed security room and typed a few commands on a keyboard, causing a buzzing sound as a door to the right slid open.

Maggie felt the chill of the place. After a short walk, they came to another door the warden unlocked with her keycard. Before pulling it open, she looked at Maggie for a long moment. "On the other side of this door, I hope you find the answers to whatever you are looking for." Before she pulled the door open, Maggie stopped her by placing her hand on it.

"Is this safe? I mean, will there be someone in there with me to make sure this doesn't get out of hand? The whole reason this man is in jail is because of me, and I'm sure he holds some kind of grudge."

"It's a little late at this point to be having second thoughts, don't you think?" the warden said in an authoritative tone. "As for your safety, that is my job. Not just for you, but for the men housed here and my officers. If I were worried, I wouldn't have allowed this to ever happen. Understood?"

Maggie nodded nervously and found that she once again was unable to make eye contact with the woman. Seeing the nervousness on Maggie's face, the warden offered some reassurance. "I don't come down for visitations. However, this being a rare scenario, I will stay in the room, out of the way.

Nonetheless, I can tell you that you will not see this man as the person he once was, but I'll let Mr. Packton speak for himself."

She opened the door and stepped inside as Maggie followed closely behind her.

CHAPTER 10

Maggie entered into a long room with only one other person and the warden with her. She looked at the man who had turned her dreams into nightmares. Now, however, this nightmare had a warm smile spread across his face as he put down a Bible that he had been reading. As he stood, Maggie slowly approached, not quite sure what to say or do now that she was actually in the same room with this man. Packton appeared to be in good health. He was no longer the large, intimidating figure from her dreams. He was now a bit on the chubby side. He offered his right hand to Maggie but stopped himself when he noticed her bandaged right hand.

"Pardon me," he said, then offered the left, which she accepted.

"Thank you for agreeing to meet with me, Mr. Packton."

"Please, call me Joe," he said with a smile. "I feel that we can be a little less formal, if that is okay with you."

Maggie gave him a nod.

"Would you like to sit down?" he said. "It would make for better conversation if we were a little more comfortable despite the cold metal stools."

Taken aback by his charm, Maggie wondered what the catch was as she sat across from him.

Packton seemed to pick up on how nervous she was. "Thank you so much for asking to see me. I learned who you were after that miserable night. I know that I can never make up for the pain and stress that I inflicted on you. So instead of offering a hollow apology, please let me tell you what I am doing to better myself. Maybe it will offer a glimpse into why I preyed upon you that night."

Maggie was shocked by the sincerity in his words. She gave him another nod, indicating he should proceed.

"After turning myself in and being sentenced for the crimes I had committed, I found that I was actually at peace with how things had turned out," he said. "I realized I was being given a second chance to start over and do things right." He paused for a moment, wanting to find the right words. "I am not your typical criminal. I grew up in an amazing home with a loving family. I don't drink nor have I ever taken any form of drug, besides aspirin. My problem is that I always saw myself as an outsider who didn't fit in anywhere. I had no friends and was bullied all through school. It made me a bitter person. I was book smart but socially awkward. I couldn't talk to my classmates. Any time I attempted to, I would begin stuttering. My anxiety would spike and sometimes I threw up in front of the person I was trying so desperately to reach out to. I dove into books because they didn't judge me. They didn't ask me to impress them. They simply offered information that I feasted upon."

He stopped, looking at Maggie, and lowered his head. "Want to hear something that will truly blow your mind?" he asked. Not waiting for Maggie's response, he continued. "I was reading at a college level at the age of nine. I skipped most of elementary and middle school. At age eleven I was coming up with solutions to calculus problems that the teachers hadn't covered yet. I have a bachelor's of science in engineering and a master's in chemical engineering. I did all this by the age of twenty-one."

Maggie was not only impressed but somehow knew that he was telling the truth. He wasn't bragging about his accomplishments, just informing her that he had made bad decisions that brought him to his current predicament.

Packton raised his head and looked at Maggie. "Of course, I had a lot of job offers when I graduated. But for once in my life, I decided I wanted to live a little. Which is what brought Mike into my life. One thing led to another, and before I knew it, I was enjoying what I thought was living and being free for the first time. I could do what I wanted without consequences—which, of course, was wrong because now here I sit. We partied when we had money. When the funds ran out, we stole so that we could continue that lifestyle. The sad part about all this is I knew I could manipulate Mike. I guess you could say he became a social experiment of mine. Mike would think up a plan to steal something, but then I would come up with a way to do it better.

"I know I used him like a puppet, and now I'm paying for it with this five-year sentence. I will never be able to live one day without remembering how I took advantage of him. He thought of me as a friend. He was easy to manipulate. I could mentally confuse him and he would do whatever I told him to. In my opinion, that is far worse than physically abusing someone."

Maggie surprised herself, finding that part of her wanted to believe him. Oddly though, she couldn't stop focusing on his face, especially his teeth, which were perfectly straight and bleached a pearly white. This brought back the painful memory of that night. One thing she clearly remembered was the smell of Packton's diseased, rotting gums. His teeth had been a disturbing shade of yellow, not the white ones she saw now. Taking her eyes off his, Maggie looked down at the table and asked softly, "You know what I remember?"

"I'm guessing the angel that saved you," Packton answered.

Maggie suddenly looked up. Why had he referred to Jonathan as an angel? Did he mean an actual angel? She didn't believe in angels or any form of religion. She sat there stunned for several seconds before remembering where she was going with her line of questions. His damned pearly-white smile had distracted her. But no matter, he was still the person who had viciously attacked her that night. She felt her anger rising at the thought.

"I remember the smell of you!" she spat. "And the yellowness of your rotting teeth. You pulled a gun on me and threatened my life. You were going to rape me! And now you want to talk to me about your childhood and your insecurities that led you into a life of crime!" Her voice had grown harsh, but at this point she didn't care. She hadn't come this far, or stooped to this level to be duped by this guy.

Maggie saw the warden out of the corner of her eye looking at them with concern. Quite frankly, at this point, Maggie honestly didn't care as the hurt and anger poured out of her.

Packton remained calm despite her outburst and now looked at her sadly. "They are dentures," he replied softly. "One of the reasons I was bullied my whole life was because of my hygiene. I honestly didn't give any thought to my appearance. And I stuttered. It alienated me from people." He then reached inside his mouth, removed the top denture, and then held it out to Maggie as proof.

Maggie visibly cringed at the sight of it. Seeing that she seemed to be speechless, he put it back in, somewhat embarrassed.

"As for hurting people, you are right," he continued. "Seems kind of odd that I would go from being a smart kid from a good family, to wielding a gun. I'm really sorry about that night when we attempted to rob you and hurt you. When that huge guy showed up, he was the biggest thing I'd ever laid eyes on. I didn't know what to think. The way he so easily threw us around, I thought he must have had some kind of supernatural powers. My only thought was getting the hell outta there alive. Then he looked at me like I was nothing. Before I knew what happened, he had me on the ground rendered helpless. I thought death was staring at me with those cool blue eyes."

Packton had to stop for a moment and gather himself.

"He is the only reason that I turned my life around. I have never known what true fear was until that day when he looked not just at me but through me. Everything happened so quick. I'm just thankful he showed mercy. I'll never forget that he told me I had to turn from my ways, admit to my crimes, and start a new life. From that day forward I have done just that, to the best of my ability. After I ended up here, I started to read the Bible. My parents were Christians and we went to church quite often, so I vaguely remembered hearing about angels. The more I read, I learned that angels are mentioned quite often in the Bible. One story intrigued me most. It's in the book of Daniel when King Nebuchadnezzar asked Daniel to interpret dreams for him. This is the verse that I believe points out to what that guy really is."

Packton then quoted the scripture without opening the Bible. "'I saw in the visions of my head upon my bed, and behold, a watcher and a holy one came down from heaven.'" He stopped and looked at Maggie. "This probably doesn't mean anything, so let me clarify. The king is describing his dream to Daniel hoping to get an interpretation. I've been thinking about those words, 'holy one,' and 'watcher.' I know this sounds crazy, but just you being here confirms that we both have questions and I hope this will help in your search. I think those words, 'holy one' and 'watcher' are what we would call an angel, maybe even a guardian angel. I read that guardian angels sometimes choose to take on a human form and live here among us. But it means they have to stay here."

Gooseflesh appeared on the back of Maggie's arms and neck. She shuddered. Packton reached across the table and placed a reassuring hand atop hers, then quickly withdrew it, casting a worried look in the warden's direction to let her know that the move was involuntary, before continuing.

"My buddy, Mike, knew he was heading for death row, but didn't care, or try to fight it in court. What he witnessed that night shook the very essence of his soul. I later found out that he had killed several people. He came from a broken everything. His childhood was hell. It really messed him up. He got to the point that he wanted to punish other people because of what he had been through. He just didn't care."

Maggie lifted her bandaged hand to her mouth. She didn't know he was on death row. "So, he is really going to be put to death one day?" she asked.

Packton didn't make eye contact with her. "Yes, he will be executed next year. I cannot talk to him and I don't know how he's doing. There are ways to exchange notes in here with bribery and such, but I can't make myself write the note to ask his forgiveness. Mike didn't even want a trial. He pleaded guilty to three counts of murder, then asked to be executed, which of course raised a lot of eyebrows. His first lawyer had tried to get him to plead to insanity, but Mike fired him on the spot and told the judge he was guilty and deserved death. But the judge ordered him to be assessed by a psychiatrist who confirmed Mike was sane and knew what he was doing and was making an informed decision. The judge reluctantly granted his request and that was the last I ever heard after the newspapers quit talking about it." Packton paused and looked down at his hands. He shook his head. "Many sleepless nights have visited me. I constantly beg God for forgiveness."

Feeling the tears start to fall, Maggie wiped at them and saw Packton doing the same.

"Are you wondering why we turned ourselves in?" he asked.

Maggie nodded. If she had been in their position there was no way she could have ever done what they did, especially knowing that she would be headed for death row.

"When that man, that angel, or whatever he was looked at me, really looked at me, it was like I was paralyzed by his eyes. They were such an odd shade of blue and then they turned a dark purple—a shade I've never seen before. At first I saw rage there. They were so powerful, but then I could see and feel the presence of peace behind those eyes. Maybe Mike saw the same thing. I swear, those eyes held the promise of peace and that is why we did what we were told. Afterward, when he took you away, Mike was the first one to talk. He said, 'I know I'm stoned, but did you just see that?' When I told him yes, he began crying and said, 'You really saw those eyes go dark?' and I said, 'Yeah, they were a dark purple.' But he said they were almost black, that the purple was subtle but they were actually black."

Maggie shuddered.

"Call it being naïve, but I pray that Mike goes to God with a clear heart," Packton said, "and that he has received forgiveness for his sins so he can be welcomed with open arms."

The tears fell easily now and Maggie did not bother trying to conceal them. This whole time she had been looking for some confirmation or assurance that what she had come to suspect—that Jonathan was not of this world—was true. Somehow he had influenced these two men, her assailants, to willingly confess to their crimes, with one of them knowing he would be heading for death row.

She still didn't know if she believed there was an actual god. She didn't grow up going to church. However, she desperately wanted to believe in a life after this one and at the same time hoped that there wasn't one—because she couldn't imagine such an amazing person as her mother being tortured for eternity, if there was a Hell, simply because she had never been a church-going person. Maggie had a lot more questions but didn't want to continue.

"Thank you for meeting with me. I'm sorry to cut this short but—"

Packton completed her thought for her. "You just needed to know if we saw the same thing as you. The answer is yes. That man, whoever he is, is not of this world, that much I know for sure. If it weren't for him, I have no idea where I would be today. I assume that I would have hardened even more over time, until eventually, like Mike, I committed crimes that would have left me hollow and more than likely dead. So, despite the overwhelming guilt I feel, I know I'm lucky to have a second chance at life. When my time is served and I finally leave this place, I will go into ministry in some capacity. Maybe I can help stop wayward youth from making the same mistakes I did and let them know that whether they are bullied or outcast, and no matter their race, background, sexuality, or whatever, that we all serve a purpose and that every life matters."

This actually was similar to the message Maggie once told all her new hires—before she went on her hiatus, that is. How odd that the man who had once tried to harm her now shared the same ideas and values she once espoused.

"We all matter," Maggie replied softly. Then with her good hand, she reached out and took Packton's. "Thank you again, Joe, for seeing me. Can I do anything for you? Anything at all?"

Packton offered a polite smile. "Ms. Gregory, just be safe in your journey. I believe that now the pieces will start falling into place for you."

He then stood and Maggie followed. They smiled at one another, knowing this would be the last time their paths would ever cross. Maggie looked over at the warden to let her know she was ready to go, then looked back at Packton. He had sat back down and seemed to be praying. Maggie turned and proceeded out of the visitation room.

Closing the door behind them, Warden Smart didn't bother asking if the meeting went well. Instead, she resumed the same confident stride as she led Maggie back the way they had come. Maggie looked down, deep in thought as they walked along. Once they reached the administration building, she felt a little relieved knowing that the first part of her search was over.

"If there is anything I can do to help Mr. Packton, please let me know," she said, looking up at the warden.

Warden Smart nodded and gave her a polite smile and then turned to walk away.

"You probably think I'm just someone who uses her money and influence to get what she wants," Maggie called after her, "but I don't want you to think I am that shallow."

"Ms. Gregory, all I have to judge you for is what I have been presented," the warden replied. "I was told to be here to let a visitor in after hours. I'd rather be home with my daughter. Now have a good evening and please go have your hand looked at." Then she turned once more, leaving Maggie alone in the lobby.

Maggie exited the building, hearing the door lock behind her. Packton had confirmed what she had already guessed, or hoped, about Jonathan not being from this world. But was Jonathan her guardian angel? It wasn't exactly something she believed in. Why had he chosen to intervene that night? Why her? Did he know she had done nothing over the last year but search for him? It was all too much for her to comprehend.

CHAPTER 11

Sitting in a rocking chair, Lucifer waited patiently as Legionaries's soul slowly took human form. This is what Lucifer enjoyed most about the souls damned to spend eternity in Hell—he could give them back their human form and then destroy it any way he pleased, over and over and over again. The skin and bone came together, then the eyes, ears, and tongue materialized as the powers of regeneration worked their way down, rebuilding Legionaries's human form.

Lucifer reached down to stroke one of the hounds that sat beside him licking its lips in anticipation of its next feeding. "Not yet," Lucifer purred. Then he looked at Legionaries. "Oh, how the mighty have fallen," he mocked. "Earlier you were so defiant, so self-assured, that you would actually rule over me. And you know how I feel about blasphemy."

Legionaries no longer had the capacity to speak. He just lay on the floor in a fetal position, occasionally twitching. *Just like a child in a womb,* Lucifer thought. He stood up and adjusted his jacket, then he blew out a breath, causing the cage that once separated them to sway for a moment and then disappear. With only a few feet separating them, Lucifer rubbed his chin as he looked down at the pathetic creature laying before him.

"You've always been a simpleton, but how dare you think you could ever dominate me!" He crouched down in front of Legionaries's face. "You belligerent, insignificant little man!" he spat. He grabbed both sides of Legionaries's face and squeezed it. The bones cracked and then shattered under the pressure, sending out a red mist. Lucifer released his hold, then slammed what remained of Legionaries's head to the floor with a squash. He calmly removed a handkerchief and wiped at the remnants of blood from his white jacket.

Exasperated, Lucifer fell back into the rocker and began waiting for the regeneration process to begin all over again. Finally, Legionaries got up on one knee. "Good God. I really thought you were going to make me sit here all day," Lucifer berated him. "Although I have the time to spare, in truth I really do have forever. But you, you miserable lackey, do not!" Lucifer held his thumb and forefinger apart an inch, igniting a yellow flame that danced between them.

When Legionaries didn't respond to the threat of once more being set ablaze, Lucifer stood from the rocker and stroked the head of the hound closest to him. The hound showed no sign of interest as it stood, vigilantly watching Legionaries with anticipation of his next move. Legionaries, finally able to form words, spoke with haste, the words falling quickly from his lips with the hope that they would be enough to satisfy Master. "All those years ago when I was sent to overtake a human soul but was intercepted by a guardian angel, we fought a long, hard battle for the soul. When he pulled the soul back from me, I was able to grab just a bit of his power, and I held it tight inside myself before I was banished. I held it deep within, knowing it would serve me well in the future."

"Hell, I already know this!" Lucifer shouted. "Who do you think was the one suppressing it!" he hissed. "I knew what you were capable of, but I didn't fathom you would ever dare to try and get inside my head." He stopped rocking and leaned forward. In front of him was a Pandora's box that, if opened and controlled, could greatly benefit him in capturing what he wanted most. That wretched fallen Jonathan. "Tell me, what else are you capable of, Legionaries?"

Still kneeling, Legionaries wrestled with how he should answer. What if Lucifer could read his thoughts? He had done it before. Seeing Lucifer's eyes turn black, he knew he had to be careful. "Master, I will do anything you ask of me. My mind is clear and I will forever be loyal to you. Please allow me to prove it." He bowed his head. "Please, tell me what you desire most and I will see to it that it is yours before the end of the week."

Lucifer was fuming. "You already know what I want, you fool! I want that damned Fallen and his little friend, Riley. After two thousand years you should know exactly what I desire. However, if you fail, I will send you to the deepest pits of Hell where there is no word for the level of pain I will inflict upon you and what's left of your damned soul!"

Legionaries cowered in terror at this threat. In the past, Lucifer had sent him down to the pits to collect souls for him. He could still hear the screams and pleas from those begging to be freed. Hordes of worms crawled inside victims' heads and throughout their bodies. Nothing could drive one crazier than knowing millions of microscopic worms were feeding on your insides. Victims felt them move right beneath the skin as they clawed helplessly at them, tearing away their own skin. Hell was a living being and the black souls that occupied it quickly learned that its appetite would never be quenched. It was a place of utter derangement and unending pain and torture.

Legionaries shuddered. "Yes, my master. I will bring you the Fallen and the human, Riley." Not wanting to overstep, but knowing he needed to strengthen the point, Legionaries continued. "I will never be as powerful as you. I know my place. My purpose now is only to serve you."

"Do not patronize me!" Lucifer screamed. "All I want to know is that, unlike those two worthless sons of mine, you can get the job done. You do not want to fail me," he hissed. "Not if you want to avoid the pits."

Legionaries groveled. "Yes, Master. I assure you, I will freely walk on the other side and, unlike Abel and Bryce, will not be limited with my powers. I can take whatever form is most useful for the task at hand. Master, I have already begun to appear to a woman who is bent on locating the Fallen. I warned her to stay away, but she will not listen. She is getting close to understanding what the Fallen is." Legionaries paused for a moment and dared to look at Lucifer, whose eyes were still as black as a raven's.

"Go on," Lucifer said.

"Yes, Master. Her name is Mary Allison Gregory. In short, she will be the undoing of the Fallen."

Lucifer leaned forward. "One week is all it would take you, and then the Fallen would be mine and Riley would be dead?"

Legionaries nodded. "Yes, Master. I assure you."

"I don't need your promises. I need action. But you're not getting a week."

Legionaries was caught off guard. He knew he was about to be set up for failure.

A maniacal grin spread across Lucifer's face. "Don't seem so glum, lackey. I have a scenario far better for you. I'm being mocked by this Fallen and his idiot human. There will be no time table. Time is of no concern to me. Eternity, Legionaries, eternity is mine. However, this will be our little secret. Understand?"

Legionaries nodded, not exactly sure what he was agreeing to.

"Beware, though, that I will be closely monitoring you. Do not try me. And know there is no way to evade me. You will accomplish this task. Otherwise, I will not tarry in sending you into the lake of fire."

Legionaries bowed his head. "Your will, my hands, Master."

"Tell me, how do you plan to achieve this little task?" Lucifer asked impatiently.

Legionaries had already given great thought to this and had a plan in place. However, not wanting to tip his hand, he replied simply and hoped it would be enough.

"Fear, Master."

CHAPTER 12

Jonathan and Riley assisted as many of the injured people on the highway as they could, working alongside the first responders. But Riley's thoughts were preoccupied with why and how the catastrophe happened in the first place. He was terrified to think that Jonathan's powers were now making him a danger to the public. What was going on?

The officer who had pulled them over was being rushed to the hospital in critical condition. Riley guessed her proximity to Jonathan was what had almost killed her. Whatever energy or aura Jonathan sent out had caused so much pressure on her body that her brain had hemorrhaged. Jonathan had finally been successful in flagging down an ambulance. Still, Riley was hesitant to let the officer out of his grasp until a paramedic told him he was in the way. When they had asked what happened, Riley answered truthfully, "I don't know."

Jonathan had tried to assist Riley before the paramedics arrived, but Riley had yelled at him and pushed him away. "You've done enough already!" As soon as the words had left his mouth Riley wished that he could take them back. He'd been about to apologize but Jonathan had hurried off to assist others.

Now Riley just stood shaking his head. Every woman, man, and child around him was asking for help. It was all because, for some reason he didn't understand, Jonathan had lost control of himself. Looking around, Riley saw that the highway now looked like a war zone. He hurried from car to car, praying as he went, and reassuring them help was coming. The day quickly gave way to night as the horror slowly faded from the scene, leaving only the remnants of abandoned vehicles, blood-stained pavement, and a fowl stench of piss and vomit.

Jonathan limped over to where Riley was standing next to the truck. The limp had become far worse in the past few hours, but Jonathan had done his best to help paramedics load the wounded into ambulances. Neither spoke as they knew this could be the end of their journey. Riley leaned back against the truck. He desperately wanted to ask Jonathan what had happened but decided to wait until he was ready to explain himself. Minutes passed before Jonathan spoke.

"I can't protect you anymore, Riley," Jonathan said solemnly. "The powers I once had are not mine anymore. I can't control them. Whatever the two demons infected me with during our fight back at the lake house is now growing quickly within me. Instead of the peace I once had, now I only feel anger taking the last bit of my sanity."

Riley knew what Jonathan said was true. He feared that this beautiful friend and guardian standing next to him would, in fact, kill him one day and then afterwards wouldn't understand why he did it. Still, Riley believed that God allowed Jonathan to come to him for a reason and grasped for that thread of hope. Riley could see that Jonathan was fighting back tears. His friend, this mighty hulk of man, had been reduced to a frightened child, crying for someone to help him. Riley threw his arms around Jonathan, hoping that his clutch would help hold him together.

"Listen to me and hear what I say," Riley said. "You are my friend, my family. When one of us struggles, we both suffer. I am not giving up on you, ever. I love you with every fiber of my being. You protected our Allison, and I know you will protect me because I believe in you." He looked up at Jonathan and placed both of his hands on the side of his face, making his friend look at him.

"Will you grant me one favor?"

Jonathan nodded. "If I can, yes."

"Let's go to Granny. She may hold the answers to help us. If not, then you and I will figure out the next part of our paths. You are good-hearted, Jonathan. I know we can figure this out. I know it."

"You are a good friend, Riley," Jonathan said.

The two got back in Riley's truck, with Riley behind the wheel. He carefully drove among the wreckage and made their way to the hospital, parking a few blocks away. As they made the long walk back to the hospital entrance, Jonathan finally spoke.

"This place holds bittersweet memories for both of us," he said. "We both lost something here that we loved very much."

"Yes, but I also met someone who quite possibly loved my Allison more than I ever could," Riley replied, looking over at him.

Jonathan gave a half smile as they continued walking toward the hospital, with his limp slowing them down a bit. Riley stopped when they found themselves at the entrance to the emergency room. They stood there for a few minutes watching as people entered and exited. Most walked in with the hope that they would leave again, but Riley knew different. These walls held their own kind of hell and frustration. Stopping by his old house was one thing, but returning to the place where he lost his Allison along with his dreams was another. Just imagining taking the elevator to the third floor where Allison died, in room 317, sent dread throughout Riley's body.

Jonathan was able to read what was going through Riley's mind. "I am here," he said. "I am not good for much anymore, but

I will offer you my shoulder and will cry with you. Believe in me just a little longer."

Feeling the push he needed to continue, Riley allowed himself to be escorted in by his friend. The waiting room was the definition of chaos. Dozens of people stood, as there weren't enough chairs available. Riley heard someone call out, "Don't send anyone else up. The hallways are jammed waiting for a CT scan."

Disappearing into the crowd, Jonathan led Riley, without being noticed, into the emergency room area. Riley was stunned by what he saw. Despite the intensity of every hurried order given, it was clear the nurses and doctors were prepared for moments such as this. Not one staff member complained as they worked as a unit, helping patients with urgency and care.

Amidst the chaos, Jonathan and Riley spotted Granny at the same time and spoke in unison. "There she is!" Granny was holding the hand of a child and whispering something that made the child smile. Returning the smile, Granny spoke to a doctor, who nodded while scribbling something on a chart. The doctor motioned to a nurse, who jumped to attention. Removing her gloves, Granny headed straight toward them. Jonathan began shifting from foot to foot and was caught off guard when Granny embraced him.

"My fellow Fallen, it is so good to see you despite the circumstances." Releasing him, she looked at Riley and read the concern on his face. "You are afraid, but trust that your questions will all be answered soon." She took Riley's hand. Then she spoke to both of them. "I won't have a break tonight, but if you can hang around in the cafeteria, I can find you soon enough."

Without waiting for a response, Granny placed a kiss on Riley's cheek, then Jonathan's. As she looked back at them, Riley saw an extreme sadness in her eyes instead of happiness. Before he could ask if everything was okay, she excused herself and went to see another patient. Riley felt a bit of reassurance that Granny may have some answers, but at the same time, there were questions he wasn't sure he wanted answers to. He remembered her as a rock, the one person he eventually latched onto when he was going through the worst night of his life. She had been the one to hold his hand when he finally had to tell Allison goodbye. Now it was strange that once again he was reaching out for her help and guidance, knowing that this could well be the end of their story.

CHAPTER 13

Riley chose a booth near the back of the dimly lit cafeteria, away from others who were searching for caffeine at these late hours. The cafeteria was closed for the night, but there was a constant string of customers who kept the coffee vending machine busy. Meanwhile, the rain continued its soft, rhythmic pattern on the windows, causing Riley to fight to keep his eyes open. Jonathan appeared overly exhausted as he stared at his hands. Riley and Jonathan were both drained from the day's events. Riley was certain this was it for them. He had taken notice lately that his friend seemed to tire more easily. It came as no surprise when Jonathan's eyes fell shut as sleep found him. Not long after, Riley, too, welcomed sleep as he laid his head down on the cool table top.

After slipping into sleep, Riley found himself being dragged along by his legs by something he couldn't see. His captor was wheezing loudly like an asthma patient. He spoke with a ragged tone. "Give, give, give. You must think I'm an idiot! You blame me for everything that has happened to you. Why don't you take some responsibility for yourself? Do you have any idea what I had to give up?" He dropped Riley's legs and grabbed his left foot in both hands and squeezed until the bones in Riley's ankle crackled and snapped. The scream Riley let out was deafening. Just on the verge of passing out, he was slapped hard on the side of the face. "Not yet, life-sucker. You will not pass out until I'm done with you." As close as they were in proximity, Riley still couldn't see the figure's face.

Once again, he was being dragged with his head bouncing off the ground as the concrete ate at the back of his head. His ankle was already beginning to swell, stretching the cuff of his pants, which caused more pain than Riley imagined possible. Looking up at the night sky, he tried to locate the moon only to find a dark, blood-red sun in its place. It didn't produce light, as if he now existed on a planet that was too far away to receive the warmth from its rays. Now the only colors of his surroundings were dark and gray.

I'm dreaming, Riley tried to tell himself, although the pain he endured was very real. Riley felt he was falling further into whatever was taking place. The strangest thing, other than the sun appearing to be too far away, was that he was beginning to hear chanting all around. Although he couldn't see anyone, he could hear several were coughing. Then he heard someone puking. The noise of the crowd grew, but he could still hear his captor wheezing as he pulled Riley along. Wanting to cry out for mercy, Riley tried his best to remain quiet. Occasionally, the pain became too much and he would have to scream until his back bounced along a sharp edge of pavement, doubling the pain.

At last, his captor came to another stop, slamming both of Riley's legs down onto the pavement with such force that Riley couldn't stop himself as he pleaded, "God help me, please help me!"

The chanting now gave way to cheers and mockery, as if the crowd had been waiting this whole time for him to speak.

"Oh, false god, please help me!" someone mocked from just a few feet away. "I'm just a victim of my own stupidity." This brought laughter from the crowd as several others now cast their lots in ridiculing him.

How did he get trapped in this nightmare? Riley searched for a glimmer of hope that he would hear Jonathan telling him to awake. He was then jerked upward as his captor spoke directly into his face.

"You are pathetic. I have given everything I know how to give. And yet you ask for more. *More! More!* Well, I'm tired of giving, and I have made a deal that will end this. My trial is done. In your eyes I failed, but I will be given a second chance."

He was thrown to the ground like a rag doll. Although he still couldn't make out the man's face or voice, he quickly realized his tormentor was none other than Jonathan. The crowd fell silent. Then someone began laughing. Rolling from his stomach to his side, Riley's mangled foot gave him a sharp jolt of pain. His eyes finally focused on where the laughter was coming from.

The man was strikingly beautiful and stood only a few feet away from him. Riley knew at once who it was. Regardless of the white suit he wore, the darkened soul could not be hidden by his garments. Riley's heart sank as he realized the fight was over. And at this point, he no longer cared. Death would be welcomed, just as long as all of this could stop—the constant fear about whether this would be his last day when he awoke in the morning, the fear of not knowing what was happening to Jonathan. He thought about all those who had suffered. Death would be merciful at this point.

"What's that?" Lucifer whispered. "You think death is the answer for this to stop? Tsk tsk tsk," he teased. "Riley, I knew you were stupid, but the pain doesn't end with death. It will never end. You are mine for eternity. You were sold out by none other than your so-called guardian. He had the foresight to know when to give up. So what if he's a little batshit crazy? Hell, I thrive on the insanity of others." He then turned and addressed Jonathan. "Oh, guardian angel. How are you, big fella? Do you need to sit down? I'll be honest, you really do sound like an asthma patient. Now sit!" Lucifer commanded as though he were a dog.

Jonathan immediately collapsed and began coughing and then spitting out wads of blood. Unable to draw in a full breath, he asked in a strained voice, "Please let me go. You have what you want. I need to leave this place. It's killing me!"

Lucifer walked over to him and kicked him in the side. Riley could actually feel the ground tremble beneath him. Jonathan grabbed not at his side but at his throat as if it had just closed off the last of his air supply. He struggled to gasp in air. Once he was able to draw in a half breath, his wheezing returned, followed by soft sobs. Riley saw that his friend was now truly a broken Fallen. Lucifer began to taunt Jonathan, seeming to feed off his suffering.

"If I allow you to leave now, how could I ever hang you on one of my beautiful walls? You'll be the latest in my collection. You are going nowhere except in a frame but only after I suck every bit of power out of you. Now shut up before I disembowel you."

The crowd roared, giving its approval. Riley could sense more than he could see that the group had drawn much closer to where he lay. Now his vision cleared, allowing him to clearly see Jonathan as if this were further punishment for him, making him witness his friend's final downfall. Wanting to comfort Jonathan, Riley called out. "I love you no matter what, Jonathan. I—" He was cut off as a boot smashed into his face, almost causing him to bite the tip of his tongue right off. He spit blood and a couple of teeth out. Then the pain had become too much and blackness overtook him.

Riley thought he would awake realizing that it had been just another nightmare. Instead, several hard slaps brought him back around as a woman crouched next to him. Giving him a disgusted look, she spoke over her shoulder. "He is coming back around, my Savior."

"Thank you, Esperanza," Lucifer said, as he entered the room carrying two small boxes.

Riley felt his vision returning to normal as he now found himself in a large living room. Lucifer set the boxes down on the coffee table next to Riley, then took a seat across from him, giving him a radiant smile. "I can't explain, or even put into words how happy this night has made me," Lucifer cooed. "I am literally glowing with pride from my catch. Took thousands of years, and now here you both sit." He mused. "What's that ignorant verse? Something about lambs and wolves? Well, regardless, just know I am so glad that the hunt is finally over."

Riley coughed several times and leaned forward, spitting out blood onto the black-tiled floor. He could see his reflection, and hardly recognized the gaunt-faced man staring back at him. Jonathan was sitting beside him. He had both hands covering his face. The wheezing was gone, but was replaced by breathless shame. Reaching over, Riley placed a hand on Jonathan. "I love you even still. You are my friend. My family."

Jonathan's hands remained covering his face, as if hoping he could somehow hide his shame as his crying grew in volume.

"Touching, very touching," Lucifer said, looking at the two of them. "Let me relish in the fact that you both, finally, belong to me," he said with a sneer. "Oh, stop your sniveling and sobbing, the both of you!"

Riley closed his eyes. "This is not happening. This is not happening. Wake up, wake up." Another hard slap to the face sent a jolt of white-hot pain through his broken mouth.

The woman standing behind Lucifer glared down at him. Although his vision came in and out of focus, Riley could still make out the disgusted look on her face. "Don't ever close your eyes on Master," she said. "I simply will not tolerate it! Do you understand me?"

"Thank you, child," Lucifer said.

Riley knew he was defeated. "Okay, you win. Now what do you want?"

Lucifer's eyes turned black as coal as he looked at Riley. "I want you both to open your boxes!" he said, pushing the boxes closer to Riley and Jonathan. "There is a present inside."

Riley looked down at a beautiful blue box edged with silver. It triggered a strange sense of warmth and comfort inside him. He took the box in both hands and pulled it onto his lap. Jonathan wiped his face and then took the other blue box and placed it on his lap. He and Riley exchanged quick looks, as if asking one another, *Are you seeing this?* They needed to know what was inside. They tore the paper and lids off their boxes to find a simple silver picture frame inside. Removing the frames, they tossed the boxes on the floor and then gazed at the delicate details of their frame.

"Look deeper," Lucifer whispered into their thoughts.

Following the directive, Riley focused his eyes even more intently as a small image started to drift in and out of focus in his frame.

"Deeper," Riley heard a voice say from inside his head. "Much, much deeper."

"I can vaguely make out something," Riley said. "It's there and then fades out of focus."

"That's not all," Jonathan replied. "There seems to be some kind of writing when I turn the frame ever so slightly."

"Just a little deeper, my dears," Lucifer whispered softly into their thoughts. "It won't be long until you can see it all." Lucifer's fingernails ripped at the leather armrest of his throne as he leaned forward, barely able to control his excitement.

CHAPTER 14

Riley jerked to his feet, water dripping down his face. Granny stood next to him, holding an empty cup in her hand. "I want you to listen to my voice," she said. "Breathe in and out slowly with me." She inhaled slowly then softly exhaled, telling Riley with her eyes to just follow her instructions. Riley could feel his heart racing and knew he was about to hyperventilate. As his legs turned into jelly and he was about to fall face-first, he was brought back around by a rush of peace that poured over him. Opening his eyes, he saw that Granny held one of his arms, keeping him upright until he found his footing.

"You were dreaming a very dark dream, but you are safe now. Do you understand?" Granny continued flooding him with a river of peace. Riley couldn't take his eyes off her. Hoping she was real, he reached out and touched her wrinkled cheek. Satisfied, he took a seat across from Jonathan. He reached across the table, but Jonathan slid his arms off the table onto his lap, not looking at Riley.

The dimly lit cafeteria came back into full view as a streak of lightning flashed across the windows, followed by loud cracks of thunder that shook the window panes. The tempo of the rain increased its rhythmic drumming, but instead of the calming effect from the earlier rain, now it seemed to have a life of its own and was angry. Riley shook his head to make sure he was back where his eyes told him he was. He looked over where Jonathan sat staring at his hands.

"Are you okay?" Riley asked him.

Granny took the seat next to Jonathan. "Jonathan is fighting something internally that he may not ever recover from. Let's give him some time before we dive into what is happening." She looked at Jonathan for a moment and then back at Riley. "Please tell me what you just experienced."

Riley wasn't exactly sure where to start. Pausing to stop his thoughts from bouncing around in his head, he took several more deep breaths and willed himself to concentrate. Finally, he was able to speak of the nightmare he had just come out of.

When he finished recalling the nightmare, he looked at Jonathan, who sat like a statue staring down at his lap.

"I don't know. I can't believe that Jonathan would ever offer me up like that. It was like someone or something had some kind of hold on him."

Jonathan sighed. "Riley, because I can read your thoughts, I also experienced that awful dream. I wish I could have prevented it from happening, but I couldn't." He paused. "We were on a couch," he started. "Lucifer was there, along with a woman named Esperanza. We were each given a small blue box. When we opened them, there was an empty picture frame inside."

From his tone, Riley could tell it pained Jonathan to relay what happened. It showed him at a weak moment, bending and making a deal with the Devil so that he could be rid of Riley. Yet what Riley wished Jonathan would understand was that it was just a bad dream and wouldn't actually happen.

Jonathan let out a soft groan of pain, then began massaging his temples. Dropping his hands to the table, he blew out a long, frustrated breath. "Honestly, I can't remember anything else. It's like you said, it's starting to fade from memory. Either it's something that we aren't supposed to remember or it's being wiped away."

Coming to Jonathan's aid and wanting to show him that they were still on the same side, Riley jumped in. "I imagine, like most dreams, if you don't write them down you forget. In an hour, we will only know that we had a nightmare."

The three sat in awkward silence, wrestling with what to do next. Then Riley spoke. "Granny, please tell me what is happening to Jonathan."

Jonathan looked up for the first time, making eye contact with Riley. Then, as if defeated, he dropped his head and stared at the floor. Jonathan's look was of shame, and it hurt Riley to think he had overstepped. He desperately wanted more than ever to assure Jonathan that he didn't fail him and that he had only asked the question so that maybe he could help.

"He has become infected by what the demons did to him, which has spread a sickness throughout his mind and body," Granny explained. She turned to Riley. "Jonathan called me a few months after he defeated the two demons and told me what had happened. When he came to the part of the cat-of-nine-tails being lashed around his leg and the blade that was broken off in him, I feared that it was just a matter of time. I prayed that maybe his powers wouldn't turn against him, but we now know that was wishful thinking." Granny then placed her hand on Jonathan's leg for reassurance and continued. "The poison from that whip and blade are now running the last part of their course. Jonathan will lose a little more of himself each day. I only know this from prayer and talking with God. He is using me as a vessel since Jonathan can no longer hear Him."

"What? Why can't he—what do you mean?" Riley implored Granny, but deep down he already knew the answer. It was because of him. Jonathan had only been doing his job, looking after him. And now the Devil was close to reaping the reward he most desired. A Fallen.

Granny now broke eye contact and politely asked, "Jonathan, would you mind getting me a cup of coffee?"

Standing without saying a word, Jonathan slowly made his way to the coffee machine. Riley was shocked to see he was partially dragging one leg.

"It's not that he can't hear God, it's his soul choosing not to listen," Granny said quietly. "All his powers, as you like to call them, are now turning darker by the hour. By my estimation, I would say he will no longer be the Jonathan that you once knew—probably in less than a week." She had a deep sadness growing in her eyes and lowered her voice. "I must tell you that eventually he will turn on you and will offer you up to make the unimaginable mental and physical pain he is experiencing go away. He truly will have no choice. That is the trial he is being put through and the path he must follow. I believe the dream you had is your future if you and Jonathan continue to be in each other's lives."

Leaning back in his chair, Riley had so many thoughts playing out in his head.

"How can we help him?"

"Unfortunately, you can't help him. There is a very small chance I may be able to, as a fellow Fallen, but I don't know if it will work. Frankly, Riley, I would rather not discuss it as I'm afraid it may give you false hope."

Riley looked at Jonathan, who was over by the coffee machine holding two cups in his large hands. Granny gave him a nod signaling it was okay to return. Jonathan walked back slowly. Settling into his seat, he placed the cups in front of Granny and Riley. Jonathan offered them an apologetic smile, then reached across and took Riley's hand. The peace that had once come from his touch was completely gone. However, Riley was more than grateful to hold onto it for as long as he could. He looked back at Granny.

"Listen, what happened earlier on the highway when everyone was affected in some way or another, for some reason I wasn't. Jonathan spared me, so surely he still has a little control. Besides, if Jonathan wanted to hurt me, he could have done so. I can help him. I know that I can help him," he said earnestly.

Granny gave him an appreciative smile, reminding Riley of how she had remained by his side with Allison. Throughout all of his angry outbursts and bitterness towards everyone, she not once ever wavered with her compassion. "Riley, I think that is probably going to be the last time Jonathan will be able to protect you from himself. I don't know that for sure, but let's play it safe. For now, I think it is best that Jonathan go far away from you. I will go with him. I've already told my coworkers and the hospital that I will be taking an immediate leave of absence. Quite frankly, they were more than surprised since I haven't taken a vacation in the last thirty years." She smiled. "However, now I am needed elsewhere so my time here has come to an end. It's all I have known for so long, but when one chapter of life ends another begins."

Riley wondered how much she had seen in all the years she had served here. How many thousands of people had she helped during their time of need? They probably had no idea she was an actual Godsend. He could see the pain in Granny's expression. But he also knew there was no changing an angel's mind. He was certain she was far too stubborn to be talked out of something once she had made her decision. It was just such a shame that she felt she needed to say goodbye to this life she had built for herself. But she was set on helping a friend. As if knowing what he had been thinking, Granny laid her hand atop his and smiled, letting him know it was okay.

"Well, I guess the only question now is: What do I do?" Riley said. "I mean, I'm still a marked man and I can't see going back to the lake house just to wait for the Devil to come for me."

Granny smiled at him. "I think something will come along soon enough that you will find comfort in. In the meanwhile, be on your guard and remain safe. Remember everything you have been taught and don't second-guess yourself. We will find you when we can. Now, if you both wouldn't mind waiting outside for me, I would like to say goodbye to a few more colleagues. I won't be long."

As they parted ways, Riley and Jonathan walked out into the drizzling rain and found refuge under the emergency room awning. Riley wanted desperately to grab Jonathan and never let go. They had been through too much to be forced to walk away from one another now. Would Jonathan return? Would he survive? What would become of them? The questions piled up until a female voice broke in.

"Jonathan!" They both turned to find an attractive woman standing behind them. "I don't know if you remember me, but my name is Maggie."

CHAPTER 15

Lucifer wasn't impressed with Legionaries's plan.

"What, exactly, is feeding into the human's dreams going to accomplish?" he mocked. "You're wasting my time."

Holding up his hands in a sign of surrender, Legionaries spoke quickly. "Master, please give me a chance to explain. I will use the tool of fear. What you just saw is only the first part of my plan. Did you see what happened after I released them from the human's dream?"

His question fell on deaf ears. Lucifer only scowled down at him.

"It's a matter of time at this point, Master," Legionaries assured him. "However, with your permission, I will go to Earth to do the rest of my work—I can be much more efficient if I am closer to the problem."

Lucifer decided who was allowed to come and go, and Legionaries was asking politely if he could be excused for the time being. Lucifer wasn't surprised by the request; he knew it would come sooner or later. He had made the mistake of entrusting his two idiot sons with accomplishing the task of ending the human and his Fallen. This time, he would dedicate all of his attention to monitoring the situation.

"Do not fail me, Legionaries," Lucifer growled.

"Yes, Master, I understand. I shall bring them to you."

Legionaries trembled as Lucifer glared at him with his blackened eyes. Then, without another word, he turned and walked out of the room, leaving Legionaries alone. He let out a sigh of relief. Now he needed to get busy. He closed his eyes and focused on a mental image of Riley. There was a loud popping sound that made him cover his ears.

When he reopened his eyes, he found that he was no more than two hundred yards away from the entrance of an emergency room.

An immediate stench made his eyes water. This meant the Fallen was very close. Legionaries looked back at the emergency room entrance and noticed three people standing underneath the awning. He knew exactly who they were—he would soon lay out the next part of his plan to manipulate, capture, and kill them all. He was glad to see how sick the Fallen was now that the poison had almost run its course.

"Thank you, Bryce and Abel, for managing to do one thing right," he said to himself.

Now he would have to focus once more on the task at hand. He trained his ears in the direction of the trio standing outside the emergency room doors to pick up every word they were saying.

CHAPTER 16

Jonathan and the other man turned to face Maggie. Jonathan neither smiled nor gave any other sign of recognition that he knew who she was. But the stranger standing next to Jonathan looked in shock and then disbelief.

"I know it's been a while, but I wonder if you remember me," she said, looking hopefully at Jonathan. "I haven't been able to get you out of my mind." Maggie was aware that she looked and sounded like an obsessed woman. The man standing next to Jonathan looked completely dumbfounded.

With the silence growing between them, the man standing next to Jonathan took the initiative. "My name is Riley," he said. Then looked at her bandaged right hand and offered her his left hand.

Reluctantly, Maggie took the outstretched hand. She noticed he had tears welling in his eyes, ready to slide down his cheeks. "My pleasure, Riley. My name is Mary Allison Gregory, but I go by Maggie." Odd, but she immediately took a warming to Riley and became aware that she was interrupting something. She glanced at Jonathan, who was just staring at her, and then back to Riley.

"Um, I'm so sorry, Riley, but would you mind giving us a moment?" she said as politely as she could while giving a slight side nod toward Jonathan.

"Of course, please, take your time," Riley quickly replied.

"Jonathan, I'll just wait over here." Then he walked away, leaving them alone.

Maggie watched Riley walk off, then looked at the man whom she remembered. He looked different now. Something was wrong. Was he sick? Then, as if confirming her assumptions, Jonathan turned his head and coughed into his arm.

"Are you okay?" Maggie asked. The blue eyes that she saw every day in her thoughts now looked to be a soft gray. "Do you remember that night when you found me in the alley and saved my life? Those . . . those men were going to rape me, maybe even worse," she said with emotion rising in her voice. "You saved my life. And then you made sure I got to the hospital safely, but then—but then you were just gone. I wondered if I would ever see you again. I have searched for over a year to find you," she said, omitting the fact that she had actually turned her life upside down in order to pursue him. Confusion lined her face as a feeling of helplessness found her. She couldn't read the look on Jonathan's face as he stared at her and then looked down.

After a long moment, he finally spoke. "Maggie," he paused. He looked in her eyes. "I do remember you," he said softly. "Of course I do. But my situation is far too difficult to even attempt to explain. I'm glad you are okay. And I would love to sit down and buy you a cup of coffee, but for now I just need to ask you to please just let me go. It's for the best, truly." He looked at the ground again.

"You want me to leave you alone?" Maggie asked in disbelief. "Do you have any idea what has happened to me since that night? I know I sound crazy, and we only met the one time, but my life changed so drastically after our first encounter." Maggie grabbed Jonathan's hand and clutched it like a little girl hoping her parent wouldn't leave her. She knew she had to maintain her composure, but strangely was unable to as she pleaded. "Can't you please talk with me?"

When Jonathan only responded by looking over to where Riley was standing, Maggie understood that her journey had come to an end. It wasn't the ending she had hoped for or felt that she deserved, but she knew it was time to let Jonathan go. Giving Jonathan's hand one final squeeze, Maggie turned and slowly walked away from the hospital.

Reading the confused expression on Riley's face, Jonathan knew he could have handled the situation better. It had been less than a minute since Maggie let go of his hand and now watching her walk away, Jonathan closed his eyes, feeling a new anger begin to build inside him. With the rest of his remaining will power, he shoved the anger back down, knowing that Maggie deserved an explanation. "Okay," he said calmly. "We can sit down for a minute, but only for a minute."

Jonathan watched as Maggie turned to face him and struggled with the allotted time frame before reluctantly agreeing. Jonathan led her over to the closest bench, then practically collapsed under his own body weight when he sat down with a thud, causing the frame to shake for a moment. Maggie followed, but Jonathan felt her eyes judging his current predicament, so he redirected her attention with a question of his own, hoping she wouldn't notice how bad of a state he was really in.

"What happened to your hand?" he said, nodding at the hand she still held clutched to her chest.

"I broke a finger," she responded dismissively. "How are you? You don't look well. Is there something I can do?" Jonathan just looked down at the ground. "Listen," Maggie continued. "I know how strange this must sound, like I'm stalking you, but truly, that's not the way it is. I know I sound desperate and probably came across wrong, but—"

Jonathan put a hand up. "Listen to me, Maggie. I'm glad you are okay, I really am. And you're right, I'm not feeling well, but it's a long story. I think I've found someone who can help. But it means I need to go away. But I need someone to help my friend." He nodded in Riley's direction. "He's been through a rough time and doesn't have anyone else."

"Riley," Maggie repeated, glancing over to where he stood. "Listen, if you need money, I've got plenty of resources and I can find you whatever you need."

"No, no, please," Jonathan said hurriedly. "There's nothing you can do. Just, please, would you help my friend while I'm gone?" Jonathan gave her good hand a squeeze, only to be bit by a quick, burning pain. He hoped his grimace didn't reveal the degree of discomfort he was in. "If I can be healed, then I will gladly sit down and tell you more about myself. But for now, could you just trust me?"

Jonathan could see her confusion and reluctancy to let him go once again. He expected an argument that he was too weak and tired to deal with.

"I will do anything you need, just promise me you will come back," she pleaded, surprising him. She threw her arms around him, holding him in an awkward embrace.

Riley couldn't understand how Jonathan knew the business tycoon, Mary Allison Gregory. He had never mentioned her and seeing them together offered so many unanswered questions. Her face had been on every news outlet imaginable. Even in his small lake town of Potogi, she was such a recognizable figure.

At the grocery store checkout, several of the magazines featured Maggie's face, with similar headlines.

"Where is Mary Allison Gregory?" Riley had remembered commenting, "What do you suppose has become of her?"

Jonathan hadn't replied, busying himself with unloading the rest of the groceries out of the shopping cart.

This brought Riley back to his current situation, as Maggie gave Jonathan a sideways hug, then attempted to pull him to his feet. Jonathan's face twisted into a grimace as he allowed himself to be pulled upright.

"I will come back and we will have that cup of coffee, I promise." He kissed the top of Maggie's head, and limped over to Riley.

Riley pulled Jonathan's head down and whispered, "I love you, Jonathan. Please always remember that." Before Jonathan could reply, Riley saw out of the corner of his eye that Granny was standing only a few feet away and went to her. Taking both of her hands, Riley looked solemnly at Granny.

"This is more than likely the end of our story, isn't it?" Riley asked, hoping it wasn't true.

Granny nodded and gave him a sad smile in response. It took everything Riley had not to break down and fall into her arms. However, he restrained himself and put on a brave face. He looked at Granny and then Jonathan. "I love you both. Thank you for everything you've done for me. I hope you know how important you are to me."

"You are a blessing, Riley," Granny replied. "One day we will meet again."

Jonathan put a hand on Riley's shoulder. "I would have loved to have more time with you, my friend. Just know that you were worth the fall. I would do it all over again. Please forgive me for not being able to save your Allison. Know that I will always carry both of you in my heart."

Riley could no longer hold back the tears as he wrapped Jonathan in what he knew would be their final embrace. *Time is cruel and always constant in its torture,* Riley thought as he let go.

Jonathan put an arm around Granny's shoulder for support. As they turned to leave, Riley saw that his friend had tears falling down his face. Watching them go, Riley whispered, "I am witnessing the death of a Fallen."

CHAPTER 17

I n human form, Legionaries watched from a distance. Granny assisted Jonathan's leave from Riley and Ms. Gregory. He smiled to himself. His plan was falling into place far too easily.

"So that's what became of you, Granny." He wanted to move closer so he could get a better look at how worthless the old woman's life had become. He knew he needed to be patient and stopped himself from following after them.

"Oh, how I would love to be there when you truly cry out for mercy," Legionaries chuckled. "The fires of Hell await your doomed soul—all because of a little betrayal. It is so satisfying watching you shuffle under the weight of that giant Fallen who will soon be by your side in Hell," he mused. "Yes, now that will be a glorious day."

Now for the issue of Riley. Legionaries knew that in order to get close to him he would need to play on sympathy and guilt. The fear would come later. And now with Ms. Gregory inserting herself into the mix, he had the potential to bring one more soul back to Master.

Closing his eyes, Legionaries concentrated on the woman officer who had been injured when Jonathan went borderline insane during that little traffic stop. Several images flashed in his mind until, at last, he saw the officer's name tag.

B. PATTERSON

Legionaries spoke aloud. With his eyes still closed, Legionaries used his telepathy to focus in on where the cop was located. Success! He was delighted to discover he was standing right outside the very hospital she had been taken to. Yes, things were looking up for him. He honed his focus on her location. He could feel the pressure begin to build inside his head, knowing that if he kept this level of intensity up he would pass out. "Come on, just another moment," he whispered. Finally, he located her on the third floor of the hospital.

His vision blurred as he panted and waited for the pressure to subside. Despite being able to walk outside of Hell with all his abilities supposedly intact, Legionaries quickly learned that there was something else at play that limited him where the mortals lived.

When he could finally breathe normally and his vision returned, he cried out: "You have got to be shitting me!" The third floor was where Riley's wife, Allison, had died. He couldn't believe his luck. He couldn't have asked for a better scenario.

Laughing now, he made his way into the hospital and headed straight toward the elevator. Noticing a group of cops around an elderly man, he could overhear them offering words of encouragement.

Ah, this must be that cop's father, he mused. He took a few steps closer.

"Just hang in there, Mr. Patterson," one of the cops said. "Your daughter is going to be all right. She is young and strong . . ."

Blah, blah, blah, Legionaries thought and snorted. He took a seat not far from the group, hoping the cops would take off soon. After a half hour they finally left, assuring the old man everything would work out for his daughter. Legionaries was always amused by these sentiments. *Your child is dying, but it will all work out for the best. You just found out a family member has cancer, but it will all work out for the best.* Or, *the country is heading for war, but it will all work out for the best.* Then they would invoke their god. Ha!

"Excuse me, sir." Someone was speaking to him. Looking up, Legionaries now found the old man, Mr. Patterson, standing before him. The man still had a full set of hair that had turned gray over the years. Green, puffy eyes, and a small-sized body that had lost its fight with gravity as he stood slightly bent over at the waist. "Sorry for interrupting, I just thought I would see if you would like anything from the vending machine."

Legionaries snapped to attention. "Oh, uh, no, there's nothing to apologize for, I was just deep in, uh, prayer." He almost laughed aloud but gave himself a mental kick. He scrambled to his feet, stuck out his hand, and introduced himself. "My name is . . . Luke."

The man took his outstretched hand and shook it. "My name is Griffin Patterson. My daughter is in surgery. I'm just waiting."

"Sorry to meet you under these unfortunate circumstances," Legionaries replied. "I sure could use some fresh air. How about you?" He hoped the guy would take the bait.

"Sure, yes, that's a good idea. But I shouldn't be away very long," Patterson replied as his right hand instinctively went up to pat his left breast pocket. Not finding what he wanted, he dropped his hand back down to his side. Legionaries knew what this gesture meant. Slipping his own hand into his pocket, he produced a pack of cigarettes and held them out.

"I can't seem to quit these things," Patterson said. "When I get completely stressed, it seems to help calm my nerves." He gave a small smile.

"I'm the same way," Legionaries said. "I've tried to quit for over forty years, but after the hellish day I've had I need one more than ever. Shall we?"

The old man nodded, and they turned and walked toward the exit.

How easily humans can be manipulated with just a little bit of addiction, Legionaries thought.

"We'll have to walk a pretty good distance from the hospital for a smoke," Patterson offered.

"The farther the better," Legionaries said. "I really need to walk for a while and hope that my troubles won't be able to find me." He gave a small laugh, hoping to find camaraderie with him. He held out the pack of cigarettes. Patterson eagerly took one and placed it between his lips, sighing with relief even though it wasn't lit.

Must really need a fix, Legionaries mused, then placed one in his own mouth and lit it, not caring that they were only a few feet out of the hospital. Out of the corner of his eye, Legionaries caught Patterson staring at him curiously.

"After the day I have had with the accident on the highway and everything, well, I welcome a confrontation if someone really wants to try to screw with me about rules," Legionaries said. Then for dramatic effect, he inhaled deeply and exhaled through his nostrils.

Patterson nervously looked around as Legionaries forced the lighter into the man's old, arthritic hands. Seeming to give in, he lit up with ease. As they walked farther away from the hospital, Legionaries tried to listen in on the man's thoughts, but they came through like a radio tuned in to an out-of-range frequency. What he could make out was Mr. Patterson asking for his daughter to make it, but then repeatedly hoped he wouldn't have to hear any more hollow, encouraging words. The thoughts became unreadable for a moment before he visibly heard, *God, I hope I can get one or two more cigarettes just to help me through the rest of the night!*

Acting on that thought, Legionaries finished his cigarette, then lit a new one, flipping the old one into the street. Patterson finished his about the same time and then stared at the butt, seemingly disappointed that it had gone so quick.

Legionaries took several long drags, making sure to exhale directly in Patterson's direction. "I can just feel the stress from this day beginning to dissipate. Can't you?"

Patterson's tongue licked at his bottom lip as he watched Legionaries. It was crazy that nicotine had this effect on humans. He could see the guy beginning to squirm. Finally, the old guy couldn't take it anymore.

"Would you mind if I had maybe one more?" Patterson asked.

They were now a couple of blocks away from the hospital, which Legionaries believed was far enough. Nightfall had completely set in and no one else occupied the sidewalks.

"Absolutely, you can," he purred. Then he turned into an alley, hoping Patterson would follow. Legionaries held the pack out to his side and continued walking. "Please keep it. I have another pack in my car."

Taking the pack, Patterson removed another cigarette and lit it, then took a long drag as if it had been days since his last one. Legionaries found that the time was right to say goodbye, but before he could carry out the first step in his plan, a woman's voice interrupted him. It was very small, making him strain to hear. He looked around, but then it stopped. Legionaries stood completely still and closed his eyes. The voice returned, sounding like a chant. Turning off the outside world and focusing only on the woman's voice, he realized she was praying. She was praying for the idiot next to him.

"You all right over there?" Patterson asked.

"Shut up!" Legionaries yelled in the direction of the woman's voice.

Patterson took a few steps back, giving Legionaries an odd look. "Are you okay?" he asked, nervously looking around. "Look, I don't want any trouble, maybe I should—"

In a blur of movement, Legionaries closed the distance between them and now held Patterson by the throat. Looking into the old man's frightened eyes, Legionaries whispered, "Tell Master that you are the first of many gifts to come." Then he gave Patterson's head a jerk, hearing every vertebra in his neck snap at once. His head now hung unnaturally to one side. Legionaries dragged the body over to a trash dumpster. Just then, a woman appeared in front of him, stopping Legionaries from going any further. He knew that this was the guardian angel who had offered up the annoying prayer. Now she stood defiantly before him, her eyes locked on his.

"Whatever you have to say, I am not interested," Legionaries said. "This insignificant man was a simple means to an end."

The angel said nothing. She simply knelt down and placed a kiss on Patterson's forehead. "I am sorry I could not help you. I failed you, my beloved, and wish I could change places with you. I will never forget you, for you were my first." She stood once more, locking eyes with Legionaries. "I pity your kind and the eternity that awaits you." Saying no more, she vanished.

Annoyed by the delay, Legionaries threw back the lid of the dumpster, heaved Patterson's body up over his shoulder, and tossed him inside, letting the lid slam shut. He walked back to the hospital, amused by how easy humans were to manipulate, and frustrated by what the angel had said to him. Back at the hospital, he stepped into the empty elevator. Once the doors closed, Legionaries noticed his marred image in the matte finish. He still carried a large frame but the rest of his appearance was to distorted to make out. He changed his appearance and morphed into the recently departed Mr. Patterson.

All I need to do is sit and wait, he thought. *Eventually, Riley will arrive. I can't wait to see his face when he comes to stand outside the very door where his beloved Allison died.* He laughed to himself as the elevator doors opened to the third floor.

CHAPTER 18

Maggie was unsure how to start the conversation with this complete stranger, Riley. What was his relationship with Jonathan? Did he know who Jonathan was? He had asked her to watch over Riley, but she didn't believe it would go over so well to just tell him that he was now her responsibility. But she also knew they needed to get off on the right foot.

"So, how long have you known Jonathan?" Maggie asked.

Her question brought him out of his daze. "Oh, um, just a little over fifteen months," he said. "I shouldn't keep you. You must be here to get that checked out," He nodded down at her hand.

I guess I can wait a little while longer, Maggie thought. She needed to keep him with her. "Oh, yeah, right," she said and gave him a small smile. "You know, I really hate hospitals. Do you think, maybe, you could go with me? Would you mind?" She prayed he would agree.

As strange as the question was, Maggie was more surprised with Riley's response. "I don't mind at all."

Maggie took the lead and began navigating them through the crowded waiting area of the emergency room over to the nurse receptionist desk. They were greeted by a disgruntled nurse whose nametag read K. Bradford. Before Maggie could ask a question, nurse Bradford spoke in an exhausted tone.

"Fill out these forms front and back, when you have finished bring them back to me. A doctor will see you soon as possible, depending on the severity of your situation." Nurse Bradford handed Maggie a clipboard. Thumbing through the forms with her good hand, Maggie was confused by why there were so many.

"Look, is this really necessary? Can't I just give you my insurance card?" Maggie said, somewhat exasperated. "I don't want to sit here all night." The nurse gave her an indignant look.

"Look, Miss," she said. "We've got a lot of people in here who have already been waiting. We've been overwhelmed by all the people being transported from that accident out on the highway. You're just going to have to take a seat. We'll get to you as quickly as we can."

Before Maggie could respond, Riley stepped forward and quickly intervened. "Not a problem at all," he said, then looked at the name written on the nurses' smocks before continuing. "Nurse Bradford, I'll help her get these filled out right away. Thank you. I know it's been a long day, and probably night, for you," he said, giving her a charming smile.

The nurse sighed and turned back to her computer screen. Riley led Maggie to a spot in the corner where there were two empty chairs. Maggie slumped into a chair, exasperated. She fumbled in her bag and struggled to dig out her wallet with her left hand. She handed the clipboard to Riley with a sigh.

"Sorry," she said. "I'm right-handed, and clearly I can't write, so would you mind—?"

"Oh, of course!" Riley said.

They spent the twenty minutes filling out the paperwork. Riley returned it to the nurse behind the desk. When he sat back down next to her, Maggie leaned her head back against the wall and closed her eyes, massaging the bridge of her nose with her good hand. "I'm sorry," she said, raising her voice to be heard over the noise in the room. "I'm not very good company. It's just been a really bad day."

"It's okay," Riley said.

But it isn't okay, Maggie thought. Her mind was a jumble. She had done a shady deal—paid off Miles Jackson, one of the most corrupt people in the state—for a chance to interrogate the men who had nearly raped and killed her a year ago. And then there was that bizarre dream or hallucination with the mirror and then breaking her finger. She couldn't even remember how that happened. Oh, and then the most incredible part, finding out that the man she'd been searching for throughout the past year might be a guardian angel? It was all just too unbelievable. Who would ever believe her? Now, here she was, sitting in a noisy, overcrowded emergency waiting room with this stranger, Riley. A stranger whom she had promised Jonathan, who also was a stranger, to look after. What had happened to her life? Several people in the waiting room started to notice her, trying to place where they recognized her from. Maggie let her eyes find the floor, not daring to look up at anyone to confirm their suspicions of who she was.

"Tell me how you broke your finger," Riley said, interrupting her thoughts.

"Oh, it's nothing, I was just clumsy," she offered. What else could she say, that some supernatural being appeared in her bathroom mirror and had done this to her? The less said, the better.

Before Riley could say anything more, a voice called out, "Maggie Gregory?"

Wow, that was good timing, Maggie thought as she looked up to see a nurse standing in the doorway to the examination rooms.

She jumped up, relieved that she didn't have to say anything more. Not just yet, anyway. Keeping her head down, she started to walk toward the nurse, then heard Riley.

"Should I wait here for you?" Riley asked.

"Actually, would you mind coming with me?" Maggie said, then whispered, "I just really hate hospitals. It would be nice to have a friendly face nearby." Maggie could tell by his facial expression that he was wrestling with the response. "Will you come?" Maggie asked again.

"Yeah, sorry, I'm coming." He followed Maggie and the nurse and let the doors close behind him.

Once in an examination room, a nurse came in and hooked Maggie up to take her blood pressure. She then removed the bandages around her hand, which was now heavily bruised. "Oh dear," she said. "That does look painful. Are you doing okay?"

"Yeah, I'm okay," Maggie said. "How long do you think before the doctor will come in?"

"Well, we are awfully busy tonight with a major accident that happened a couple of hours ago. We're working as quickly as we can. We've called in a few off-duty docs to help out. Hopefully, someone will be here soon." She turned her attention to the laptop station next to the bed and typed some notes. Then she turned to Maggie and lightly touched her arm. "Just hang tight here for me, okay?"

Maggie tried to engage Riley in some light banter to pass the time, but he wasn't very talkative. Clearly, he had a lot on his mind. Thankfully, it didn't take long for a doctor to come into the examination room. "Ms. Gregory," he said. "I'm Dr. Ramsfeld. It's such a pleasure to meet you, although I'm sorry it's under these circumstances."

"Hello, Dr. Ramsfeld. It's nice to meet you as well," Maggie said. It sounded like he might recognize who she was. She really hoped he didn't want to ask a lot of questions about her or the business. It would make things go so much more quickly if she didn't need to make a lot of small talk.

The doctor said, "So, from the notes it looks like you may have a broken finger." He then reached out and delicately took Maggie's hand in his, concentrating hard on her broken finger. "I can confirm that it is a break just from how the finger is positioned. However, the good news is that I don't believe you'll need surgery. Still, I want to get an x-ray just to give us a better look. Then if that looks good and it's a clean break, we'll bring you back down here and do a splint to immobilize it for six weeks. Whoever put this one on did a great job."

Maggie hoped he wouldn't ask her who had done the splint. That was a story she didn't want to get into.

"Just wait here," the doctor said, "and someone will be in to take you up to x-ray. Then they'll bring you back down here."

"Okay, thank you, Dr. Ramsfeld," Maggie said. "Thank you for seeing me so quickly."

"You're welcome. I'll see you when you're back," he said, giving her a smile and nodding at Riley before leaving the room.

Maggie wondered if her so-called celebrity status had influenced how fast they had gotten to her. Well, she had too much on her mind to worry about it now. She laid her head back and closed her eyes. "Thank you for staying with me, Riley," she said.

"Sure, no problem," Riley replied.

"Are you good friends with Jonathan?" Maggie asked with her eyes still closed.

"Yeah, I am," Riley said. "How do you know him? I don't mean to be rude, but I've spent a lot of time with him and he's never mentioned you before."

Maggie wondered if what Joe Packton said about Jonathan

being a guardian angel was true. This wasn't something she could just ask someone about their friend. She would have to get to know Riley and make him comfortable with her. "Oh, um, well, we met a little over a year ago, probably about the same time you met him, it sounds like. Some guys were giving me a hard time and he came along almost like a knight in shining armor and rescued me. He made sure I was okay, and then he just disappeared. I've spent the last year trying to find him to thank him. I couldn't believe my eyes when I arrived at the ER tonight to have my hand looked at and found him here, practically in the same spot where we parted ways that night."

Riley smiled. "Yeah, that sounds like Jonathan. He's a good guy."

"Riley?" Maggie said in a soft voice. "There's something else—" she paused and looked directly into his eyes. "I found it odd, and I'm not quite certain I should tell you."

Riley looked at her curiously. "What? What is it?"

"Jonathan asked me to look after you. Do you know what he meant?"

Before they could say anything more, an orderly appeared at the door. "Mary Allison Gregory?" she asked, looking up from her clipboard.

"Yes, that's me," Maggie replied, sitting up.

"I'm here to take you to x-ray."

Riley followed closely behind the orderly, telling himself that he needed to be there to support Maggie while she got her hand x-rayed. However, in actuality, he knew that it was time to let go of a little more of his past.

As they ascended, he closed his eyes, trying to take his mind someplace else. Moments later, the elevator dinged again. He opened his eyes and watched the doors open. He realized they had arrived at the third floor—the floor where his beautiful Allison had died. To anyone else it was just another hospital floor with the white-tiled floor, walls painted light green, and the smell of powerful disinfectants. However, for Riley, this was the place where his terror and sleepless nights began. Granny, the kindly nurse who had looked after Allison, had been his only strength and constant. She helped him prepare to tell Allison goodbye. He thought his own life was over. But then he met Jonathan. And now, he was gone too.

A swift feeling of dread swept over him as a wheel rolled over his foot, making him stumble. He put his arm out to catch himself but fell to the floor, wincing as he reached back and touched his foot. The orderly had pushed Maggie's gurney out of the elevator and looked back. "Sir, are you okay?" she said and quickly pushed the elevator button to keep the doors open.

"I'm okay," Riley said, getting gingerly to his feet, trying to hide his discomfort. "Just kind of clumsy, I guess." He knew that wasn't the case. His mind immediately went to the demons he and Jonathan had encountered months before. *Oh God*, he thought. *Are they back?*

As the orderly turned the gurney and proceeded down the hall, Riley felt Maggie's eyes studying him. The orderly positioned her gurney outside a door marked, *x-ray*.

"Okay, Maggie," said the orderly. "One of the technicians will come out for you when they're ready, and when you're done, I'll get you back downstairs."

"Thank you," Maggie said as the young woman walked away. Then she turned and looked at Riley with a look of concern on her face. "Riley, are you okay?"

Riley walked closer to her, limping as he did, and nodded. "Yeah, I think I'm just overly tired. Like I said, I was just clumsy."

Strangely, Maggie placed her good hand to his chest and held it there for a long moment. A tear fell from Riley's eye, but he wiped it away before it ran down his face. "You know, I think I just need to take a short walk. But I'll come right back and will wait for you by the elevators." Without waiting for her to respond, he turned, ducking his head, and walked with ease back down the hallway. A moment later, the door to the x-ray room opened and the technician stepped out.

"Mary Allison Gregory?" she said.

"Yes," Maggie replied, still watching Riley walk away.

CHAPTER 19

Riley was glad for a chance to be by himself. His mind was racing with thoughts and questions—and fear of the unknown. Where had Granny and Jonathan gone after they left the hospital? What was going on with him and this brewing anger that was so unlike the Jonathan he knew? Could Granny help him? He was terrified that he may never see his friend again. There were just so many unknowns. And now, with the incident in the elevator, he had passed it off as clumsiness to Maggie, but he knew better. There had been something else in that elevator with them.

And then there was Maggie herself. Obviously, Jonathan knew her, but who was she? Outside of being the number one sought-after person by the media. Why had Jonathan never mentioned her to him? He knew that she was concerned and wanted to help if he would allow her, but they were strangers. Besides, he would only be placing her in harm's way. Why had Jonathan asked for her help? Had he forgotten that everyone they came into contact with ended up severely wounded or dead?

Then again, Jonathan was no longer himself. Who would have ever thought that he could actually get sick? Riley contemplated this for a moment, then remembered what Jonathan had said about no longer being Allison's guardian angel: he had the choice to return to Heaven or fall to Earth to take care of Riley. If he chose to become a Fallen, he would give up many of his angelic powers. Riley had to remind himself that as a Fallen, Jonathan was vulnerable to physical harm. It was all too much for Riley to take in.

Knowing he wasn't going to find any answers in the hallways of the hospital, he returned to the x-ray department, but Maggie wasn't done yet, so he walked to the elevator bay to wait for her there. A moment later, as he was deep in thought, an elderly man walked up next to Riley and asked politely, "Are you coming or going?"

His question brought Riley out of his thoughts, and he realized he had stopped directly in front of the elevator doors. "Oh, sorry. I guess I do look kind of strange with my back to the elevator."

"Thought did cross my mind," the man said with a smile. "I figured maybe you were stalling, as I did earlier today when I learned that my daughter had been brought here. I drove like a maniac to get here then found myself stuck in all that mess out on the highway after that bad accident. Once I arrived at the hospital, I couldn't seem to move and found myself doing what you're doing."

"I was on the highway when the accident happened too," Riley replied. "How is your daughter doing?"

The man looked down at the floor and went quiet for a moment. "Well, she was brought in with what the paramedics believed was a concussion. Turns out that her brain had begun to swell, which led to calling in a neurologist. They took her in to emergency surgery to do whatever it is they do to relieve pressure. Now she is in the ICU on this floor."

"Oh, I'm really sorry," Riley said.

"No change yet. They put her in a medically induced coma until the swelling subsides. I keep hoping that she will just wake up and walk out the door with me, but the doctors have told me that—" Not able to continue, the man broke down.

Offering sympathy, Riley placed a hand on the man's shoulder, all the previous questions he had been struggling with now long forgotten. It was as if God had placed this stranger in his path to remind him that no matter how big a problem may seem, that He was always in control.

The man looked over at Riley. "I am so sorry to burden you with my troubles. I just wish my wife were here so I had someone to lean on," the old man said, shaking his head. "But it would break her heart to see our daughter in this state."

"Would you like to sit down?" Riley asked, gesturing to a nearby bench.

The man nodded. When they sat down, he pulled a handkerchief from his pocket, blew into it, then returned it back to his pocket. Riley thought back to how his dad did the same thing. Riley always found it disgusting when he saw him do it, but now it was strange how much he cherished that memory. He hadn't thought about that in years.

"Sorry for you to have to be my shoulder when we don't even know each other's names," the old man said, not quite able to meet Riley's eyes.

"I am glad to be your shoulder," Riley assured him. "I'm just waiting for a—a friend. She's getting an x-ray."

"Well, my name is Griffin. Griffin Patterson," the man said, offering his hand. Riley shook it and introduced himself. Again, a small pulse of electricity, or maybe it was adrenaline, shot into him, immediately leaving after their hands separated. Riley felt a jolt of great energy for a moment, and then the next he was completely drained.

"Where were you on the highway?" Patterson asked. "It took

me a couple of hours to get here from the detour through all the side streets and traffic lights."

Riley shook his head, trying to snap himself back out of the sudden sleepiness. Just as quickly as it arrived, it was now gone, making him wonder if it had even happened. Knowing what little he did about the paranormal, Riley became suspicious of Mr. Patterson, now that this jolt had happened twice in a short amount of time. Then he felt silly for jumping to conclusions, since Mr. Patterson had just opened up to him about his daughter. "I was actually one exit up from the hospital."

"Oh, how were you not affected? I heard that the police traced the point of origin about half a mile from here. They found one spot that wasn't disturbed at all, as if something, maybe a vehicle, had been sitting there. Everything around that spot had been completely destroyed. Apparently, everyone within a mile radius seemed to have some kind of medical issue. The news is reporting there was some kind of lightning strike that hit the ground and caused an earthquake. Can you believe that?"

Riley felt his mouth go dry. "I—I'm not sure why I wasn't affected," he heard himself say, worried that his trembling voice betrayed him.

The old man eyed him a moment too long. "Well, thank goodness you made it out safely."

"Where was your daughter when this happened?" Riley replied, finding a bit more control over his voice.

"My daughter is a police officer. Her cruiser was parked right behind the area that hadn't been touched by the devastation. I was told she had informed dispatch that she was making a routine traffic stop. After that she was unreachable, and then all the dispatch lines were flooded, reporting a strange event taking place in that very location."

Riley felt his palms and forehead break out in a cold sweat. "Your daughter is a police officer?"

"Yes, she's been on the force for six years now. Couldn't have been prouder when she graduated. I never regretted her decision to help protect and serve this great community. Only now, of course, I'm terribly conflicted. I am a father after all." He sniffled and reached for his handkerchief again, blowing his nose. "The memories just keep flooding back. I remember when she first learned to crawl. All the diaper changes. All the late nights when she was colicky and I'd walk the halls hoping she would just sleep. I remember the first time she told me she loved me as she wrapped her arms around my neck. And teaching her to drive. Then she was off to college. Oh, it goes so quickly, Riley."

Riley remembered that the officer's badge had read PATTERSON. This was her father. He felt a flood of guilt pour over him, knowing that Jonathan was responsible for this man's daughter being hurt and now lying in a hospital near death. He wanted to apologize to him, to explain what happened, but it was too surreal, too wild a story.

He cleared his throat. "Griffin, I'm truly sorry about your daughter." Down the hall, a nurse was wheeling Maggie in their direction. "Listen, I've got to go, but if you ever need to talk, this is my cell phone number." He pulled out his wallet and handed the man one of his business cards. "Call me anytime day or night, okay?"

"I appreciate you just hearing me out, Riley, thank you. One can always use another friend." They shook hands, except this time Riley didn't feel a surge of energy passing between them.

Leaving the old man on the bench, Riley walked to the elevator as the orderly swiped her badge at the control panel. He smiled at Maggie as he stepped in and they followed. Riley needed time to reflect on what he and Jonathan had done to Mr. Patterson's daughter. He closed his eyes and leaned his head back against the wall, hoping Maggie would understand by this gesture that he had no interest in conversation. Both her and the orderly seemed to pick up on his mood as silence became deafening on the ride down.

CHAPTER 20

Crammed into Granny's small car, Jonathan was relieved to finally be out of the city and out in the countryside. His thoughts were on Riley, whom he wasn't sure he would ever see again. To have come so far, only for it to end like this, simply wasn't fair. At least if he was gone, Riley wouldn't have to take care of him. Jonathan couldn't bear that. It was supposed to be the other way around. This was one more way he had failed Riley, just as he had in failing to protect Allison.

Sweat was pouring down Jonathan's forehead. "Is this air conditioner working?" he said with an edge in his voice. When Granny didn't reply, he rolled down his window and took several deep breaths. "The air outside is cooler than in this piece of junk!" he said angrily. "Is this really the best you can do?"

Granny slowed and then pulled off onto the shoulder. Jonathan waited for her to reprimand him. "This spot holds bittersweet memories for me," she said. "Would you like to walk around for a bit and enjoy the scenery?"

Not waiting for him to reply, she got out of the vehicle, crossed over to his side, and opened his door. Still frustrated, Jonathan stepped out, wondering what Granny was up to.

They were now a couple of hours away from the city. Although the scenery of dark green meadows and rolling hills was beautiful, it didn't improve Jonathan's mood. Granny listened patiently to his rants and didn't interrupt or scold him for the foul language and abusive tones that were a product of his uncontrolled frustration. She recognized that Jonathan was sick to the point that he could no longer distinguish between right and wrong.

"What are we doing here? I thought you were going to help me," Jonathan seethed.

"Walk with me Jonathan," Granny said, slipping her small hand into his and lightly pulling. Jonathan started to pull his hand away from her, but her grip was stronger than he expected. Her grip tightened, and with it came a flood of warmth and peace.

"The reason this place is special but painful for me is because this is where I lost my human, Cristal," Granny began. "I wasn't given the luxury of spending more time with her as you were with Riley. It took less than a month for tragedy to find us. Cristal died right in front of me as I begged for her forgiveness. While Lucifer didn't do the deed himself, he did show up after I had been beaten into submission by one of his demons. After Cristal had been ripped from me and taken out of this world, I wanted it all to be over with. I remember Lucifer mocking me as I crawled on the ground, broken, wanting to touch Cristal once more."

Hearing the agony in Granny's voice as she talked about the painful memory silenced the rage within Jonathan, replaced by overwhelming sadness. No longer able to look directly at her, Jonathan dropped his head in seek of solace among the blades of green grass beneath him.

"Shame doesn't begin to describe how I felt," Granny said, shaking her head. "In my defeat I asked Lucifer to kill me—begged, actually. I was so distraught that I had failed so easily. He placed his hands atop my head and started chanting. I felt what little life I had left begin to slip away. But then he suddenly let go of me and began coughing uncontrollably. After he had control of himself again, he gave me a look that still haunts me, though not as much as what he said to me."

Granny stopped walking and released Jonathan's hand. The peace left at once, replaced by pain that immediately sent Jonathan crashing to the ground. His whole body felt like it had been set ablaze, causing him to cry out for mercy. As his vision blurred, Jonathan knew he was on the verge of passing out until Granny's distant voice broke through, rescuing him from the darkness.

The physical pain was crippling, but seemed manageable as he listened to Granny talk about her past. As though completely unaware that he was no longer holding her hand, she took two more cautious steps away from him. She knelt, running a hand over a spot on the ground, leaned down, and actually kissed it before rising once more.

"Lucifer told me that the power I willingly gave to him was my downfall and that I now belonged to him. He said he would welcome me into Hell once I tasted death, all because in my darkest hour I had asked for him to end my life."

Jonathan was shocked. He had only ever seen Granny as a pillar of strength. "Why did you continue to serve God if you thought you were destined for Hell?"

"Do you think the souls who are trapped in Hell cease to pray?" she asked.

Jonathan shuddered at the thought.

"In the beginning," she said, "I was so scared that I prayed continuously, begging God to hear my cry to be given one more chance. However, my connection seemed to no longer exist no matter how much I begged. The sounds of praise that resound through Heaven were absent to me until you showed up in the hospital that night with Allison." Granny paused and smiled at him. "That's when I heard a glimpse of what I once knew. Our

Father whispered to me in that moment: 'My good and faithful servant, I have and always will love you. Never question what you mean to me.'"

She stopped and looked at Jonathan. "You see, that was my trial. I was basically in Hell even though I never occupied it. I was tested by the Devil, who is the king of lies, and overcame him because I always believed that I would see Heaven once again. But while I waited, I wanted to be of some kind of service while I was here. That's why I became a nurse. I believed that's where I was needed most."

Even though the pain he felt was intensifying, Jonathan smiled at Granny. She was better than he would ever be because of how she handled the trial that was forced upon her. "You are the definition of purity," he said as he gazed at her. "I have never met anyone like you."

Granny just smiled up at him.

"I am honored to have known you," Jonathan said, returning her smile.

"Come sit over here," Granny said, taking him over to her car and tapping the hood. Jonathan obeyed. She placed her hand on his injured leg. A warming sense of peace came immediately, pushing out all the pain.

"Close your eyes, Jonathan. I want you to block out everything and just feel yourself breathe in and exhale slowly, and then I want you to listen."

He closed his eyes and focused on his breath. He breathed in and then out. And then again, and again. There was nothing other than the sound of his own breath. Then he heard soft voices in the distance. They grew louder and louder until he could make out the words of a song. He could distinguish individual male and female voices. The praise eventually became so intense that

Jonathan smiled at what he once could hear before his sickness had taken hold of him.

Someone took his right hand and kissed the back of it. He opened his eyes, believing he would see Granny. But it was his Allison standing before him, smiling. He felt a lump in his throat. He couldn't believe his eyes. Was this a dream?

"Jonathan," she said gently. "Yes, it's me. And I know who you are. Thank you for being my guardian angel and watching over me." She pulled his head down and kissed him lightly on the forehead. "I will always love you, Jonathan." And she faded from view.

Tears flooded his eyes. Then he heard a soft whisper from the voice he had longed to hear. "I have not forgotten you, my son. I will be with you all of your days."

Jonathan was just about to cry out when he heard a cough that brought him back to himself. When he opened his eyes, Granny was on the ground several feet away from him, coughing so violently that when she pulled her hand away from her mouth, droplets of blood stained her palm. Jonathan rushed to her side.

"It's okay," he said. "Just try to catch your breath." He patted her softly on the back. As he looked into her eyes, he could see that Granny didn't look worried or confused. Jonathan held her in his arms. Her eyes had gone from their normal bright blue to a dull gray. Her breathing became more labored.

"I am so cold," she said weakly. "Would you help me back to the car?"

He scooped her up into his arms and stood. He felt as strong as he ever had. He was amazed to find that the crippling pain in his leg was gone. Looking down at his beautiful friend, he saw her condition was rapidly worsening. Beads of sweat formed at her brow and she shuddered. Arriving at the car, Jonathan opened the door and placed Granny in the passenger seat. He hurried to the driver's side, asking God for help.

Granny spoke in a strained voice. "Please, just take me to my home. There's nothing in this world that can help me." Jonathan knew she was right, but he hated it. He didn't want to lose her. He held her hand tightly and got back on the road. As the landscape blurred by the tears in his eyes, he realized that he was no longer sick. He felt his strength coming back. But why now?

"There is no need to hurry," Granny said. "I would like to look at the scenery once more, and enjoy the smell of the outdoors before this chapter comes to a close for me."

Jonathan wished that the physical pain would become his once again, instead of having to watch this great angel suffer on his behalf. "Granny, I don't want it to end like this."

She let her arm rest on his. "I knew what I was doing when I healed you," she whispered. "I will finally taste death, and I just ask that you stay with me until the end. Please consider this the last request of an old friend."

Jonathan looked over with tears on his face and saw Granny's eyes pleading with him. He nodded his head.

"Okay, I'll take you home."

CHAPTER 21

O nce back in the emergency room, it didn't take long to get Maggie's broken finger put back into a splint. Dr. Ramsfeld said the x-ray showed a clean break. She would wear the splint for six weeks and then see her internist to check that it was healing properly.

Riley contemplated how to remove Maggie from this equation. By simply being near him, he felt certain her life could be at risk too. The thought kept running over and over in his mind that anyone who got close to him was eventually hurt or killed. He thought about the quaint little lake community where he and Jonathan had spent the last year together and how his presence had changed it forever. Two of his friends had been killed there. And now the lives of dozens of innocent people had been forever altered by that horrible incident on the highway. Unbelievably, it wasn't at the hands of the Devil or his loyal demons, but rather his best friend.

He looked over at Maggie and gave her a small, forced smile. "I'll see you outside," he said. However, he didn't plan to hang around. It would be best if she never saw him again. Before she could answer, Riley slipped out of the room and hurried for the exit.

With Maggie's hand now splinted, Dr. Ramsfeld scribbled out

a pain prescription and handed it to her. Without offering an apology, Maggie grabbed the prescription and ran out of the room, leaving him shaking his head. Maggie made her way to the exit near the ambulance bay. She was forced to a stop by an ambulance pulling up. Making her way around it, she frantically scanned the parking lot but saw no sign of Riley. It had only been a couple of minutes, but he had already vanished into the night. Her heart sank.

"Not now, not like this, this wasn't the plan!" she cried out. Her year-long search now seemed to have been in vain. Why hadn't she thought to get Riley's cell phone number, or last name, even a damned address! *I can't go through another wasted year of putting my life on hold for another search*, she thought.

Collapsing onto the same bench where she had last seen Jonathan, Maggie placed her head in her hands and began cursing her ignorance, which broke into loud sobbing. Her breathing quickened, causing her to gasp for her next breath as her world closed in around her. She frantically pulled at the collar of her blouse, which suddenly felt too constricting.

A few pedestrians hurried past. As she looked up, she saw a young boy all alone across the parking lot, pointing his finger at her and laughing. Maggie's vision began to blur from the tears and lack of oxygen. As she looked at him, his face began to change. His mouth became disfigured, then grew so wide that he looked like a cartoon character. Knowing that she was hallucinating, Maggie attempted to cry out for help but made no sound. She began tearing at her collar to stretch it even wider.

"He's coming for you, Maggie," the boy teased her, in a high tenor voice. "He's going to chew on your face, and he'll bring you down to where I live so I can play with you."

Maggie found her voice and let out an ear-piercing scream as the boy trudged toward her, dragging his left leg behind him.

Maggie tried to stand up, but she had no control over her body. The boy was now ten feet away, then in a blink he was directly in front of her. Small worms crawled all over his face. They wriggled underneath his skin.

"Won't be long now, Maggie; not long at all. He's not far from you. He tried to warn you." He looked at her bandaged hand and sneered. "Do you want to learn how hard the damned can bite?"

Maggie quickly pulled her splinted hand to her chest, but the boy snatched it first. His tongue protruded from the side of his deformed mouth and began licking the parts of her exposed hand in a slow methodical movement. Then he stopped and grinned up at her. Maggie saw pure evil staring back at her. She tried to pull her hand away, but the boy's strength was far greater than her own. He opened his mouth wide and then bit down hard. Maggie's blood shot out, spraying her. The boy's eyes bulged cartoonishly. He winked at her before his eye popped out, sending a jelly-like substance onto her blouse with little worms wiggling back and forth in search of their next host. Maggie swiped furiously at her blouse to get rid of them. Then darkness overtook her.

Now she heard a man's voice but couldn't make out the words. Someone was lightly patting the side of her face. "Wake up, Maggie. You're okay, just listen to my voice and focus on your breathing. In and out, in and out. Nice and slow."

Her lungs burned as if she had been sprinting. She moved her head from side to side, trying to open her eyes, but a bright light flashed in front of them.

"Just listen to my voice; just inhale and exhale. I want you to feel more relaxed and calmer with every breath."

Maggie tried slapping at the light.

"She's coming around," the voice said.

When she could finally open her eyes, black dots clouded her vision. Blinking several times, Maggie could finally make out the face of the person who had been speaking to her.

"Do you know where you are?"

Still not in full control, Maggie answered, "The emergency room entrance of a hospital. I met an angel here not more than a few hours ago."

People began to chuckle. Blinking hard, her eyes finally focused.

"Wow, I've never been called an angel before," the voice said. Others around her chuckled again.

"No, I mean I really met an angel," Maggie persisted.

"She's okay. Give us some room, please," the voice said.

"Riley?" Maggie said, attempting to sit up.

"Whoa, let's go a little slower! Don't need you moving too quickly," Riley said.

It really was Riley. Maggie was angry.

"Why would you run off and leave me!" she yelled. "Do you have any idea what I have been through? I've been searching for over a year to find Jonathan. The moment I do, he asks me to look after you and then disappears on me again. I don't even know you!"

"Well, it seems that you're feeling much better now, so let me help you up."

"I don't need or want your help!" Maggie barked. She quickly stood up, only to find that the ground shifted underneath her, propelling her once again into darkness.

Now that he was outside, Riley quickened his pace toward the direction of his truck parked a few blocks away. Each passing step brought with it a sense of dread, telling him that he was making a coward's choice by leaving Maggie behind, without so much as an explanation as to why. Feeling guilty, Riley tried to rationalize his behavior.

I am doing the right thing, and I shouldn't feel guilty for being the only sane individual of our group, outside Granny. This situation was forced upon me because Jonathan was obviously too sick to think clearly. Besides, I am doing both Maggie and Jonathan a huge favor by walking out. One day they will both thank me for being the level-headed, considerate person that I am.

His argument fell flat. His pace slowed until he was standing still, only a block away from his truck. Looking down at his boots for answers, Riley thought of a bible verse that his father had always quoted. He said it more than once, any time Riley began to complain about something not going his way.

"Cast all your anxieties on him, because he cares for you."

Riley smiled, knowing that if his dad was still alive he would tell him this word for word. Turning around, Riley walked more calmly back to the hospital, hoping that Maggie would understand why he had tried to leave her. Hopefully he would be able to convince her to stay away despite Jonathan having asked her such a foolish request, that most certainly would lead her down a dangerous, painful path.

A few minutes later, as Riley approached the emergency room entrance, a woman who looked a lot like Maggie sat on an outside bench. Riley wasn't certain it was her until the woman lifted her bandaged hand in what appeared to be a wave. Returning the wave, Riley thought, *Well, least we are being cordial to one another.*

With only twenty feet separating them, Riley strategized how to begin what would surely be an awkward conversation. A simple apology would not be sufficient and Riley wasn't sure about how much to tell her, since his goal was to convince Maggie that it was in her best interest to stay away.

Drawing closer, Riley opened his mouth to speak until

Maggie interrupted his line of thought, slapping at something on her blouse. *Must be a bug,* Riley reasoned, until he realized how ghostly white Maggie had gone. Her expression was one of terror as her body went completely rigid. When he rushed over to her, Maggie looked directly at him before her eyes rolled back, revealing the whites of her eyes.

Catching her before she went face-first into the ground, Riley carried her to a nearby bench, wondering what she meant by Jonathan asking her to look after him. Why would he do that? He decided it might be best to try to explain himself to her, although she was a total stranger. But then again, the last year had been nothing short of crazy.

Coming back around, Maggie rubbed at her temples as Riley once more coaxed her back through the breathing exercises. When she was better, Maggie gave him a hateful look and continued where she had previously left off. "Explain yourself right now!"

"Okay, okay," Riley said, trying to calm her. "Maggie, I need you to listen without interrupting. Can you do that?"

She shrugged her shoulders.

He began. "You know the Jonathan that once existed. He's changed a lot. He's very sick and will probably never be the same. I've tried my best to help, but really, there's nothing I can do." Riley paused as he thought about the poison those demons had unleashed on his friend, breaking him down. Taking in several breaths to keep his composure, Riley's voice broke as he struggled to continue. "He is sick and rapidly falling apart because of me." He stopped there. He couldn't tell her any more than that.

Maggie listened patiently and then looked at him with a straight face as if nothing he said would deter her.

"Seriously, Maggie, you don't want to be involved. The

only reason I came back was because I believed I owed you an explanation. I'm glad I did because you were having a severe panic attack. So, please, it's for the best that we part ways. I'm not going to hold you to agreeing to look after me. Okay?"

"No," Maggie answered firmly. "That is not going to happen."

Now Riley was convinced she was stubborn, and possibly even slightly insane.

"You have no idea what's happened to my life since I first encountered Jonathan," she said. "That night he came to my aid? Those guys in the alley weren't just giving me a hard time, like I told you before. They were about to rape and kill me. I've never been so scared." She paused as tears welled in her eyes. Then she looked at Riley again. "But then this giant of a man came along and threw them off me. I didn't know what to think. At first he terrified me, but then he assured me he would do me no harm. And he made sure I got out of there safely. He even insisted I go to the hospital to get checked out. And then he just disappeared. I've been searching for him ever since to thank him."

Riley watched fresh tears come to the surface as Maggie paused to catch her breath and get herself back under control. Then she looked at him hard. "Riley, I turned my entire company over to my best friend to manage because I've become so obsessed with finding Jonathan. I don't know why. I've never done anything like that before. I have alienated everyone in my life. So don't sit there and tell me to walk away as if all of this is anything resembling normal. My life will never be normal again. Those days are behind me. I am in this no matter what you say, or wherever you think you can run off to. I will find you. Believe me, if I can find Jonathan, I can find you. Now, I don't want to spend another year of my life doing that. But I will, Riley; so help me I will."

This time the look Riley gave her was empathetic. However, he also knew he had made the wrong decision in returning. He was not going to be able to convince her to stay away.

"Riley," she begged, "please don't shut me out. I am not some extravagant rich girl looking for a thrill ride. When Jonathan came into my life, it all changed for me as I am sure it did for you. So, please, don't walk away. Please let me help." She reached over and took his hand in hers, staring directly into his eyes. "I don't know where this road will lead, but I want to be along for the journey."

Still holding her hand, Riley broke eye contact and looked back at the ground. He knew this was a mistake, but clearly he didn't have much choice in the matter. "Okay, Maggie, you win. Just remember I warned you. I don't know why Jonathan invited you into my life—I'm just sorry that he did. If we do this, you need to trust me and you need to do as I tell you. Do you understand?"

Riley could tell that his words were beginning to create a sense of fear in Maggie, as a worried expression drifted across her face only to be replaced a moment later by her confident tone. "You know, this could be interesting." She smiled. "I've never taken orders from anyone. I'm always in charge, but okay, we'll do it your way."

"No, Maggie." Riley now looked directly at her. "This will definitely not be interesting. You may think that now, but eventually you will realize that Jonathan actually placed you in harm's way. Look, I can't explain it all to you now. I'll do everything I can to protect the both of us, but that is the reality we're dealing with."

His eyes bore into her until she had to look away, watching her as she wrestled with the question of what she was getting herself into.

Several minutes of silence passed between them until Maggie held up her injured hand. "Looks like the danger you speak of has already found me."

Riley shook his head and replied in a defeated voice, "A broken finger is the least of your problems. I just hope I don't fail you the way I have everyone else in my life."

CHAPTER 22

L egionaries transported himself directly from the third floor of the hospital and straight into Griffin Patterson's home. He shed the old man's clothing and morphed back into his normal human form. Upon seeing his reflection in the hall mirror, something seemed off. Slowly turning his head from side to side and leaning forward into the mirror for a closer look, he saw something odd about his eye color. There now seemed to be a red tinge to it.

A pain formed in his temples, interrupting his thoughts. Reaching up with both hands, he began to massage the sides of his head, only to find that the harder he massaged the more the pain seemed to amplify. He stopped, but the pain continued to intensify. The pounding became so extreme that his legs buckled and he collapsed helplessly onto the floor. Legionaries pressed the palms of his hands against the sides of his head, hoping to stop his skull from opening up. He curled into a fetal position, whimpering for mercy.

"Legionaries!" a voice thundered, causing him to tremble. When he opened his eyes, he saw dark circles that blocked his vision.

"I have just given you a taste of what will come if you ever try to ignore me again," the voice said.

"Master, I would never ignore you," Legionaries groaned. "I didn't know this is how we would communicate."

"Well, now you know to listen for a soft ping inside that thick head of yours. If you don't answer immediately, the pain will grow until it cripples you where you stand."

Legionaries knew this could be counterproductive—in the middle of luring Riley and Maggie into their own personal place in Hell, only to have to stop and give Master a damned update. As soon as the thought occurred, Legionaries wanted to take it back. He knew that Master could tap into his thoughts at any time. He held his breath as seconds passed.

"Well, what have you accomplished?" Master asked, clearly irritated.

Surprised that the pain hadn't returned, Legionaries quickly updated Lucifer, sparing no detail of what he had accomplished. Once he finished, he wondered if Master had heard his other thoughts.

"All right. Go ahead with your assignment," Lucifer replied. "And don't forget—listen for the ping," he instructed, as if he were talking to a child. Another jolt of pain hit Legionaries between the ears, though it wasn't nearly as bad as the last one. Lucifer left his thoughts without another word. However, Legionaries felt the sensation that something was now missing from inside his head. It was as if the fear that usually accompanied his thought process, anytime he was around or heard from Lucifer, was now missing.

He wondered how his thoughts hadn't betrayed him. Every soul in Hell was under control. No one was given any sort of freedom, let alone the ability to actually think for themselves. Perhaps Master had decided to give him a longer leash. Or maybe—he was afraid to even think it—freedom? Or could it be that his powers were growing? He shook his head. *No, don't get ahead of yourself*, he thought. It wasn't so long ago that Lucifer had locked him in that damned cell and had him torn apart by his hounds bit by bit.

One thing Legionaries knew for certain was that he would never rule Hell or be able to inflict the kind of torture that Master had unleased on him for thousands of years. Still, he wondered what it might be like for the tables to be turned. He allowed the thought to run around in his head for just one moment before willing it away. Those were dangerous thoughts to entertain.

Getting back to his feet, Legionaries took a walk through the rest of Patterson's house. It was small, yet everything seemed to have a place. *I guess Mr. Patterson was a tidy man*, Legionaries mused. Then a photo on a nearby table caught his eye. It was Patterson down on one knee next to some massive wall. Looking at it more closely, he saw that the old man was crying as he held a hand against the wall. *Why would anyone want a picture of that?* Legionaries wondered. Wasn't the idea of photos to commemorate times of happiness in one's life? Giving it no more thought, he slapped the picture frame face down on the table and went to explore the rest of the house, only to be interrupted by the doorbell.

Ignore it, Legionaries thought, but then changed his mind. *What if it was Lucifer trying to trick him?* He rushed to the door and quickly transformed himself into Patterson's image before jerking the door open. He looked out at a small, middle-aged woman.

"Yes, Master?" Legionaries quickly said, fully expecting that Lucifer had taken on another form. The woman looked up at him with a quizzical look on her face. Legionaries could feel that the energy surrounding her was not that of Lucifer. Surprisingly, he was able to tap into the woman's thoughts quite easily:

I thought this might happen, given the strain of his daughter suffering such a grave injury. Griffin has gone through so much. Lord, how can I help him, especially if he goes back to drinking? That road was hard enough the first time.

So, our Mr. Patterson has two vices: alcohol and nicotine! Legionaries grinned, then remembered he was supposed to be deeply worried about his daughter.

"Hello, Griffin. It's me, Pastor Beth," the small woman said in the sweetest voice. "Are you all right, dear? I know you've had a terrible shock. I thought I would drop by to see what I might do to help."

"Oh, yes. I'm so sorry," Legionaries quickly responded, trying his best to sound meek and vulnerable. "I take it you've heard."

She eyed him a moment longer. "Yes, I thought I should come by and check in on you. Is now a bad time?"

Legionaries couldn't contain his smile as an evil idea came to him. "Now is a perfect time. Won't you please come inside?" He pulled the door back, hoping she'd take the bait.

"Thank you," she said and walked in somewhat cautiously.

Once she was inside, Legionaries slammed the door behind them, watching with amusement as the pastor jumped and put a hand to her chest.

"How about a drink?"

"Yes, water would be fine, thank you." She dropped her hand back to her side and composed herself.

"Water it is. Now, please have a seat in the living room," Legionaries said, pointing a finger toward the couch.

Pastor Beth gave him another suspicious look, making Legionaries want to snatch the life right out of her. Instead, he headed to the kitchen. Sure, he would be breaking the rules and going beyond Master's strict instructions, but he felt like having a little fun. Why not put a little doubt in the good pastor's head? He filled a glass with water and headed back to the living room.

"Here you are," he said, handing his guest a glass before seating himself in an adjacent recliner.

"I have no words to put you at ease in this difficult time, Griffin," Pastor Beth said. "But I do know that your daughter loves her job and has been a devoted Christian. She once told me that the proudest moments in her life were becoming a police officer and getting you to come to church with her. And I must say, it's truly remarkable how your life has changed in the past few months, being able to finally reconnect with her after so many years estranged from one another. I know Vietnam, um— changed you, but God is bigger than all of our hurt."

"Really? You honestly, truly believe that?"

"Yes, Griffin, I believe that whole-heartedly." Pastor Beth nodded.

Remembering the picture of Griffin crying next to a wall, Legionaries realized it was the Vietnam Memorial. This could be fun.

"Pastor, can I ask you where God, Jesus, or this Holy Spirit was when my whole platoon was wiped out by a bunch of gooks in Vietnam? Young men were drafted and forced to fight a war that everyone protested. I was lucky to have survived!" he paused and stared at Pastor Beth, who was looking uncomfortable. "And you know what I got when I came home? There wasn't any parade. No one said, 'thank you for your service.' No, what I got was people spitting at me and calling me a baby killer. I changed out of my uniform, put on civilian clothes, and grew out my hair just so I wouldn't be harassed," he said, really getting into the act.

"Despite the shame I felt, I still wanted people to know I lost good friends in that hell hole. Those of us who made it back were being mocked and ridiculed by people who believed we were the actual problem, all because we were drafted and forced to fight! So, tell me, where was your precious god then?" He was really on a roll. Why stop now? "Where was this god when my wife was taken from me because of cancer? And where is God now when my daughter is lying in a hospital bed fighting for her life? She was just doing her job and then some bizarre accident—"

"I am not here to debate with you, Griffin," Pastor Beth interrupted. "I know there is evil in this world, but we have to believe in something bigger than ourselves."

"Why pray or believe in a god who obviously doesn't care about us?"

"Griffin, we have spoken about free will countless times. It's God's greatest gift to his children. If He had not given us free will then we all would be forced to think and believe the same way."

Ahh, Legionaries thought. *This is just like Master. He gives us a choice to do his will or not, but the consequences are a thousand types of torture and being banished to the deepest pits of Hell.*

"Tell me more of this free will," Legionaries said. He was intrigued.

Pastor Beth stared at him with an idiotic look, making him wonder if maybe his rant had gone on a little too long. However, now he wanted to learn as much as possible about this free will humans had so he could exploit it better.

"I am so sorry, Pastor Beth," he said, speaking more softly and hoping she couldn't see the gleam in his eyes. "I'm just under so much stress. Please continue and I promise I won't interrupt. I need to learn more about free will."

The woman's face once more had that annoying do-gooder look from before. He could see that she was pleased with herself, believing she had reconnected with him.

Pastor Beth took a sip of water and looked like she was gathering her thoughts. "Well, Griffin, God gave us this gift so that we could make our own choices," she began. "We know when we are making a bad choice, but we are free to explore and make our choices, understanding that there will be repercussions for the decisions we make. We learn and grow from our faults. It's what makes us human." She stopped and searched Griffin's face to see if he agreed with what she was saying, hoping that her answer was what he needed to hear.

Legionaries couldn't contain his smile. "Thank you so much for explaining this to me." He could see that the pastor was quite pleased with herself. *Oh, you are truly pathetic*, Legionaries thought as he smiled politely back at her. Regardless, she did give him perspective on the current situation that he found himself in. Now he just needed to see what he could do with this so-called "free will."

Giving him a sympathetic smile, Pastor Beth asked, "Would you mind if I prayed with you?"

Legionaries wanted to slap her right off the couch. But why not play along? "I would be honored. But first, do you mind if I dim the lights?"

She appeared pleased by the suggestion and responded eagerly, "Yes, please dim them. It always seems right to pray and thank God for the day," she said. "It's how I close out my day, on my knees, with the only light coming from the lamp on my nightstand."

Well, whatever works! Legionaries thought as he turned off the lights and switched on a nearby lamp. She was already on her knees with her eyes closed. Legionaries assumed he was supposed to follow suit, so he knelt down and took her outstretched hands in his. She gave a small jerk when he sent a small pulse of adrenaline through her hands.

"Father, we come to you asking for guidance for our good friend Griffin," she began.

As he listened to her pray, Legionaries felt a strange discomfort and realized that he was now the recipient of pulses and shocks. He tried to pull away from her grasp, yet for some reason he was unable to. Then a low voice spoke to him with an air of authority. It definitely wasn't Master, but something far greater than he could comprehend. In fact, this new voice struck a fear in him unlike any he had ever experienced despite his long confinement in Hell.

"I know of you, just as you know of me, so listen and heed my warning: If you carry out your plans and harm those who have declared themselves to me, you will feel my wrath."

The voice left just as quickly as it appeared, and Legionaries once again heard Pastor Beth rattling on.

Finally, Pastor Beth said, "Amen," and gave him a light squeeze of his hands, letting him know it was his turn.

However, Legionaries was feeling panicked. He sat with his eyes open wide, looking frantically around the dim room. Would the voice take on a form? He felt another squeeze in his hands, startling him.

Pastor Beth opened her eyes and smiled at him, looking serene as she made eye contact with him.

"Griffin, I am sorry to have to visit you under these circumstances," she said quietly. Then she leaned forward and wrapped him in a warm embrace. "Please call upon me at once when you get any news at all about your daughter. I want to be here for you, so don't hesitate to reach out to me."

She stood and took notice that he didn't move. She offered her hand and pulled him to his feet. His legs began to shake under his own weight. She noticed.

"My goodness, Griffin. You don't look well. Please sit and I will get you a glass of water."

Legionaries collapsed onto the couch, staring after Pastor Beth as she turned on the lights and disappeared into the kitchen. A moment later she was back, handed him the water, and continued speaking as if everything was perfectly normal. "Please, Griffin, call me for anything. I am here for you. For now, please just try to rest. I will see myself out, but before I do, is there anything else I can do?"

Legionaries had become so disoriented he was barely able to give a shake of his head.

"Just remember that you are loved and I am here for you. I will see myself out, you just try to relax and know that our god works in mysterious ways."

Pastor Beth left. Hearing the front door open and close filled him with a sense of dread. What was wrong with him? He let the glass of water fall from his hand and asked the empty room, "What the hell just happened?"

CHAPTER 23

As Jonathan pulled into a run-down neighborhood defiled with graffiti, he wondered if Granny's GPS was faulty.

"Is this the right neighborhood?" he asked.

Granny gave him a sad smile and nodded. Jonathan thought about how hard her life must have been all these years with no one to open up to through her Earthly trials as a Fallen. Somehow, she continued to put others before herself despite no longer being able to hear the songs of angels, let alone God's voice. It was the price she paid when she chose to fall to Earth.

Pulling into the driveway, Jonathan found that Granny's house fit right in with the rest of the neighborhood. Looking closer, he noticed that Granny's home seemed to have been singled out—it had been spray-painted all over with graffiti, even the roof. A logo, likely from a local gang, had been drawn on the front door. It consisted of three fingers—the pointer, ring, and pinky finger—with the word "REAPERZ" underneath it.

"I usually put the car in the garage, but I won't be needing it any longer," Granny said quietly. Her voice was so faint that Jonathan could barely understand her. Her face had become ashen and her eyes had gone completely light gray, almost white.

Jonathan got out, hurried around to the passenger side, and opened the door. He quickly caught Granny before she fell out.

She gave him a pained smile, as if apologizing for the current state that she was in. She whispered, "Would you mind doing an old lady a favor and carry me inside?"

"It would be an honor," Jonathan responded. Then he took her in his arms, knowing that he was in the midst of the most beautiful woman he had ever seen. She stared past him up into the night sky, as if knowing it would be the last time she saw the stars with mortal eyes. Jonathan stopped and looked up too, just happy to share this moment with her. He wished it could go on forever.

Granny gave him a pat on his chest letting him know she was ready. He wanted to say something about how much he appreciated, loved, and respected her and was humbled just to be in her presence, but he couldn't get the words out. Once more she gave him a pat to his chest. He looked down at her and she gave him a knowing smile. As he approached the front door, he could see it was a metal security door, the type that was more difficult to break through. It angered Jonathan to think about Granny and all the good she had done in the world, only to be preyed upon by those who couldn't see it. "You know it is wrong to think that way," Granny murmured, hearing his thoughts. "They are lost souls who need guidance. They don't like me because I've helped so many over the years to find a different path. The ones who didn't want my help see me as a nuisance because I stuck my nose where it didn't belong."

She coughed several times, misting Jonathan's shirt with blood. Her breathing had become so strained that even through the pain she tried to apologize. Holding her like a small child in one massive arm, Jonathan placed a finger to her lips, letting her know it was okay. He took her inside and found her bedroom, which was sparsely furnished. He pulled back the covers and gently laid Granny down, then used part of his shirt to dab her lips and chin. She tried once more to smile, thanking him for his kindness, but now even that had become too much for her.

Jonathan knew why she had to experience this pain. It wasn't because she had healed his leg. It was the choice they had made to become fallen angels. Because of this choice, they had to experience death and its cruelty the same as mortals did.

"I'll be right back," Jonathan said. "I'll get you some water." He went to the kitchen and filled a glass and was making his way back to the bedroom when he noticed a table with only one chair. He stopped dead in his tracks. This would one day become his own fate—Riley would eventually pass from this world, leaving him to sit alone at a table. It was his payment for choosing to fall to take part in a mortal world. Knowing that his time would far exceed his human, since he aged so much slower.

Granny once more began coughing, pulling him away from his thoughts. As he returned to her room, he was dumbfounded by what he saw. Granny had aged ten years in the few minutes he had been gone. Her hair had started to fall out, leaving visible bald spots. Her face and neck now had red splotches of the disease that was taking her life. Jonathan grabbed a towel from the bathroom and wiped the blood from Granny's face. Her breathing rattled in her chest.

"Mercy, Father. Please show your loved one mercy," he pleaded. He took hold of Granny's hand and tried to flood her spirit with peace.

Then Granny spoke in a clear voice. "Remember when we first met? I told you it wasn't a waste to fall." She tried to contain her cough but it won out, causing her body to shake violently from the strain.

"I remember," Jonathan said. "Please, just try to relax. I will stay with you."

Granny ignored his plea. "We love our humans so much—we feel honored for the chance to be a part of their lives. Hang on to Riley and love him without end. Make the most of every moment you are blessed to have with him and hold onto every memory you are given." Then her body arched as it tried to draw in one last breath.

Jonathan clutched her hand and spoke softly. "Thank you for giving me your gift and for healing me. You were selfless for what you did for me. I will do as you have said and will never regret making the decision to fall."

Granny's body relaxed back onto the bed as her mouth opened and closed slowly. Jonathan bowed his head. Sobs shook him at the helplessness of the situation. There was nothing more he could do for the soul who had done so much for him. His sobs turned into cries for mercy as he watched Granny's features relax and the light in her eyes slowly diminish.

"I am sorry, God, that she had to sacrifice her life to save mine," Jonathan quietly prayed. "She has taught me what it is to be pure, selfless, and humble. Forgive me, Father, for my failings." He fell across Granny's body, wanting to hold her for as long as possible.

Hours passed until Jonathan felt strong enough to get up. Blowing out several shuddering breaths, he regained his composure, reached over, and closed Granny's eyelids. Getting to his feet, he looked down at Granny, knowing he would never see anything so beautiful again until he returned home.

Then he was aware of another presence in the room. He turned to see St. Peter standing before him, smiling. To any mortal eye, St. Peter had the appearance of someone who worked behind a desk for long hours. He was small-framed, carried a notepad in his breast pocket, and to complete the typical eight-to-five office-worker look, had a pencil stuck behind one ear. Anytime Jonathan had encountered the angel, he was constantly jotting something down in the notepad. However, that was only his outside appearance. This small angel was not to be taken lightly, for he alone guarded the gates of Heaven. Jonathan knew that in his notepad listed the names of the dead, with either a check mark next to the name if the person was allowed to enter, or an "X" if the person was to be turned away.

"Peace be with you, brother," he said. "I have come for our sister." Jonathan was unable to hide his smile before embracing the smaller angel. They stood that way for several seconds. "Thank you for coming," he said.

"You said it best when you called her pure," said Peter. "Even though she was unable to hear our Father for years, it was her trial to work through. She has been welcomed home and has reunited with her human, Cristal. I am here to collect her mortal body, but I must also inform you that you must be patient. The sickness that was inside you has left you vulnerable to temptation. Granny healed you, but you need to relearn how to control your powers. If you return too soon, you will harm those whom you swore to protect. So be still and trust God."

Although Jonathan wanted to return to Riley's side that very moment, he knew the words St. Peter had spoken were true. He must be patient.

"I know what your heart desires. Riley is eager to see you too. Just pray and listen for God to tell you when it is time. A demon has already made its way into Riley's life. He is using the manipulation of fear. But beware, Jonathan. If you return to Riley too soon, it will not be the demon who takes his life. Do you understand?"

"Yes," Jonathan replied.

St. Peter smiled at Jonathan, then placed a reassuring hand on his shoulder. "Be patient and know that the Father's design is always perfect." He disappeared, leaving Jonathan alone.

The sound of shattering glass jolted him out of his thoughts. It came from outside the house. In the blink of an eye, Jonathan stepped from Granny's bedroom and onto the front step where he found a group of teens totaling thirteen. One of them was behind the steering wheel of Granny's small car, trying to figure out a way to start it.

"I have no clue how to get this piece of crap started," the teen yelled from behind the steering wheel. Jonathan glared down at him from his position on the front step, pinning the teenager with his eyes. Receiving the message, the teenager slowly held up both hands as if Jonathan was holding a gun.

A skinny kid started to say, "Jesus C—" until Jonathan interrupted.

"Never take the Lord's name in vain!" he barked. He looked around at the group. "Let me introduce myself. My name is Jonathan, which literally means 'Gift from God.'" He took the car keys from his pocket and tossed them on the ground in front of him. "The car is my gift to you."

Jonathan knew they were intimidated by him. He could hear a couple whispering that they wondered if he was human. "Come, retrieve the keys, and the car is yours. I no longer need it. Neither will the woman who once lived here. I assure you that I won't call the police to report it stolen. All you have to do is come and retrieve the keys and the car is yours."

Not surprisingly, no one moved. They appeared to have been frozen in place after Jonathan had cast down not a gift but a challenge. "If someone doesn't volunteer then I will choose the lucky individual." No one took a step. Several looked at the ground, hoping they wouldn't be called upon. Jonathan could hear each of their thoughts and knew they were all wanting to flee from the place and never return.

"All of you are a test of my patience," Jonathan said, irritation rising in his voice. "You see, the woman you bullied for so many years is now gone. She was very special to me and always will be. She asked me to show you love and kindness even while she was dying." The thought of how much pain Granny had to endure at the end caused Jonathan's muscles to bunch on top of one another. He knew that without Granny's healing, he could fall into the clutches of the demons and tear these kids apart one by one. Jonathan could hear their collective thought: *Run!* He could smell the rank, musty smell of fear in the air—that alone nearly drove him back over the edge, but then Granny's words hit him like ice water.

You know it is wrong to think that way. They are lost souls who need guidance.

Once more, Granny had pulled him back from the edge even though she was gone. This was his first test. He took in a deep breath and closed his eyes to calm down. He pointed at the teen behind the wheel of the car. "You, come here!"

The teen reluctantly exited the vehicle and looked around at his friends for help, but all eyes were on the ground. Making the short walk to Jonathan, he stopped a few feet away, not daring to look up.

"I promise I will not hurt you," Jonathan said. "I give you my word that no harm will come to you by my hands."

Bending down, the teen picked up the keys and quickly backed up several feet.

"Please look around at one another and remember each face you see. A year from now, several of you will be in the ground because of stupid choices you will end up making just because you want to fit in. This willingness to bend to peer pressure will only take you down a path that leads to pain. People you once called friend will eventually betray you. The woman who lived here only wanted the best for each and every one of you. You took her kindness for granted and abused the one person who truly wanted to help you."

The smell of fear dissipated, bringing forth shame and understanding. Listening more intently to the group's thoughts until he found what he needed, Jonathan singled out each individual, shocking them even more as he called them by name. "James, Taylor, Michael, Trey, Mallory, Brittany, Chad, Julia, Sarah, Adam, Scott, Daniel, Marshall. All thirteen of you are guilty of negligence, and furthermore, just being naïve and reckless with your life choices!"

Several of the teens began crying, as the former bully persona was now exposed for what it really was. Just frightened teenagers afraid to be loved and terrified of rejection.

"I will offer you some advice and hope it will resonate with you," Jonathan said. "Turn away from your evil ways and seek refuge and hope in God, the one true savior. If you don't, then know that on your day of reckoning, you were warned by a stranger." He then took several quick steps, causing the group to cower, before vanishing in front of them.

Jonathan now found himself sitting under a large oak tree. He looked out across a meadow, taking in its beauty. As he watched the tall grass sway in the breeze, he understood why Granny had brought him here. It really was peaceful. As he sat there thinking about the lessons he learned from Granny, and the words spoken by St. Peter, he realized this was where his new life would begin.

CHAPTER 24

"**I** take it you drove here?" Maggie asked Riley.

"Yes, I'm parked a few blocks away," said Riley.

"Well, I'm in the parking garage," said Maggie. "I grabbed a spot reserved for staff. I probably shouldn't have done it, but I really didn't expect to be here this long. Why don't we leave your vehicle here and you can ride with me? I can call someone to tow you back to my office." She moved to head toward the parking garage.

"Okay, stop. Let's get one thing straight," Riley said, sounding a little annoyed. Maggie turned and cocked an eyebrow at him. "You will not order me around. I don't work for you. You're only here because Jonathan asked you to be. I don't owe you anything, so we will treat one another as equals or I will leave you right here. Now, do you understand?"

Maggie tried to hide a grin. She hadn't noticed until now, but when Riley became frustrated his brow furrowed, making him appear like a pouting child. "Well, I was only trying to think logically. You would need a vehicle placard and an ID badge in order to get into my office building."

"Why do we need to go to your office?" Riley asked with irritation.

"It's where I live—well, the thirteenth floor. It's my private apartment. We can stay there while we figure things out."

"Before we came back to the city, Jonathan and I were at my

lake house in Potogi. I think we should go back there. It's pretty isolated and Jonathan transformed it into the safest place that I can think of. He set up heavy-duty sensors, a security system, a safe room, and a large arsenal of weapons."

"Jesus, what were you guarding against?" Maggie asked jokingly, which he ignored.

"The place is a little over four hours away. I'll explain as much as I can while we drive. I think we should take my truck and leave your vehicle here."

Maggie decided to give in. "Okay, yeah. I can have someone retrieve my vehicle in the morning." She would call Spencer and direct him to keep things to himself. "At least the conversation won't be boring," she said lightly. "But I would like to pick up a few items before we go. Toiletries, clothing, and a few other things."

Riley looked at her as if she had just spoken a foreign language.

"I'm sure you can buy whatever you need when we get out of town. We do have stores out there."

Riley smiled as he headed to where he had parked.

Quickly catching up with him, Maggie asked, "Will we bicker back and forth until we finally decide which one of us is in charge? I mean, it's fun. I just want to make sure you can come to terms with the fact that Jonathan asked me to protect you."

Giving her a sideways glance, Riley let out a long, loud laugh. She was, indeed, a strange woman. He expected a little more concern from her knowing that she had consented to hang around with a stranger.

As they arrived at Riley's truck, Maggie stopped and looked at him. "How did Jonathan end up in your life?"

"It's a long story. Get in the truck." He started the engine and got them on the road, taking a detour around the highway where all the trouble had begun earlier that day. Riley was silent, keeping his eyes on the road. He needed to come up with a plan. And this time he didn't have Jonathan to help him.

After driving the first several miles in silence, Maggie asked her question again. "How did Jonathan end up in your life?"

"God, you are relentless," Riley said, irritated. "I heard you the first time. It's just a painful topic to talk about."

"I'm sorry, Riley. It's just the business side of me coming out. I always want to know as much as I can as soon as possible. You know what they say about how time is money. It's true."

Once again, she had caught him off guard with yet another apology. Riley looked over at her only to find her staring out the passenger window. They drove in silence for a few more miles. He knew he had to tell her something, since she had cast her lot next to his. He took a deep breath.

"Jonathan came into my life after my wife passed."

Maggie didn't offer a hollow apology. Instead she continued to look out the passenger window, quietly waiting for him to continue.

"Jonathan felt he was responsible for Allison's death—it's a long story, which I won't go into now. I was angry. Angrier than I'd ever been in my life. But not at him. When I met him, I was mentally and spiritually broken and I didn't want anything to do with God—or anyone else for that matter."

Now that he had started the story, he found himself continuing on, as if opening up about his past was a way to let it go.

"There were times when I wished Jonathan would just leave. He was constantly talking about God. Eventually, I learned to see him as someone who truly loved and cared for me. He became a very dear friend that I would gladly give my life to protect. He became like family to me."

Maggie turned to look at Riley. "I don't know what to really think of him. I just know he is someone who I want to have in my life. I began my search for him almost immediately after the night he rescued me from being raped and possibly murdered. He made sure I got to the hospital to get checked out. But then he just disappeared. I've always wanted to find him and thank him for what he did. I mean, at first he scared the hell out of me. I've never seen anyone so big. He had this incredible strength. You wouldn't believe it, but he grabbed these two grown men and threw them like they were rag dolls."

"I believe it," Riley said with a small smile.

"Anyway," Maggie continued, "I became so obsessed with finding him that everything else fell to the wayside. I decided to turn over the helm of my company to my most trusted colleague and friend, Stuart. I pretty much became a recluse. I mean, up until then I was constantly being photographed and interviewed as a rising tech star. I actually kind of liked it, but after a while it became too intrusive. When I disappeared from the public eye, the newspapers and tabloids thought I'd suffered a nervous breakdown or something. Maybe I did."

"Oh, I'm sorry," Riley said, turning to look at her. "I had no idea."

"When I first bought my building, I had the thirteenth floor converted to a condo so that I would never have to leave. That's how much of a workaholic I was. After the attack, I didn't leave that floor for over a year. I only spoke with my receptionist and my friend, Stuart. However, in my search for Jonathan, I learned about the two men who had attacked me. They had been apprehended on a long list of crimes and eventually sentenced. One of them is actually on death row. Anyway, I was so desperate for even a tiny fragment of information about this mysterious man who had rescued me that I was finally able to pull some strings and talk with one of the inmates. So, yesterday I drove out to the penitentiary. He told me he turned his life around because of Jonathan."

"Wow, that's pretty amazing," Riley said. "Was he able to tell you anything else about Jonathan?"

Maggie paused. "Actually," she began, "he said he believed Jonathan was not of this world and it wasn't just because of his superhuman strength. He saw something in Jonathan's eyes. And you know, I did too. Then he told me about what he'd been reading in the Bible, about angels and that sometimes they come to Earth and walk as holy ones among us. I mean, he went so far as calling Jonathan an angel!" She stopped and looked at Riley.

Riley fell quiet and stared at the road. Listening to Maggie's story, he could understand the logic behind what he thought at the time was a rash decision to throw away her life by coming with him. Not only was she in the correct mindset for the journey ahead of them, but she was far braver than he had given her credit for. She had given up the comforts of her life to seek out the truth of who Jonathan was, despite the fact that the media, as well as those who worked for her, would never understand what drove her.

"What do you think?" Maggie said. "Do you believe in angels?"

Night was finally giving way to morning as the sun peeked over the horizon. Glancing at the fuel level, Riley saw they were running low and took the next exit.

"I think we need to fill up or we will have to push the car the rest of the way," he replied, relieved that he'd found a way to change the subject. He would need to figure out pretty quickly what he would tell Maggie about Jonathan. Could she handle the truth?

"Well, we don't want you having to push while I steer," Maggie said, shooting him a wicked grin. This conversation was not over. They both knew it.

Riley pulled up to a gas pump and jumped out. He inserted his card and began refueling.

"I need food," Maggie said. "Anything I can get for you while I'm inside?"

"I would love a couple of energy drinks to help keep me alert."

"You know those are bad for you."

Riley tried not to laugh out loud. She was offering health advice when he knew their lives were at risk. "I think falling asleep at the wheel takes precedent."

"True, but don't blame me if your heart explodes."

Riley shook his head, knowing that trying to debate with her was pointless. He would have better luck arguing with the gas pump.

"I'm just having a little fun with you," Maggie said. "I'll get us some breakfast and then you can feel free to wash it all down with a heart-stopping energy drink. Not my fault that you want to be a cardiologist's dream!" She walked away before he could reply.

Forget the energy drinks. That woman will be the death of me, Riley thought. *Lock me in a room with her for a few days and I will save the Devil the trouble.*

———

Upon entering the gas station, Maggie was surprised to find that it housed a small chain fast-food restaurant. After placing their order, Maggie went to browse the energy drinks, finding one that actually read HeartPump. Laughing aloud, she picked up two of the cans and headed up to the counter to pick up her food order. Then she heard her name called out over the intercom at the pumps. *Damn!* She hurriedly pulled out some cash and tossed it on the counter. "Sorry!" she said. "Gotta go, keep the change!"

She snatched up their food and drinks and hurried out to where Riley was waiting. She held her bag in front of her face as she ran to his truck.

"Ms. Gregory!" someone called out. "Over here!"

Maggie quickly glanced over to see someone pointing his camera phone at her and she hid her face again with the bag.

"Hey, is that really you?" he called out again.

Jumping into Riley's truck, she yelled, "Go, go, go!"

Riley did as she asked.

"Did I just participate in a robbery?"

Her embarrassment was replaced by a smile as she fastened her seatbelt.

"I mean, seriously Maggie. If you needed money, all you had to do was ask. I'm all for helping the needy," he laughed. "In fact, I was once a Boy Scout—even earned a merit badge by helping out in a soup kitchen, so I can sympathize with your struggles."

"No, don't worry. Let's just say they made a big profit off my order. I think I threw down a fifty before running out of there." She laughed and playfully punched him in the shoulder. Then she pulled out two large energy drinks from the bag and held them up so Riley could read the label.

"HeartPump! Perfect. I wonder if it's any good."

Maggie popped the top on the first can and handed it over. "Of course they're good. Start chugging. I'm anxious to know what fate lies ahead!"

Shaking his head, Riley took a sip. "Wow! I don't think you needed to buy two. I am officially wide awake!"

"I got you some breakfast too. If the energy drink doesn't kill you then the grease should." Maggie dug in the bag and handed Riley a breakfast burrito.

He tore off the wrapper and took a large bite. "Thank you," he mumbled.

"Don't thank me. I'm going to be the reason for our deaths."

Her comment didn't make Riley laugh. Maggie quickly picked up on the fact that she had said something wrong.

"Sorry, Riley. Very poor taste on my part."

"No, you're fine. I just hope that isn't the case for either of us. Lately I seem to focus on how dark things are instead of just trying to live a normal life."

Maggie played back the events of the night, remembering the warning from the bizarre and surreal image in her bathroom mirror. It had to be some kind of hallucination. Regardless, she couldn't help but think her life may never be normal again.

CHAPTER 25

H ours later, Maggie and Riley finally arrived at the lake house. It was strange to have her in his truck, knowing that reporters would probably pay large amounts of money for the opportunity to be in his shoes. Apparently, the world wanted to know why she had closed herself off for the past year, only to resurface now. He found it rather humorous.

Since it seemed they were going to be attached to one another for better or worse, he needed to figure out how to keep the two of them alive. But without Jonathan, he had no clue how to fend off supernatural threats. For now, he was simply too exhausted to think straight and needed several hours of sleep to recover.

Maggie had reclined her seat and had been softly snoring for the last hour. She had offered to drive at the halfway point, but Riley was too wired at the time. Now he had trouble even remaining alert. Putting the truck in park, he reached over and placed a hand on Maggie's shoulder. "Maggie, we're here. Time to wake up." She stirred for a minute, wiping at her face, then sat up quickly, confused at what was going on. Then she found Riley's face and stared at him as if he were a strange bug.

"Everything is okay," he assured her. "We're here." He stepped out of the truck, raised his arms above his head, and stretched his exhausted muscles. "I would show you around, but for now let me show you the room you'll be sleeping in."

Nodding, Maggie hopped out and followed Riley to the

house. After unlocking the door, Riley led her down the short hallway.

"This will be your room," he said, opening a bedroom door. "Mine is just across the hall. The bathroom is just down the hall next to Jonathan's room."

"Okay, thanks," she said, giving him a small, awkward smile.

"Sure. Well, good night," Riley replied, then let out a loud yawn.

"Actually, good morning," she corrected.

Riley was too tired to smile at the joke. Shuffling like a zombie into his room, he fell onto the bed without bothering to get undressed or pull the covers over himself.

Riley found himself back at the hospital. He was standing in front of the elevator in the lobby. The doors opened and several people hurriedly pushed past him. He felt himself drawn to getting on the elevator. An elevator attendant asked what floor and everyone replied in unison, "Two, please." The elevator attendant made eye contact with him. "You will be going to the third floor." He said before turning to face the elevator doors.

Riley wanted to tell the man he didn't want to go to the third floor, but found himself compelled to follow along. When the doors opened, everyone hurried off. As Riley was about to follow, the attendant put his arm out to stop him.

"Riley, you are to go up one more floor. No one wants to see you here. These souls are still alive." He pushed Riley, who slammed against the back of the elevator. "Next floor up. She is waiting for you." Riley thought he saw the man's eyes turn red.

The doors closed and the elevator began to shake as it ascended to the third floor. Like clockwork, the doors opened as several people began to enter until they noticed Riley. Then, as if they all knew who he was, they smiled and stepped aside, waiting for him to exit. A nurse stepped forward and spoke to Riley. "She has been waiting for you. Not much time now, so go quickly."

"Who is waiting? Where do I go?" Riley asked her.

The nurse smiled at him and took one of his hands in hers. Upon contact he received a shock, the same shock that had jolted him when he had touched Griffin Patterson. He felt the same surge of energy followed by extreme tiredness, causing him to let out an over-exaggerated yawn. The nurse dug her fingernails into Riley's hand as he tried to pull back. She smiled politely at him while crushing his hand in the process. "You can rest after you're gone," she said. Riley opened his mouth to ask what she meant only for a distant cry to interrupt him. "Hurry along now," the nurse replied, releasing his hand. As she turned to walk away, he saw her eyes turn a shade of red just as the elevator attendant's had.

The crying seemed to intensify and he clearly heard someone call out his name. Riley thought he recognized the voice but couldn't put a face to it. He slowly walked down the hallway, but then his pace quickened as hospital rooms flew by. He felt he was being pulled toward his destination. He suddenly came to a stop in front of room 317. This had been Allison's room the day she died. Sobs and screams were coming from the other side of the door. Riley now knew who they belonged to. He wished he could turn and leave but knew there was no way he could turn his back on this woman. He gently pushed the door open a bit, but another force swung it completely open and Riley fell facedown. The door slammed shut behind him.

"Riley, why did you let this happen to me!"

Pushing himself up to one knee, Riley looked up only to find the room dark as night. Struggling to his feet, Riley held out his arms, cautiously searching his way through the blackness that now enveloped him. The screams and cries that had been so evident before had now gone silent. A beeping sound helped him locate the bed.

"Granny?" Riley asked the dark. "Talk to me. I can't see anything."

"Still having trouble finding the path laid out before you?" Granny's voice snickered, followed by several sharp coughs and loud wheezing.

Saying nothing, Riley stepped toward the noisy gasps of air. The coughing had stopped, but the wheezing had intensified to such a degree that he had to cover his ears. Squinting from the awful sound, he took several steps before bumping hard into what he presumed was the side of the bed. The room went eerily silent and Riley removed his hands from his ears.

"I'm here, Granny. Please tell me how I can help." A light pierced the dark and brought everything into focus—except for the bed, which remained shrouded in darkness. Reaching out his hand, Riley felt what he thought was the side of Granny's face. "Granny, please talk to me. I'm right here. Tell me what I should do."

Moments passed as Riley contemplated asking the question again. The lights poured from the ceiling so brightly that Riley could only see purple spots before his eyes.

"Can you raise the dead?" Granny screamed, spraying warm spittle across his face.

Riley fell backward. His vision was distorted for a few moments, until Granny's face came into focus. He blinked several times, then rubbed his eyes. He was horrified to see that Granny's face had been eaten away and tiny worms wriggled underneath the mangled flesh. Part of her face was severely burned. Riley could only be certain that it was Granny because of her eyes. They remained the same for a moment until her right eye seemed to protrude. Without warning, the eye gave way to a small white worm crawling out of the socket. The worm groped blindly and slid halfway down the side of Granny's cheek, tail and all.

Riley scrambled to get away but couldn't find his footing. Granny slung both of her legs over the side of the bed, then stood upright in one smooth movement. Burns ran up her legs, stopping at the bottom of her hospital gown. As she walked toward him, the flesh on her body rippled just beneath the surface, swishing back and forth as she took each step. As she came closer, Riley could make out the shapes of worms attempting to push their way to the surface of her skin. He let out a reflexive scream at seeing what had happened to Granny. He violently kicked at the floor but to no avail. A pair of hands grabbed him by the shoulders and shook him vigorously.

"Wake up Riley, wake up. You're having a nightmare."

Riley opened his eyes to see Maggie's concerned face.

"You're dreaming, Riley. It's just a dream. It's okay."

Understanding that he was now back in his room, Riley couldn't stop himself as he broke down sobbing, turning away from Maggie. Not from embarrassment, but because of the terror that had dripped into his dream. He felt her hand tentatively touch his. Then she rubbed his back with her other hand, trying to assure him that everything was going to be okay.

"Just let it out, don't hold back on my account," Maggie said. "You were having a severe nightmare."

Lying on his side, facing away from her, Riley let the tears run down his face. He wanted to ask her to leave—not just his room but back to the life she knew. To forget about Jonathan as well as him.

"Would you like to talk about it?"

He blew out a shaken breath and wiped his face on the pillow adjacent to him. He wasn't ready to tell Maggie the truth just yet.

"I started having nightmares after Allison died. They stopped a long time ago, but now they're coming back. During the last one, Jonathan had to restrain me so I wouldn't harm myself."

"It's okay," she said softly and continued to rub his back.

Rolling over to face her, Riley couldn't believe how calm her demeanor was. He wanted to scream at her that this was far from okay and to tell her that if she knew what was best for her, she would listen to reason and leave.

Maggie gave him a reassuring look as her hand continued to rub his back. "I don't know what to expect on the road ahead of us," she said quietly. "But I do know that we will walk it together. Okay?" She wasn't asking for permission.

Riley finally broke eye contact with her saw that the clock on the night stand read 3:00 p.m. However, he had no desire to fall back to sleep. Sleeping would only bring an unknown fear that, if he wasn't careful, death would come to visit as well. "I need a shower and to get out of these damp clothes," he said, sitting up.

Maggie, perched on the side of the bed, stood up. "You get a shower and I'll strip your bed. These sheets need to be washed; they reek as badly you do!"

Riley forced a smile, headed toward the bathroom. Stopping halfway down the hall, he called over his shoulder, "Did you at least get some rest?"

"A little," Maggie replied. "That is, until I heard you across the hall."

Feeling sheepish that he was the cause for her lack of rest, Riley replied sincerely. "I'm sorry about that."

"Don't worry about it," she said, coming out of his room with his bedding and pillows in hand. "Thought we should wash the pillows as well, since they smell of—" then stopped herself.

"Me," Riley said with a grin. "They smell like me. I smell."

Maggie smiled back at him. "Well, to be quite frank, I wasn't raised on a farm, but I am pretty sure that this is what pig farmers deal with."

Riley found that now his smile wasn't forced. For some reason, she was able to give him a bit of hope that this would all be okay. "I think you might be right. But who would've thought that one day I'd have a millionaire doing my laundry?"

"Riley, I passed that years ago. I think you should put a B where that M is." She gave him another smile and turned and walked towards the laundry room.

Hopping into the shower, Riley felt the tension of the situation seep into him again as his muscles tightened up. He closed his eyes and tried to calm himself back down. A knock at the door interrupted his concentration.

"Since there's only one bathroom, would you mind not taking all the hot water?"

"I'll be right, out your majesty!" Just at the sound of her voice, he loosened up a bit and quickly finished showering. A few minutes later, he wrapped a towel around his waist and left the bathroom, almost walking directly into Maggie, who stood there as if she had been eagerly awaiting her turn. Thanking God that he had wrapped the towel firmly around him, Riley fired off a snide remark. "Don't worry, madam, I made sure you have plenty of hot water for your bath."

She gave him a wry smile, then walked into the bathroom, calling over her shoulder, "Please start dinner, peasant, since I am forced to draw my own bath." She closed the door before Riley could reply.

CHAPTER 26

Legionaries felt quite pleased with himself despite holding hands with that little Pastor Beth woman and praying to her god. His plan was working with Riley—and it was all achieved through his greatest power: telepathy. He was able to get under Riley's skin with the nightmares that he poured into his sleep. He would slowly drive him insane, and Maggie too. She was a bonus. However, there was a fine balance to be wary of. If he pushed too much too soon then Riley would shut down, making the next step of the plan impossible to carry out. If Master truly had given him an unlimited time frame, then Legionaries knew that Riley and Maggie would eventually beg for their sanity back. When it didn't come, they would take their own lives and Legionaries would find himself in Master's good graces.

Though it was a bit strange that Master wasn't micromanaging him. Legionaries found that he could simply sense an event about to occur, and then it would come to pass. This new talent affirmed that he was growing in power as he surpassed another boundary. Once Lucifer realized the mistake he'd made in letting him out of Hell to fulfill his tasks, it would be too late to close the Pandora's box that he himself had opened. A wide smile spread across Legionaries's face.

Honestly, Legionaries couldn't care less about Riley, Maggie, or capturing the Fallen. They weren't the real prize. They could go on the rest of their days doing whatever they pleased for all he cared. He just longed for the day when he would finally take control over Lucifer. He would command those damned hounds of his to tear their pitiful old master apart as he begged for mercy. Lucifer would finally be on the receiving end of all that Hell had to offer.

The thought of the pain he would inflict, not just on Lucifer, but on every black soul in Hell that had abused him and laughed at him, or called him "lackey," made him smile. Leaders of the regions that took delight every time he screamed for mercy would more than pay for their transgressions. The thought of watching every one of them cry out as he looked on in amusement made him chuckle. Before he knew it, he was laughing hysterically. But then he suddenly struggled to catch his breath and the laughter quickly turned into violent coughing as sweat poured off him. He fell to the floor on all fours like a dog. *Damn, this must be Lucifer's doing.* His thoughts had once again betrayed him. Now he would suffer the consequences.

Clutching at his throat, Legionaries saw that his hands had changed into large, cat-like paws. *I'm losing control!* was his last coherent thought as he fell facedown on the floor. The view of the room started to fade away. Then the roar of a sinister voice startled him.

"You pathetic loser! You've never been in control of anything."

"I am sorry. Please don't punish me, Master." Legionaries begged.

"He is not your master!" the voice screamed, making Legionaries wince. "Now *he* is the lackey! *Your* lackey!"

Confused, Legionaries cowered on the floor, afraid to say anything.

"Do you know why I can hear your thoughts?" the voice said.

Legionaries remained quiet.

"Why don't you stand and tell me what you see," the voice commanded.

Legionaries cautiously looked around until he spotted a mirror on the wall in the front entryway. He got up and walked over to it, looking nervously around him. When he reached the mirror and peered into it, he saw a strange beast staring back at him. "Because I am *you!*" it roared.

An odd feeling overtook him as he studied his image in the mirror. He'd never seen his own true image before. Lucifer had kept him under his thumb for so long that he had no idea what he himself looked like—perhaps not even what he was capable of. He'd always been dependent and subservient to Master and it blinded him. Now he was seeing himself for the first time.

He bore the head of an eagle. When he opened his beak, he saw an arrow-shaped snake head slither out just a bit, but then quickly retract as his beak clamped shut. Looking himself up and down, he had the body of a lion. Toward the back he wore the scales of a snake that rippled from top to bottom, causing pulses of electricity to flow over them. *Why have you been hiding from me?* Legionaries thought.

"Thousands of years ago, you were forced into slavery by the one whose name I will not say. He knew the threat you posed to him. Do you remember?"

Legionaries said nothing.

"Let me help you focus," the voice said. "Now, what was the last thing you remember of how you came into existence?"

"All I have ever known is Hell," Legionaries said cautiously.

"Search deeper," the voice said.

Closing his eyes, Legionaries tried to focus, but all he could see were Lucifer's hounds tearing him apart every chance they got. Even when he was forced into the depths of Hell to chew on the flesh of others, he tore at his own flesh, futilely trying to stop the worms that ate away at his insides. He nearly panicked just at the memory of these ordeals. He was still worried Lucifer would throw him back and sentence him to spend all of eternity there. He couldn't bear it—not now when he had tasted freedom.

"Calm yourself, Legionaries. I'll tell you exactly what happened when we came into existence. Our so-called master sent us to a kingdom called Gadarenes to watch over it and keep it his. The inhabitants quickly learned they didn't have to abide by the laws of their false god. They could live as they pleased and feared no consequences. But one day, their false god arrived on our shores to cast us out and reclaim his people. He ordered them to bind us and imprison us until a great judgment day. However, after their false god cast us out, the inhabitants realized what had been taken from them—their freedom! They demanded that he leave, but he would not listen to them."

Legionaries sat down on the floor, dumbfounded. Now, it seemed, a glimmer of memory was coming back to him. He struggled to focus.

"You see, Legionaries, he was not welcomed where we once ruled. He did not receive the glory that he had hoped for. He was forced out and then it wasn't long before Lucifer sent his soldiers to rule with a heavy hand. We had treated them fairly. We had given them certain privileges and freedoms, but now Lucifer would rule over them without mercy. Children were sold, families were ruined, people were murdered by the thousands—and why? Because of a simple-minded false god who believed himself to be all-knowing, and a god to a few.

Legionaries shook his head. He had no memory of this, yet it was coming from himself, somehow.

"When we were cast out, we placed a curse upon their livestock. Untold numbers of cattle, sheep, and pigs drowned as the waters of the sea rose up and crashed down upon them. This led to mass starvation. Afterward, we were forced to return to Lucifer and he punished us without mercy."

"Why?" Legionaries asked. "We did what he wanted us to—"

"Because we were foolish enough to be captured and imprisoned. Because in our weakness, that false god found his way into Lucifer's territory. That was the worst possible scenario and our fates were sealed."

Legionaries sat on the floor, feeling a mix of confusion and anger fighting one another in his head.

"So, now that you have learned where you come from, do you know who you are?"

Legionaries got to his feet and went to stand before the mirror once more. He smiled at the image of the beast staring back at him. "I am *Legion!*" he roared.

CHAPTER 27

Standing in the kitchen, Riley found that he was more exhausted now than when he had tried to rest. The sound of the shower just down the hall didn't help, the repetitive thrumming of the water lulling him into a calm state of mind. He let out an exaggerated yawn Maggie wouldn't be able to hear. He stretched his arms and legs and then his back, feeling several pops along his spine. He needed to shake a few cobwebs loose. He was also hungry. He opened the refrigerator and pulled out two steaks. Then he wondered if Maggie was vegan. He went to the pantry in search of vegetables. The thought of her looking back at him, disgusted, as he informed her that she was about to eat grass-fed T-bone steak cooked to a perfect medium rare, made him laugh.

Riley realized that he had found his smile once again now that she had forcefully entered into his life. The constant banter over who was right about this or that was actually welcomed. This reminded him of the way he and Jonathan were before the sickness made him a shell of his former self. Now he wondered if Jonathan was gone forever. If by some miracle he did return, what would it be like? Could Riley feel safe around him? Could he dare hope that Jonathan would become his old self again?

Pushing the thought away, Riley began preparing dinner: seasoning the steaks, prepping the vegetable foil wraps, and making lemonade. While the food was grilling, he stared out at the lake for a moment then fell into one of the patio chairs.

From the outside, he appeared to be living the good life—grilling out on a lake property, lounging around aimlessly, and doing whatever he pleased. Yet the outside world would never understand the insanity of his life. He looked over at the dock where Jonathan had finally told him what was really happening to him. That night now seemed like a distant memory, one that he wished he could have back just to be around his friend once again.

"I think whatever is on the grill is burning," said a voice behind him.

Riley leapt to his feet and opened the grill, only to find that the steaks were just fine. He looked over at Maggie as she poured herself some lemonade and looked back at him innocently.

"I was only trying to help," she said coyly.

"Well, I hope the shower went cold on you!"

"Aww, now is that any way to treat a house guest?"

He hurled a grilling mitt at her, but Maggie caught it with ease then shook her head.

"Wow, you really put some heat on that one."

"You are a consistent pain in my—"

"So, what are the plans for tonight?" she interrupted. "I really need to purchase a few things."

Riley was about to answer until Maggie's phone started dinging. "Hold that thought," she said, holding up her index finger. She looked at her messages. A moment later, the smile slid off her face.

Wondering if it was something serious, Riley took the seat across from her and waited. She was typing furiously away on her phone when another notification came through.

"Miles Jackson, you slimy worm. How dare you try to do this to me," she muttered at her phone.

"Should I ask?" Riley said. Looking up at her, he saw a defeated look on her face.

Her phone rang, breaking her out of a trance as she quickly answered it. There was a pause. "Yes, Stuart, parts of that are true." Maggie responded as she quickly hurried back into the house.

She listened as her best friend, and appointed CEO of her company, told her everything that had happened in her absence. "Mags, I love you to death, but why did you have any dealings with that man?" Stuart said. "You know how corrupt Miles Jackson is. Apparently, the FBI has been investigating him for the last nine months for fraud and embezzlement, and they're even saying that he's turned a blind eye to prisoner abuse, including torture, at some of the prisons. Anyway, there's a massive investigation underway. He was arrested yesterday and rumor has it that he was all too happy to drop your name as someone he had prior dealings with. Maggie, he said you had $1M wired into his account just yesterday. What the hell?"

"I know it looks bad, but—"

"Mags, it doesn't look bad, it is bad. The board has called for an emergency meeting later today. I need you to come and explain your side of the story."

She fell quiet, knowing that even if she could make it to the meeting, she would be lucky if they would hear her out. What would she say? *Ladies and gentlemen, I appreciate your concern in this matter, but I wired the money to find what I believe may be a guardian angel.* "Okay," she said. "So, I will speak with the authorities and explain the situation."

On the other end of the line, she heard Stuart blow out a long, tired breath, knowing that he must be running around putting out fires on her behalf. "So, it's true?" he asked, exasperated. "Oh my god, Mags."

Maggie walked into the living room and fell onto the sofa, anticipating what he would say next. "I should resign," she blurted out. "You are already doing an amazing job and I don't know when I will make it back."

"No, Mags. Don't do anything rash. Just give me a few hours. I will meet with the board later and do some damage control. But I do need to get your side of it. And soon. For now, you just stay put wherever it is you've wandered off to."

She desperately wanted to tell him that her search had come to an end and she'd be back in her position soon, but in truth, it was only beginning. Sure, she had found the mysterious Jonathan, but he had disappeared just as quickly. And now she found herself out here in the middle of nowhere with a guy she'd only just met twenty-four hours ago. Now in the light of day she realized she had no idea what she was doing.

"Maggie," Stuart's voice startled her. "I will figure this out. It's why you put your trust in me to not only run your company but to cover you when you make idiotic moves." He sighed deeply. "Just make sure I can reach you later. Okay?"

"Yes, Stu." She only used her childhood nickname for him when she needed to get back on his good side. There was silence on the other end. She began to wonder if he had hung up on her.

"Just tell me that you are safe," he said in a quiet voice. "Despite everything else that is happening, I just want to know that my best friend is safe." There was her old friend again. God, she loved how good-hearted he was. Even when the world seemed to fall down around them, he was still her rock. Maggie wiped at her eyes and tried to keep her composure.

"Yes, I am safe. I promise."

"Are you sure everything is okay?" he asked again.

Stifling a sob, Maggie replied quickly. "Promise."

"Okay, keep your phone on. I love you, Mags."

Maggie couldn't reply. She ended the call and put the phone on the side table. Dropping her head into her hands, she allowed herself to break down. A few moments later, a hand touched her shoulder. She looked up through her tears to see Riley standing in front of her.

Wiping at her face, Maggie jumped to her feet. Riley retreated a few steps. "I take it the food is ready?" she said.

"Yeah, it's ready. You hungry?" He turned and walked back out to the patio and Maggie followed. Not knowing what to say, they busied themselves with unwrapping the foil veggie packets and eating without talking. When they finished the meal, Riley finally broke the silence.

"Do you still want to go pick up what you need from town?"

"Yeah, I still need to get a few things."

"Are you sure? I mean, we can wait until this situation dies down."

"What?" Maggie said, surprised. "Oh. You know. How did you—?"

Riley held up his phone. "When you were on the phone, I pulled up a news feed, just to see what was going on in the world, and I saw headlines with your name and photo. Oh, and 'under investigation.'"

"Well, in my experience, this kind of thing takes a while to die down," Maggie said with an edge to her voice. "When someone like me has the words 'under investigation' next to their name it . . . well . . . it's the kind of thing you can let ruin your life or you can choose to just live your life until the next big story comes along and they forget all about you."

"Well, it's a really small town, so I doubt anyone will even recognize you," Riley offered.

Not bothering to reply, Maggie walked back into the house, grabbed her bag, and then headed out the front door. Riley hurriedly cleaned up their dinner, picked up his keys, and followed Maggie to the truck. Settling in behind the wheel, he looked over at Maggie, but she was looking out her window. She still hadn't looked at him by the time they arrived at Jackson Brothers' Super Store.

Once Riley parked, Maggie climbed out and slammed the door behind her, rocking the truck with its force. Still not speaking as they entered the store, she jerked a shopping cart free and nearly ran Riley over as she pushed by.

After she had loaded the cart with everything she needed, she turned to Riley and simply asked, "Could I have the keys? I'll wait in the truck."

He tossed them over. After she left him, Riley made his way to the front of the store to pay for everything. The cashier gave him a few strange looks as she rang up the items. When she got to the bras and panties, a corner of her eyebrow went up.

"I hear they don't ride up like boxers, so I figured why not give them a try?" Riley quipped. He was rewarded for his humor with a soft chuckle as the cashier rang up the rest.

After paying and walking back outside, Riley looked out at the half-empty parking lot and saw that his truck was not where he had parked it. "I swear to God that if she left me—" he fumed.

A horn honked, and he swung around to see Maggie behind the wheel. Back in the truck he found her actually grinning devilishly at him. "Did you make sure to get everything?"

"I purchased everything you had in the shopping cart," he said a bit dryly.

"All the tops, low-cut jeans, and women's personal items?"

"I think so," Riley answered and rifled through the bags, not knowing what he was searching for.

"Did you at least make sure the cashier knew that the thongs were in your size?"

Riley's eyes shot up to her, his face going red with embarrassment.

Putting the truck in drive, Maggie burst out laughing. "Put your seat belt on. Don't want us having an accident and the cops finding your new thong underwear. I mean, how embarrassing would that be?"

Still too stunned to say anything, Riley turned his head away and thought, *She has officially lost it.*

A few minutes later, they turned into Riley's driveway as the sun began its descent into the horizon.

"You have a beautiful home here, Riley," she said as she got out of the truck. "Even though my world has turned upside down, I can still sense the feeling of peace out here."

"Thank you. How about we get this stuff inside and I'll show you around the property tomorrow?"

"Okay, I can get these," Maggie said. She grabbed the bags and ran inside.

Riley stayed behind and looked around the property. He breathed in the warm night air. He really loved it out here. He wondered how long it would remain peaceful. Noticing a few weeds in the flower bed, Riley dropped to his knees and began pulling them while he waited for Maggie to return.

"I leave you alone for one minute and come back to find you playing in the dirt!"

"Well, Maggie, this is how us common folk maintain our lawn. You see this?" He held up a fistful of weeds. "They're called weeds and they choke out these beautiful flowers. However, I don't expect you to know these things since you were born with a silver spoon in your mouth."

"I will have you know that I pulled my fair share of weeds growing up," Maggie said, crossing her arms.

"Come on, let's go in the house," Riley said as he stood up. "It's getting dark."

CHAPTER 28

Maggie awoke the next morning confused by her surroundings until the jumbled pieces of her memory fell back into place. Untangling her left hand from underneath the covers, she held her wristwatch a few inches from her face, finding that it only read six thirty.

Knowing that sleep wouldn't welcome her back, Maggie kicked her legs over the side of the bed, the feel of the carpet pulling her senses fully awake. Staring at the gray walls of her new room, Maggie finally welcomed the start of a new day.

After seeing to her hygiene and getting dressed, she embarked on an idea that didn't involve a microwave and a toaster. Finding eggs, bacon, and bread, she began busying herself with cooking breakfast. Losing herself in the process, she was startled when she heard Riley behind her.

"Wow, something smells great. Have you been up long?"

Maggie turned and smiled at him. "Not long. I hope you don't mind I made myself at home. It's not very often that I cook. And I never eat like this." She plopped two pieces of bread in the toaster.

Riley began filling two cups of coffee. "No, not at all, especially if you're going to make me breakfast." He handed a cup to her.

"How did you sleep?" Maggie asked.

"It was a quiet night. Slept like a baby."

"That's good." She gave him a smile.

A few minutes later, they sat at the table and ate their breakfast. Maggie watched as Riley devoured his, wondering if he would finally open up to her about Jonathan.

"So, what's on the schedule for today?" Maggie asked, finishing her eggs.

"I thought I would show you around the place. I know you have questions about Jonathan, so I'll do my best to answer them."

"Okay, good," Maggie said. "Where do we start?"

Riley stood up and gathered their plates. "Since you made breakfast, I'll wash up the dishes. Then I'll show you around outside. You can head out, if you like, and I'll be out in a few minutes."

"Fair enough, thanks," Maggie agreed. A few minutes later, she put on her shoes and went out the front door. The early morning sun was bright and warm. She walked down to the dock and admired the lakefront. The sun's rays bounced off the water, making her shield her eyes. *A person could get used to this*, she thought. She liked the sound of the water returning to the shore, drumming against it. The rhythmic sound could lull a person to sleep. Maybe Riley would take her out on the water. Then she stopped herself. This wasn't a vacation. This was not an idyllic getaway. She was here to learn more about Jonathan and to figure out his relationship to Riley and why Jonathan had asked her to look after him.

"Hey, Maggie!" Riley called out. She looked and saw him waving her back up toward the house. She gave him a wave back and headed in his direction, leaving the tranquil lake behind her.

"The lake is so beautiful!" she called out as she approached him.

"Yeah, I was lucky to find this place. I always thought it'd be a great place to retire."

He was standing next to a large metal building. He opened

the side door and flipped a switch. The lights flickered on, taking a moment to fully illuminate. "This is what Jonathan and I built," he said.

Maggie looked around the large expanse of the room. It looked like an Olympic training room. It was filled with everything from punching bags, to kettlebells, free weights, battle ropes, and a rowing machine. She could feel the testosterone in the place.

"So—are you and Jonathan into some crazy CrossFit exercises? Or maybe you're training for the Olympics?"

"I think CrossFit would be a kinder word for what he put me through," Riley said. "On the first day after we finished building it and brought everything in here, Jonathan told me we were going to continue our sparring. We do it all the time, but I still get nauseous when I see him putting the gloves on. You've seen him. He's a giant and far outweighs me. Besides, I haven't ever done the kind of workouts that he puts me through."

"He physically hits you?" she asked, a bit shocked.

"Yeah. It was his way of getting my attention. I mean, he didn't hurt me. I used to enjoy working out until he came along. It was like a baptism into hell. We would do circuit training for hours and then do ten-mile runs. I'd ask for a time out, gasping for air while my lungs were on fire. When I fell to my knees, he'd pull me back up to my feet and yell, 'Move faster!'"

"He could have seriously hurt you."

Riley turned and looked at her. "Nah, he knew what he was doing. I trusted him. Jonathan and I built this for one reason only, and that was to teach me how to defend myself just in case he wasn't around. He said I would have to be prepared for whatever might be coming for us."

Maggie couldn't believe what she was hearing. "What did he mean by that?"

Riley chuckled as if trying to play it down. "Well, look around, we're pretty isolated out here. You need to know how to protect yourself."

Maggie gave him a wary look. "There's something you're not telling me. In fact, I think there's a lot you're not telling me." She paused and looked at her surroundings. Recent memory was catching up with her. "Riley, things really aren't adding up for me. I've been searching for Jonathan, this mysterious man who swept into and out of my life, for over a year. I finally find him and then poof! In a flash, he's gone. But not before telling me he needs me to look after you. What is that all about? What is *this* all about?" She waved her hands dramatically about, pissed off that Riley still wasn't being forthcoming with her. If her life was truly in danger, then she felt that the moment had arrived for her to have all the answers about Jonathan.

His eyes had narrowed and were boring into her, holding her in place. Maggie realized that she may have just potentially pushed too hard and right out of both Riley's and Jonathan's lives. But if the business world had taught her anything, it was to not apologize when she knew she was right. To show weakness would only invite further manipulation.

"You know what?" he finally said. "Let's go into the garage. There's something else you need to see." He turned and walked out of the building, and Maggie breathed a sigh of relief before following.

Once they were inside the garage, Riley walked over to the middle of the floor and knelt down. Then he pushed down hard and fast on a spot that was a slightly different color than the rest of the concrete. It looked as though it had been patched. To Maggie's surprise, it was actually a spring-loaded door that popped up just enough for Riley to get his fingers underneath it. He lifted it the rest of the way open, then let go of it as it fell backwards with a loud thud. Maggie peered down into a dark hole in the ground. Riley reached inside and flipped a switch that illuminated a staircase. He descended the stairs and motioned for her to follow. "I want to show you something."

"Riley, I'm claustrophobic, and I mean *really* claustrophobic."

"So am I," he said and then descended the rest of the steps. Maggie looked down at Riley, wondering why she was subjecting herself to this, but also knew that if she didn't follow, her questions would never be answered.

"I promise, it's completely safe," Riley told her. "There's a lot of room down here, which is the only reason I'm not too freaked out." His words didn't offer any comfort as she remained standing like a statue. "It will only take a quick minute," he said.

Maggie summoned all her strength before cautiously proceeding down the steps. Finding the bottom step, she reached out and grabbed Riley's hand in a death grip. "I don't want to be down here any longer than I have to, so hurry up and show me whatever it is you need to."

Allowing him to lead her down a concrete hallway, she found that it opened into a small room. "Okay, this room has plenty of food, water, guns, and ammo that could sustain two people for quite some time. The rest of the tunnel goes about two hundred yards and comes out beyond the tree line, where an ATV is gassed up and out of sight."

"Riley, what is all this?" Maggie said, taking a step back from him. She hit him with a flurry of questions. "Are you some kind of survivalist? What is this place? Who are you running from? I'm not taking another step until you tell me."

"This is going to sound really crazy, but trust me, Maggie, it's real. Yes, I guess you could say I am a survivalist, but it's not what you think."

"Go on," Maggie said warily.

"Back at the hospital, you asked me if I thought Jonathan is a guardian angel. The answer is yes. Well, he was. After Allison died, Jonathan came to visit me—he looked as real as you or me. He told me he was Allison's guardian angel. Naturally, I didn't believe him. I thought he was crazy. But he knew things about her. There was just this . . . way about him, a genuineness. Anyway, he told me that the night of the accident, I was meant to die with Allison in the car crash."

Maggie remained quiet, hoping that he would continue, knowing that the time to push was now over.

"Jonathan said there are demons out here among us. They have the power to do awful things. They kill people. They can even take over the body of someone and use it as a vehicle for evil. That night, they wanted to kill both Allison and me. They distracted Jonathan and he wasn't able to protect her. As a result, she was gravely injured."

"I'm so sorry," Maggie said softly. "Take your time."

Riley wiped a tear from his cheek, struggling to maintain his composure. "Well, the guilt was more than he could handle," he continued. "So, he was given a choice. He could escort Allison to Heaven and remain with her there for eternity, or he could fall to Earth and look after me. I would be his new charge. However, he would lose some of his powers. For reasons I don't understand, he decided to become a Fallen. I think maybe he thought he owed it to Allison. He told me that because he had chosen to become a Fallen, he had a price on his head—"

"What do you mean?" Maggie said, looking at him.

"Well, Fallens are rare. When a guardian angel falls to Earth to walk here with us, they are considered a gold prize to the Devil. He wants them and will do anything to get them, just to spite God. He sends his demons to Earth to hunt them and claim them and if they can take down a mortal along the way, even better."

"So, it's true then, that there really are guardian angels?" Maggie said. She recalled what Joe Packton had told her that night when she went to meet with him at the prison. She had always been skeptical about religion and God and Heaven. But something deep down inside her was pushing her to open her mind and heart to what Riley was telling her. "So, where's Jonathan now? Why did he leave if he's supposed to protect you?"

Riley gave a long sigh. "Last year, I came across a group of demons who tracked us down. They killed two of my friends trying to get close to us. Luckily, we survived that first encounter. Later, two more demons found us but they were different from the first group. They attacked Jonathan and almost killed him. During the attack, he was infected by a poison of some kind, one which is now slowly moving through his system, and it's changing him in ways he can't control. Sometimes he goes into what you might call a blind rage. Anyway, he decided he was becoming a threat to me and didn't want to risk hurting me.

"That night when we met at the hospital, Jonathan was preparing to go away with another Fallen to a place where he can look for healing and where he won't be a danger to me or anyone else. I think he thought I'd be safer if he weren't around. So, for now, I'll stay out here until I figure out what to do. I honestly don't know why he asked you to stay with me or look after me."

When Riley stopped talking, Maggie looked up, already knowing from his expression what he would say next.

"It would probably be better if you weren't here, Maggie. I've lost two friends already simply because they knew Jonathan and me. I don't want anything to happen to you."

Maggie considered everything Riley was saying. Her analytical mind kicked in. As crazy as all this sounded, she wasn't as shocked as Riley may have expected. She knew deep down that Jonathan was no ordinary man. In that first instant she met him that night in the alley, she was astounded by the giant of a man he was and how he had appeared out of nowhere and threw her two assailants around like rag dolls. There was no doubt in her mind that he had saved her life. His whole being, the way he spoke, the way he was with her—she knew there was something different about him, but she didn't know how to define it. He was . . . otherwordly.

"I'm not going anywhere," Maggie said flatly. "I don't know why, but that night outside the hospital, Jonathan looked me in the eyes and asked me to look after you. I'm not sure what he meant, but he saved my life. And—whatever his reasons, I'm going to do what he asked. I'm going to stay with you. We'll figure it out."

"Okay, for now we'll stay here. Just know that this will be the safe place if there's ever a threat. This is where you should go whether I'm with you or not. It's a hiding place that nobody would be able to find. The door locks behind you, and can't be penetrated from the outside once you push the locking mechanism. Jonathan told me, if there was ever trouble, to wait as long as possible and then leave."

Looking around the tiny room, Maggie almost asked where they would sleep. But then who could sleep knowing someone or something was out there trying to harm you? Or worse. "So, where would we go after that?"

Riley looked down. "I honestly don't know. I guess we run for as long as we have to and hope to stay one step ahead of—death."

Maggie looked at Riley and nodded, fully understanding that being under investigation was the least of her worries.

CHAPTER 29

L ucifer couldn't comprehend why he could no longer hear Legionaries's thoughts. It was as though someone had changed the frequency. If he couldn't tune into what his lackey was thinking, he wouldn't be able to manipulate him. This could be a problem. His most useful tactic was his ability to know whenever a subordinate was lying or scheming, and now his lackey had somehow figured out how to tune him out. *Damn, what is that lackey up to?* he wondered. True, he always loved a good challenge, but only if he already knew the outcome. Perhaps he would have to send one of his regional leaders to babysit Legionaries until he could figure out what was going on. But he needed to be careful. Gossip spread like wildfire in the ranks, which could eventually lead to a struggle for power. He needed to keep control of things.

Lucifer knew he would have to be careful about who he selected. It would have to be someone with a lot to gain. It was his own mistake, allowing Legionaries to walk among the humans. He knew damn well what the consequences could be if he didn't keep Legionaries under his thumb. But Legionaries must have seen his own image reflected in a mirror and knew what he was. He had to make sure Legionaries never figured out the depth of his own power, which had been successfully subdued for so many centuries. Lucifer wasn't about to allow his reign to be challenged.

"Damn!" he screamed, slamming his fist into the palm of his hand. "Esperanza, come!" he said sharply.

As if on cue, Esperanza was immediately by his side, head down, making sure not to look directly at him. She knelt before him, placing her head all the way to the floor before she spoke. "Yes, my Savior, how may I serve?"

The frustration growing inside of Lucifer faded a bit as he saw how obedient and eager she was to please him. Her presence brought pure enjoyment. She was almost perfect in all that she did for him. Almost. After all, she had dared to touch him without permission back at the trial of Abel and Bryce. It was only the one time, but it was in front of all the regional leaders. They surely must have noticed. He couldn't have them thinking he was losing control of his own house. First his sons, then Legionaries, and now Esperanza. He felt himself seething. All of his subordinates knew to never, ever touch him. Ever. The anger that he told himself to keep in check moments prior boiled over.

"Never defy me!" Lucifer yelled, then stomped on the back of Esperanza's head, flattening it into the ground. Her body went completely limp and her right leg twitched for a moment before going still. Lifting his foot, he wiped the brain matter on the back of her dress. He turned away from her and felt a bit of relief. Carrying out a little discipline always made him feel better. However, no one was around to have seen him do it, which diminished some of the desired effect.

Lucifer watched the slow, methodical process of regeneration until Esperanza returned to her old, beautiful self. She neither asked him why nor looked up at him, but instead resumed the same position, kneeling with her head touching the floor once more. Yes, she was nearly perfect. Still, he felt no pity for her since, truthfully, it brought back old memories of how it used to be with Legionaries as his lackey. Only with Legionaries, he had made sure to torture and punish him daily, since he knew what his former lackey could become if he didn't constantly manipulate him.

"Bring me Tristan," he said calmly, his anger cooling. He had selected Tristan for one reason: his brains. Tristan was far more manipulative than any other regional leader and had no problem with how far he was willing to go to make sure that he received glory for his accomplishments.

Esperanza remained, unmoving, in the same position. Lucifer was once again about to lose his patience until he realized she was waiting to be dismissed. She really was the perfect servant.

"Leave me. I expect him here immediately," he said coolly.

Esperanza finally stood, head bowed, then backed out of the room, never looking up or showing him her back, out of respect. Once out of Lucifer's chambers, she walked with a quick step to the front door of the house, which led into Hell and the damned souls that occupied it. As she entered, blackened souls pleaded with her to show mercy as she passed by. Arriving at the swirling green wormhole that would take her to Tristan's region, she turned and looked at the faces pressed up against the translucent wall—the only thing that separated her from the damned.

She gave them a sadistic, unforgiving smile. "No one can hear you, and no one cares. Accept your fate and know that you are doomed for eternity." Then she stepped into the wormhole and disappeared.

———

There was a time when the regional leaders referred to Esperanza's job as a lackey. Esperanza, however, commanded more respect from these so-called leaders. Several, at first, did call her a lackey until she informed them that if they continued to refer to her in that manner, she would refer to them as replaceable. All she would have to do is whisper their names to their master, their savior, and then the consequences would fall upon their heads. She knew they were all jealous of the attention Lucifer gave her and realized that she, too, had their fate in her hands. If they knew what was good for them, they would only call her Esperanza.

The wormhole opened, placing her right in front of Tristan and several of his slaves. They were leaning over a map of his region. He looked up at her but didn't acknowledge her presence.

"You have been summoned," Esperanza said flatly.

A trace of annoyance crossed Tristan's face. But he was loyal, obedient, and smart enough to understand the importance of a summons, no matter who delivered it. He said nothing to the others as he walked over to where Esperanza stood. There was only one wormhole in Hell that always remained open. Only region leaders and Esperanza had access to it. Like the others, all she had to do was call out her destination and the wormhole would transport her to her desired location. To be transported back to Hell, she wore a necklace with an upside-down cross pendant. Holding it in her hand, she would say, "He is not risen," and the wormhole would appear a moment later.

"One day you will learn your place when speaking to me," Tristan sneered under his breath. Esperanza gave him no sign of understanding as she spoke the commanded phrase. Suddenly, a wormhole opened and pulled them both in.

Tristan's region, like the others, ran on numbers. All of his slaves knew to carry on as was expected. If they didn't, Tristan would cast them back into Hell to be fed upon by other less fortunate souls. A slave's job was to collect the dead that were marked for Hell. Each region was responsible for their own area. Tristan's region of the world was so vast that he had twice the number of slaves.

When the wormhole opened again, Esperanza walked ahead of Tristan, leading him back through Hell and the translucent wall holding the damned behind it and into Savior's home.

Esperanza stopped in front of a door and opened it for Tristan, not bothering with turning her face from his, knowing that he would see it as a lack of respect from someone in her position. After he entered, Esperanza bowed her head to Savior and pulled the door close.

Restraining himself, Tristan marched into the room and knelt on one knee. "How can I serve you, Savior?" he asked.

Listening to Tristan's thoughts play out like a bad piece of piano music, Lucifer knew for certain that he was the right idiot for the job. This demon had twisted and schemed his way into overseeing the largest region, but he never challenged Lucifer in the slightest way.

"You once asked for the opportunity to bring me the Fallen," Lucifer replied. "As you know, I decided to give the task to my two sons, who are now at the Tower of Babel, paying the price for their incompetence and insubordination."

"A most fitting way to deal with anyone who doesn't deliver what they are asked," Tristan replied.

"Honored that you agree," Lucifer replied mockingly. "So, now I have chosen to send you to not only assist Legionaries in bringing me the Fallen, but you will also ensure that Legionaries returns to me as well. You will not only work with him, but you will closely monitor his actions and report back to me any suspicious behavior."

"Suspicious, Master?" Tristan asked skeptically.

"You don't think I can handle this myself," Lucifer spat back in disgust.

"No. I mean, yes. I know you could and am honored that you would—"

In a blink, Lucifer was out of his chair and lifting Tristan up by the chin with one hand. "Are you to question that I can't control everything and everyone that serves me? You kneel before me, yet your thoughts betray your intentions. You dare question my authority and what I am capable of? I am your Savior and your master and control everything in your miserable existence. Do not question me!"

He squeezed Tristan's throat, taking pleasure in listening to the cartilage and bone crackle under his grip. Tristan's body went limp as the life left his eyes and his head fell loosely to one side. Disgusted, Lucifer hurled Tristan's lifeless body at the wall, then sat once more. He fumed at how everyone now seemed to feel they could do what they wanted, from questioning his authority to touching him without permission, and now that damned Legionaries somehow closing off his thoughts. This would not do.

"Things are going to change around here," Lucifer seethed, "even if I have to rip this underworld apart. Everyone will know their place from now on!" His eyes were blazing red as he watched Tristan's body resume its form.

When the process was complete, Lucifer screamed, "Hounds!"

Several hulking mutts appeared, and without further instruction, closed in on their target, knowing exactly what was expected of them. Lucifer was in too much of a rage to enjoy the punishment. As his flesh was being ripped apart, Tristan's screams were soon silenced and replaced with deafening howls as the hounds fought over pieces of mangled meat.

Calming himself enough to look down at the carnage, Lucifer found his mood lifting. He could always count on his hounds. Intestines were strung out across the room as two of the hounds chewed on Tristan's corpse, which rocked back and forth from each pull and jerk from the razor-sharp teeth. Lucifer laughed. He always found the hounds so entertaining to watch.

"My children, you are my perfect creation!" Lucifer said, quite pleased with himself. The hounds paused for a moment and looked up at him, motionless, anticipating the next command.

"That is enough for now, my loves. Release!"

The hounds obeyed and walked back over to their master, licking their lips. They took up positions around him and turned a dead stare at the remains on the floor, hoping for another chance to feed.

The regenerating process was taking longer this time around. When it was completed, Tristan approached clumsily and knelt down before his Master.

"Do not ever question me," Lucifer growled. "If I ever hear another doubtful thought from you, I will take everything you believe to be yours. Do you hear me?"

"Yes, Savior."

"You will work with Legionaries. If you need to take charge of the situation then so be it. I will permit you to choose the body you wish to inhabit on Earth. However, keep in mind that I will pull you back if you fail me." Lucifer seethed at Tristan. "Leave me. I have grown tired of you."

Looking around at the hounds that remained at his side, his mood lifted. He grinned sardonically at Tristan. "On second thought, my hounds seem to want to say goodbye." At that, several of the hounds let out deep growls that echoed off the walls. Tristan froze, hoping they wouldn't be given a command. After a few moments, and satisfied by the desired effect, Lucifer's eyes bore into Tristan as he watched his pupils widen with terror. He then put him at ease with a simple word.

"Leave."

"Yes, my savior," Tristan replied shakily, tripping over his feet, as he quickly backed out of the room.

Closing the door behind him, Tristan found Esperanza standing there, staring at him. His demeanor changed quickly. "Get out of my way, you damn lackey!" he glared at her. "Don't forget your place. I am the leader of the largest region. And *you*, you are a lackey."

Esperanza said nothing as she looked back at him. The corners of her mouth curled up into a smile that told Tristan everything he needed to know. She had gotten the best of him, without saying a word. "Follow me," she said. "I will show you out so you can begin your job for Savior."

Biting his tongue, Tristan followed her back to the front door of Hell. She held it open for him and closed it behind him.

"Good luck," she said in a condescending tone right before the door closed.

He wanted to beat her so badly. Instead, he walked by the translucent wall in Hell and disappeared into the wormhole to find Legionaries.

When he arrived, he stepped out onto a well-manicured front lawn where Legionaries now lived. Looking around to make sure no one had seen him appear out of thin air, Tristan proceeded up the path to the front door. He knocked until he heard a voice from inside the house call out: "Give me a damn moment!"

Tristan pounded harder until the door flew open, revealing an elderly man staring at him. He reached out and swiftly caught Tristan's fist with ease. His grip tightened and bones began to crunch under the pressure. Tristan found himself on both knees staring up at the old lackey.

"Didn't anyone ever tell you to respect your elders?" Legionaries said, glaring at him. "Even an ignorant fool such as yourself should know better." He now slowly twisted Tristan's crushed hand. "Now tell me, why the hell are you here!"

Tristan did his best to keep his chin from quivering and his voice steady. He didn't want to give the lackey the satisfaction. "Master sent me to assist you."

"Assist me?" Legionaries mocked. "Are you sure you understood him correctly?" He tightened his grip, turning Tristan's hand into putty.

Tristan grimaced. "He directed me to work with you."

"Work 'with' or 'for' me?" Legionaries mused.

"For you." He couldn't stand the pain any more. "Please, Legionaries, I will do whatever you ask."

Legionaries's eyes turned black as coal, just like Master's did. Smiling down at Tristan, Legionaries released him and walked back inside.

Clutching at his forearm, Tristan saw that not only was the hand shattered, but his wrist was as well. He stood up and stumbled inside, kicking the door closed behind him. Entering the living room, he found Legionaries in a recliner, feet up, holding a glass of wine. He neither looked at Tristan nor seemed to care that he was there. Instead, he appeared to be in deep thought. Collapsing onto the couch, Tristan grimaced at his misshapen hand. It had already started to painstakingly rebuild itself as each bone and tendon morphed back into place.

"For the love of all that is evil, heal already!"

Legionaries snorted in amusement.

"What's your plan for the Fallen?" Tristan asked, finally able to sit upright. He began massaging his hand, trying to rub out the dull pain inside his knuckles.

"Kind of ironic that you are now taking orders from me,

wouldn't you say?" Legionaries mused. "I even had you on your knees begging for mercy."

Tristan knew Legionaries may be in charge for the moment, but he would always be a simple-minded lackey. He searched for an appropriate response. "Yes, it is quite strange, but I believe if you allow me to assist you, we will easily bring down this Fallen and reap our rewards."

"Tristan, you really are an idiot if you believe the vomit that just poured out of you. Even with all of our capabilities, there is a very slim chance we will succeed in bringing down a Fallen. Don't you recall that Bryce and Abel failed miserably?"

"We are never to speak their names! Besides, you know they only failed because of their own ignorance."

"Shut up, you tiresome, pathetic imbecile."

Tristan wanted to explain his side of thinking further, but knew that Legionaries was right. Wounding a Fallen was hard enough, but to actually bring it back to Master was a nearly impossible task. He waited. Minutes passed until Legionaries's eyes finally returned to normal. Then he smiled at Tristan, causing gooseflesh to appear on his arms.

"You now work for me, correct?

Unsure where the conversation was heading, Tristan didn't bother answering.

Legionaries beamed. "I believe one of us needs to be a lamb— and I also believe that job is best suited for you."

"What do you mean?" Tristan said, but he already knew the answer. He remembered the ancient stories that talked about a lamb, but he was fuzzy on the details. Assisting Legionaries was one thing, but now he was forcing him into this demeaning role?

"Just as I said," Legionaries replied, as he leaned forward and stared right through Tristan. "You—are going to be my sacrificial lamb."

CHAPTER 30

It had been weeks, and Riley and Maggie were still waiting for what was to come next Maggie was frustrated with the way her life had taken a hard turn. Her last call from Stuart informed her that the board had asked for her to step down, at least until things had settled down.

Throwing the phone on the couch, Maggie paced around the room, her arms folded in front of her. "Dammit," she finally blurted after her third lap, throwing her arms in the air.

"How bad is it?" asked Riley.

"Well, the company my father and I built could potentially no longer be mine. The board is asking me to step down for a short while, which basically means they want my resignation."

"What does Stuart think you should do?"

"Stuart believes that I am being used as a pawn in some game. He even went so far as to informing the board that I am still the primary shareholder and that he would accept their resignations if they chose to speak out against me. Which didn't go over so well, since several of my board members did indeed resign, signing severance packages within a week."

"I'm truly sorry, Maggie," said Riley. As if reading her mind that she needed to be alone, Riley slipped out the patio door.

Once he was gone, Maggie broke down on the couch, tucking her knees to her chest.

Having to play hard ball, given the board's dissension and

their lack of confidence in her, broke Maggie's heart. She had appointed every one of them, not just because of their background and the experience they brought to the table, but because of how hardworking they were and how much they had contributed to the company as individuals. But as hard as it was to accept, when push came to shove, the business's bottom line would always win out.

But that wasn't the only thing that was troubling for her. Now both her and Riley's dreams had become so intense that sleep was a thing they feared as much as a demon or the Devil himself showing up at their door. Before they said goodnight, they would look at each other hoping they would still be alive the next morning.

To keep busy, Riley taught Maggie how to shoot and introduced her to Jonathan's workouts—or as Riley called them, a baptism into hell. Despite having a broken finger, she did almost everything that he could. The weight training, as well as the cardio circuits, were far more intense than any trainer Maggie had ever worked with. She quickly came to agree with Riley's assessment of them. She was amazed that Riley was able to go for hours, even after she had quit. At one point she had joked that she should have him drug tested. Despite her daily pleas for mercy in the gym, she was happy to discover that in just a few weeks she had become really good with a handgun. The kick from the gun didn't bother her hand as much as she thought it would, partially because she beat Riley every time during target practice. He was a good instructor, but not the best shot. After their last practice, she hit ten out of ten targets in the span of fifteen seconds. Riley simply said, "Great shooting." She knew that it bothered him that she was already so much better than him with a handgun. If she needed further proof that she was correct with her assessment, Riley now only used the shotgun or rifle when they practiced.

Finishing up the Cardio Circuit training for the day, Maggie felt as if she had been hit by a truck. She believed she was making improvements until Riley had intensified it by adding in plyometrics, making her jump around like a rodent on a hot skillet. As they were completing the cooldown, Riley's phone began to ring. As he retrieved it off the bench, Maggie took the opportunity to rush outside to begin dry heaving.

The caller ID read Unknown. Riley was about to hit Ignore, believing that it was a solicitor. But then his thoughts drifted to Jonathan, and he quickly accepted the call.

"Jonathan?" Riley answered with a little too much hope in his voice. Maggie looked over at him. There was a pause on the other end, which Riley instantly took as a solicitor. Removing the phone from his ear, he was about to disconnect the call when he heard an older male voice on the other end.

"Riley? This is Griffin, Griffin Patterson. We met several weeks ago at the hospital. You gave me your business card and invited me to call if I ever needed to talk."

Riley remembered him. It was the night of the accident out on the highway—the night he had to say goodbye to Jonathan. His daughter was the police officer who had pulled Riley and Jonathan over. Griffin didn't know it, but Riley was partially responsible for what had put her in the hospital.

"Hi Griffin. Sorry, I was thinking it may have been someone else. Is your daughter doing any better?" There was a long pause. He immediately knew the answer.

In a somber tone, Griffin said, "Well, Riley, I buried my

daughter a week ago. Doctors told me that she had suffered a brain aneurism. I guess I can be thankful that she is no longer suffering, but now I carry a pain that no father should ever have to be burdened with."

Riley's mouth went dry as if he had just swallowed sand. He was unable to form an appropriate response. How could he possibly tell the poor man that he and Jonathan were to blame for her death? He collapsed onto the bench and ran a hand through his sweaty hair. Given everything he had been through, how could it be that another innocent life had been taken?

Griffin began crying. Speaking through sobs, Riley could barely understand what the man was saying. Finally, he pulled himself together and Riley heard him blow his nose. "Riley, would you maybe want to meet? I feel strange even asking. I mean, we've only met the one time. My pastor came by, which was kind of her. But I need more than just spiritual counsel."

Riley was on the verge of breaking down from the shame he carried. Especially now that this stranger was begging him for comfort when Riley felt he should be the one begging for forgiveness. His mouth was so dry, but he managed to respond. "I am so sorry Griffin, but I'm not in the city right now. I went back to my lake house after we spoke that night."

"I understand," Griffin said. "It was foolish for me to place my burdens on you. Forgive me, Riley, but if you ever come back to visit, please look me up. I would love to buy you a cup of coffee to express my gratitude for showing me such kindness that terrible night."

"I know this will come off as strange," Riley said, "but my lake house is in Potogi. It's about four hours away from Taupe City. Would you like to come stay with me for a few nights? It wouldn't be any trouble and I would love to have you." He looked over his shoulder and saw Maggie cock an eyebrow, wondering who he was talking to.

"Well, I don't know—I would hate to intrude on you. Besides, that's a pretty long drive for an old fellow like me."

"Please come," Riley said. "I have a guest room that even has an orthopedic mattress. You can rest as soon as you arrive. I promise it's no inconvenience. Plus, I think we should talk." It was time that he told Griffin the real cause of his daughter's death. He needed to confront his own demons and accept the repercussions. Griffin was broken not only because of a freak accident by Jonathan's powers gone wrong, but by Riley's futile understanding of how sick Jonathan really was. Furthermore, in protecting Jonathan he had flat out lied to Griffin that night in the hospital. This made Riley even more guilty than Jonathan since he had tried to cover the whole thing up, rationalizing that it was the right thing to do at the time. Except now an innocent life had been taken, and he was left hollow because he knew the whole truth. Maybe one day Griffin would be able to accept his apology.

"Well, if you're sure I won't be intruding, then I guess I could make the trip," said Griffin.

"Griffin, I promise that you are welcome here. It's just me and a friend who also needed to get away from the city for a bit." Riley felt a bit guilty for not first asking Maggie if she would mind.

"Are you sure that your friend won't mind me intruding?"

"Not at all." With the pressure building in the room, Riley turned to look at Maggie, only to find that she hadn't returned. "Would you like to come this weekend?" It was only Wednesday, so that would give him plenty of time to prepare for his guest.

"I guess I could make that work," said Griffin. "I could head out early and be there around noon on Friday. I haven't been sleeping well mainly due to bad dreams. Besides, people my age are always early to bed, early to rise."

Riley hoped that Griffin's dreams didn't bring fear of the dead with them. Goosebumps prickled his skin, and he shuddered. Then he realized that he had been quiet too long. "Yes, that sounds perfect. I will look forward to seeing you, Griffin. I believe we will have much to talk to about."

"I look forward to it as well."

Riley gave him his address, exchanged a few more pleasantries, then ended the call. He then went to check on Maggie. He hoped she didn't mind him inviting someone up. Once inside the house, he got his answer. He could hear things being tossed around in her room. Walking slowly down the hallway, finding the door wide open, he found her packing her things into one of his old suitcases.

"What are you doing?"

"Packing. What does it look like? I know I'm only a guest here, but maybe you could have asked if I minded you inviting someone else up here. Someone I don't know!"

"I need you to stop what you're doing and listen to me."

Maggie continued pulling clothes and other items from the dresser, throwing them aimlessly over her shoulder toward the suitcase, with most finding the floor. He allowed her to continue until he'd had enough of her tantrum, then he spoke more forcefully than he had intended.

"Maggie, stop right now!"

Like a coiled rattlesnake ready to strike, she spun and faced him, causing Riley to take a couple of steps back from her.

Her eyes bore into him, but it wasn't just anger that he saw in them. He could tell that he had wounded her with how carefree he had been in offering up his home to what she perceived as another stranger.

"Do you have any idea what is happening in my life right now?" she said. "My company is under scrutiny and I'm being blackmailed by a complete bottom-feeder. I've put my life on hold for this crazy year-long search for Jonathan. And when I finally find him, he disappears again! But that's not all. No, he asks me to take care of you—another stranger! And now I need to get ready to meet yet another stranger? Add the fact that we're essentially hiding out from I-don't-even-know-who or what. Riley, it's too much!"

Her voice had become a scream. Tears welled in her eyes.

She had every right to be pissed at him, but he needed her to calm down and understand why he did what he had. "Maggie, I was wrong not to have asked you first, and for that I am sorry," he said softly. "Believe me, I know how much you have sacrificed. But—I'm really sorry—I really am, but there's something else I need to own up to, so please just hear me out. It's important." He was afraid of her response, but he needed her to know.

His apology hadn't had much effect on her. Her eyes didn't soften. Instead, Maggie now crossed her arms in front of her, waiting for an explanation. Riley hated that he once again had to shine the light on something that he was responsible for. He looked down at the floor, unable to meet her eyes. He cleared his throat.

"This man, Griffin. I met him at the hospital. Jonathan and I are responsible for the death of his daughter. She was out there on the highway." He decided not to tell her, just yet anyway, that the whole thing started because she pulled them over.

Neither spoke for what seemed like an eternity. Finally, Riley looked up, finding that now Maggie was the one unable to make eye contact. "You have every right to be upset with me because this is where you live too. We're joined at the hip, for better or worse, at least for the foreseeable future. Which is why I need you to understand why I did this. I have to let this man know what really happened and to beg for his forgiveness. I even plan on telling him about Jonathan and why my life is the way it is now."

Maggie looked at him like he was crazy, but she didn't say a word.

Riley held up his hand. "I know, I know. I'm probably crazy to even consider it. But I can't go through the rest of my life knowing what I am partially responsible for and not owning up to it. Keeping Jonathan's secret is beyond this. The man lost his daughter and the guilt from it is eating me up inside."

He couldn't hide his hurting from Maggie. Tears rimmed his eyes, begging to be released. The weight that had rested on his shoulders seemed to be lifting little by little with every word he said. Taking the few steps between them, Maggie wrapped her arms around Riley, saying nothing. She just held him. After a few moments, Riley went to pull away, but Maggie held on to him.

"I had no idea you were carrying this extra burden," she whispered. "I understand why you invited him to come. Please don't think I am criticizing you or trying to sway your decision, but have you thought about how this man will perceive what you unload on him? I have seen Jonathan in the flesh, and I still can't believe what he actually is. Asking this man, Griffin, whom you've only just met, to believe that a guardian angel not only killed his daughter, but that you also tried to cover it up. Riley, this won't just mean exposing Jonathan, but this could get you in serious trouble if he goes to the authorities. Whether they believe him or not, they will want to speak with you."

Riley knew she was right, but he also knew he could no longer sit idly by, holding in the guilt he felt about the man's daughter. He needed to make things right.

Maggie pulled back and looked into his face. "Riley, whatever you decide, I will respect and support you. I just want you to understand that this is a conversation that may take more than just a weekend to explain."

Again, Riley knew she was right, but at this point he had to take the risk that Griffin wouldn't believe him, may even write him off as some kind of nut, all in an attempt to help him come to terms with what he himself couldn't fully understand. "Thank you, Maggie, for trying to understand, but I have to do this. I hope he won't think he's stumbled across some Bible-thumping maniac. I just have to believe that, for some reason, he will listen to what I have to say and will understand that I am telling him the truth."

"Then I will support you," Maggie said.

CHAPTER 31

"Want to let me know what that was about?" Tristan asked. He had overheard the end of the phone conversation, his partner feigning the voice of a weak old man.

Legionaries gave him a malicious look as he placed the phone back on the cradle. "Need I remind you that you are simply serving as a sacrificial lamb?" He turned away. "You don't need to know anything else."

In the past few weeks they had been forced to work together, Tristan had come to understand that Legionaries was no longer the same lackey that had suffered under Master's boot for so many centuries. In fact, he was more calculating and more powerful than Tristan had ever imagined. For hundreds of years, Tristan had heard the stories that Legionaries may be playing a part that he hadn't asked for, similar to the one that he himself was now being forced to play. There had been a few rumors here and there that Legionaries was far different than what he appeared to be. Some had whispered that if Legionaries knew what he truly was that he could very well be the new god of Hell.

Tristan had always been too preoccupied with his own efforts to grow his region. He was working on a strategy to absorb the other regions so that he would be second only to Lucifer. There would be no more competition for his favors. However, after weeks of seeing those red eyes up close, Tristan now understood what the other regional leaders had been whispering about. He no longer saw Legionaries as some poor, pathetic lackey who begged to be shown mercy. No, what he now saw was the very essence of death and all the suffering and rage that dwelled inside it. During their first night together, Tristan went back to one of the spare bedrooms to be alone. He wasn't tired, he just couldn't comprehend that Legionaries wasn't the same individual he was before. For hundreds of years, he had mocked Savior's former lackey, even took pleasure countless times listening to the demon beg for mercy, only to see that this new version of Legionaries was self-assured and domineering.

Growing tired of contemplating what to make of Legionaries, Tristan stood from the bed and, just as his hand was on the bedroom doorknob, thought he heard two male voices coming from the living room. Pulling the door open, he walked into the dark hallway, placing his hand on the wall to help guide him.

In the blackness of the living room, Tristan found two red eyes already locked on his location, as if they could see him in the dark. When he found the wall light switch, a sinister voice that didn't belong to Legionaries stopped him from turning it on.

"Go back to your room, sacrificial lamb. Stay in there until I need you."

Then came the oddest sound of a snake hissing, followed by a ripple of electricity that half illuminated the outline of some strange beast. Instead of turning his back, Tristan walked backwards until he was back in his room with the door closed. Confined in the room, Tristan vaguely heard two male voices start up again, but the words were too muffled to understand.

Days later, after the incident had occurred, and growing tired of being a pawn in the game, Tristan's anger got the best of him. He stood up and proclaimed, "I will not be some kind of sacrifice just so you can claim all the glory for capturing a Fallen."

"Sit!" Legionaries hissed.

Tristan immediately collapsed back onto the couch. He attempted to stand again in defiance, only to find that something seemed to be forcing him down, like two invisible hands on his shoulders that drove him into the couch.

"What's happening?" Tristan asked, confused.

"You are sitting. Or are you too blind to see that?"

Tristan struggled. "Why can't I stand?"

Legionaries gave him a mischievous smile. "I don't think you really want to know the answer to that question. As soon as you quit struggling, we will continue."

Tristan continued to struggle against whatever was holding him in place, only for the force of the invisible hands to drive him even further into the couch. "Okay, I submit! Please stop what you are doing to me." Suddenly, the pressure on his shoulders was released.

"That's a good lackey," Legionaries grinned. "Don't worry, you will have plenty of opportunities to claim your so-called glory, receive all the praise you desire, blah, blah, blah. However, you will travel that road alone. I don't need the false praise of that pseudo-god. And I won't stand there and watch you suck up to him either, one idiot praising another."

Tristan couldn't believe Legionaries was openly mocking Lucifer. Had he forgotten that he could hear their unguarded thoughts? A voice whispered to him, "No, you worthless ass, I have not forgotten. Listen closely to what I am about to say. I simply don't care if he can hear my thoughts!" Legionaries was smiling devilishly.

Tristan was astonished by the outright blasphemy Legionaries had just committed.

"I'm a simple lackey, isn't that what you were so quick to call me?" asked Legionaries.

Tristan stared at Legionaries in disbelief. The rumors he'd been told from the other region leaders turned out to be true. Legionaries had been forced into the role as lackey, not for punishment, but because Lucifer was indeed afraid of him, and knew exactly what he could do if not supervised.

"I warned you, didn't I?" Legionaries said as he stood, then fell to his hands and knees in convulsions. Tristan watched as Legionaries's body started to grow, as the seams of the clothing stretched and split apart. His shoulders made a loud popping noise as they separated, followed by more loud pops as the rest of his body grew in size. Then everything came to a complete stop, as Legionaries's head collapsed to the ground.

Too fascinated by the whole ordeal to get up and check on his partner, Tristan waited, anticipating that there would be more to follow. A soft gurgling sound filled the silent room and before Tristan knew what was happening, a large beast stood over him, pinning him to the couch with one massive paw. A serpent's tongue slithered out of the creature's eagle head, striking him several times in the face, causing Tristan to cry out in pain.

The beast climbed off him and sat back on its haunches, never taking its red eyes from his. Tristan drew back, taking in what was now before him, the lion's body with an eagle's head. Electrical currents ran up and down the scales along his back. "What are you?" he asked.

The voice was one he had never heard before. "I am what your so-called Master will wish he would have kept close to his side. That worthless, mindless individual should have known this version of me would one day be unleashed. And here I am," it hissed. "You will address me as Legion, and only Legion."

"Yes, Legion," Tristan quickly replied. "Tell me how I may serve you."

"Tsk tsk tsk. If Lackey heard you speak such blasphemy, you'd be banished to the depths of Hell without a second thought."

"I can be of use to you. You know that I command the largest region. I can bring every one of my slaves to assist in taking whatever you want."

Changing back into the body of Legionaries, he walked, naked, back to the recliner. The clothes he had been wearing now lay shredded on the floor next to Tristan. The look on Legionaries's face gave the impression that he was actually considering Tristan's offer.

"You really want to help me?" said the naked demon.

Tristan groveled. "Yes, very much, Legion."

Sitting once more and picking up his wine glass from the end table, Legion took a small sip before returning the glass to its resting position.

"Then be my lamb!"

CHAPTER 32

Friday arrived faster than Riley had anticipated. Riley had tried to call Griffin before he left to come out to the lake but only got the answering machine at his house. He had been in such a rush to repair things with Maggie that he hadn't thought to ask Griffin for his cell phone number. He and Maggie were at the kitchen table, drinking coffee and reading sections of the newspaper. Maggie had chosen the sports section and Riley had the classifieds. He would occasionally glance at her and see that she was biting her nails. He knew exactly what had her on edge, which presented him with a moral dilemma.

On one hand, if he gave in and allowed her to self-indulge in the nonsense written in the business section, she would be pissed off for the rest of the morning. On the other hand, the one time he had thrown the business section of the newspaper out, believing that he was doing her a favor. She had made him go dig it out of the trash and was still pissed off for the rest of the morning after reading it. It was a catch-22 no matter what he did.

After Maggie shifted in her chair for the umpteenth time, Riley shuffled through the newspaper, found the business section, and handed it over. She snatched it from him and saw the headline that read "Gregory Portal Provider Stock Worthless" and dove into the article. She began swearing under her breath until, finally, she flung the business section across the kitchen.

Without looking up at her, Riley picked up the sports section and handed it back over. Taking it, she responded sheepishly, "Thank you." Riley didn't offer a reply because he knew what would follow, now that they had fallen into a daily routine.

"It's complete crap what they are allowed to print these days!" she said with a huff. Riley remained silent knowing that if he engaged with her, she would rant for the next several hours. "I'm serious," she continued. "Last I heard, my stock was on the rise. Despite that, everyone loves drama even though they know it's complete crap."

"More coffee?" Riley asked, knowing she hadn't heard him since she began spiraling. He refilled their mugs and placed hers directly in front of her. Then he returned to the classified ads, hoping today's tirade would be over soon.

She pounded the paper into the table. "Blows my mind that newspapers can print whatever they want without being held accountable for their negligent reporting."

Riley knew that eventually this rant would lead to the changes she would make to the judicial system. It was like a scene out of a bad movie that he was forced to partake in every morning.

"I'm serious, if I were a lawyer or judge or had something to do with the judicial system, you can bet there would be some changes."

Riley wondered how this woman had become one of the richest people in the world. One minute she was joking nonstop, then the next she was raving like a lunatic over some news that had set her off. He let his curiosity get the best of him. "How is it that you have been so successful?" he asked. "From what I see, you seem to enjoy picking at me without end and when you vent—oh dear God, you can go on and on and on and—"

"I get the point!" she blurted.

Riley cocked an eyebrow at her, doubting that she even knew

what he was asking. He could tell she was giving his question serious thought and choosing her words carefully, or so it seemed.

"It was one of the best days of my life when I bumped into you," she said.

Without saying a word, Riley cocked his head to the side and once more raised an eyebrow as if to say, *You've got to be kidding*.

"Don't flatter yourself. I am aware that we are only together because of our circumstances. What I am trying to say is that during my search for Jonathan, I decided to shut out everyone and everything in my life until I had accomplished my goal of finding him. Even though it was fate that I ran into him at the hospital just as unexpectedly as he had shown up that night to save me from the attack, I just feel . . . oh, forget it. I'm rambling."

"No, Maggie, go on. I'll hear you out."

"Well, I guess spending time with you has made me realize that this could be the start of a rare friendship, unlike any that I have had in the past. We met at a weird point in our lives, and I only stuck around because Jonathan asked me to. Turns out, I am glad that he did, despite how much I am afraid of the future. But I can tell you one thing for certain."

"And what's that?" Riley replied.

"For as long as the ride lasts, I am just happy to be a part of it. But I still want to see Jonathan again. I need to see him again. I mean, you're okay, but I searched a year to find Jonathan, not some lawn boy."

Riley laughed. "Well, I can't say I blame you. If our roles were reversed and I had searched for a year and then only got to see Jonathan for a few moments, and then got stuck with some overbearing, overconfident, self-centered—"

He stopped himself.

She cocked an eyebrow at him. Riley blushed, knowing the message had been received.

"I just want to make sure you know where you stand on the hierarchy ladder," he muttered.

Maggie was about to reply when they heard the sound of a car door closing.

CHAPTER 33

Legionaries and Tristan were just leaving Lucifer's chamber after reporting in and, for now, Legionaries would continue to play the role of his lackey. Lucifer, true to his nature, reminded him that he was an overthinking idiot, who'd better not screw up his task of bringing him the Fallen. He even reminded Legionaries of what awaited him if he failed by causing a throbbing pain in his head. Legionaries did his best to show how badly it was hurting him. He writhed around on the floor, begging for mercy, playing the part as best he could.

The pain that had once been so crippling was now only a soft pinprick inside his head. Legionaries was, indeed, growing in power and this confirmed it. Although Lucifer had controlled him for centuries and cast on him torture upon torture, his powers over him were diminishing. But he couldn't let on to Lucifer. Not yet. Legionaries secretly wondered in awe at a future of endless possibilities.

Once Lucifer had left the room, Legionaries couldn't help being disgusted about having to carry on with the charade. But he knew he just needed to bide his time. Then he heard the reassuring voice of Legion in his head. *Patience. It won't be much longer until we have it all.* Legionaries smiled, knowing that Legion would always protect him. Until then, he must wait for the day when Legion was fully incorporated in him. He longed for the day when Legion's voice would be his.

"I'm sorry, but what the hell just happened?" Tristan asked.

"Say nothing more, you idiot," Legionaries hissed, "until we are back at Patterson's house." With that, he called forth a wormhole and the two of them were instantly transported back to Patterson's home.

Legionaries went to the kitchen and poured a large glass of wine, before taking his usual seat. "For now, all you need to be concerned about is getting yourself near Riley. But keep yourself out of view. Wait a day to let me get settled into the routine of their lives. Then you know what to do."

"But I thought I was supposed to help you get the Fallen," Tristan said.

"Yes, Tristan, I am aware of that. But we have no idea where the Fallen is. We must lure him to us."

Tristan, knowing his place, remained silent.

"For now," said Legionaries, "I will go stay with Riley, serving as the bait to bring the Fallen out of hiding. If he doesn't come after the first day I am there, then your job is to kill Riley and his new lady friend. I will not stand in your way. But when the Fallen comes, we'll each have a part to play. Remember yours. If we are successful, you will get to have all the glory of bringing the Fallen back to your Master. I, however, will not accompany you."

"No?" Tristan said, bewildered.

"Just remember, if you ever cross my path again after our job is complete, I'll have you begging me to send you back to Hell. Understood? There are other things I plan to do. I will no longer serve that tiresome false god for the rest of eternity."

Tristan began to reply until Legionaries held up a hand silencing him. "Leave me before I show you what kind of pain I can really inflict upon you."

CHAPTER 34

Pulling up to Riley's lake house in Patterson's car, Legionaries was actually impressed with the size of the property. The lake sat right off the grounds, which appeared to be very well kept. He began to wonder what it would be like to make the place his own once the owner was gone. He now understood what free will was, since the good pastor Beth had explained it to him. He was free to make his own choices but needed to be aware that each choice he made came with its own set of consequences. He could do what he wanted when he wanted. But he also knew he couldn't be foolish with this gift or it would rear its ugly head and bite him hard.

The only thing that kept him on this assignment was the thought of seeing a Fallen face-to-face. This would be a test to find out just how powerful he was becoming—with the help of Legion, of course. He was now eager to fight a Fallen and see if it would bleed. That thought alone was enough to hold his interest.

He stepped from the car just as the front door of the house opened, and Riley and Maggie came out onto the wraparound porch. He smiled and raised a hand in greeting. "It is good to see you, Riley, but I feel foolish for putting you out."

Riley met him by the car, then wrapped him in a hug. "Thank you so much for coming," he said. "I think this weekend will do us both some good."

More than you think, Legionaries thought.

"Can I grab your suitcase?"

"Oh, I can do that," he replied, walking around the car to the trunk to retrieve the suitcase.

"Let me show you inside," Riley said, "but first, let me introduce you to my friend, Maggie."

"Hello, Griffin," Maggie said as she offered her hand, which Legionaries pleasantly accepted.

"It's so nice to meet you," he said. "I must say, and I hope it's not too bold of me, but you are far prettier in person than those pictures I've seen of you in the newspapers and tabloids."

Seeing the worried look on her face made Legionaries almost laugh out loud. If she only knew he thought. "Oh, I'm sorry, dear. Don't worry, I will never tell a soul that you are out here," he said, smiling at her. "You are both doing me a favor in allowing me to share this beautiful home with you for the weekend. So, rest assured, and know that your secret is safe with me."

Maggie now smiled, then hugged Griffin. Still no spark, which again Legionaries found odd.

"Let me help you inside," said Riley. "I'll show you which room I have you set up in."

"Thank you so much."

Arriving at the steps, Riley placed his hand on Legionaries's back to assist him. Playing the role to perfection, Legionaries took hold of the railing and began ascending slowly. "Go on ahead, Riley, I can manage."

But Riley, ever the good host, stayed by his side.

Once inside the house, the foul smell hit him with a force. It was like rotting meat that had been left out in the sun. Not even Hell had this kind of stench. Yes, this was the unmistakable smell of a Fallen. Any demon ever released or escaped from Hell could attest to what Legionaries was now having to suffer through.

As they walked through the house, Legionaries knew for certain what room he would be staying in.

"The room at the end of the hall will be yours," Riley said. "Maggie's and mine are just down from yours." Riley led him down the hall and opened the door. Again, a powerful stench blasted Legionaries, causing him to gasp aloud and making his eyes water.

"What's wrong?" Riley asked. He went to reach out and steady Griffin, then stopped himself as though he remembered the shocks he had received off him. He dropped his hand to his side.

Trying to breathe through his mouth, Legionaries asked, "Could we sit outside? It would do me good after such a long drive."

"Sure, if you want to," Riley said. He seemed a bit concerned. "Can I get you something?"

"I'll take a glass of water, if you don't mind," Legionaries replied, then headed to the patio door off the living room. Stepping outside, he closed the door behind him, hoping to keep the stench from following him.

Riley looked at Maggie, only to find that she seemed to be sympathetic with Griffin's situation.

"I'll grab us some lemonade," she offered. "Put his suitcase on the bed so that he doesn't have to exert himself retrieving it from the floor tonight." She hurried to the kitchen.

After placing the suitcase on the bed, Riley joined Griffin outside, taking the seat across from him. Having made the lemonade earlier in anticipation of Griffin's arrival, Maggie was already sitting next to him, holding his hand. "I can't tell you how sorry I am to learn of your daughter's passing."

Riley noticed that Griffin didn't offer a thank you, then pushed the thought away. The man had just lost his daughter, and here he was scrutinizing every move the man made. *What is wrong with me?* Riley wondered.

"We are so glad that you came out," Maggie continued. "Riley told me everything and I know there are some things he needs to open up about to you as well."

Riley had wanted to wait to broach the subject. However, now all he could envision was Griffin calling him an idiot and leaving for a much longer ride home.

Griffin turned his sad eyes to Riley. "What do you need to tell me?"

Guess this is as good a time as any, Riley thought. "Griffin, before I begin, I want to express how sorry I am for your loss. I feel more grief over it than you might imagine."

Griffin stared at Riley with a confused expression.

Riley let out a long sigh. "I don't know how to even begin, but please hear me out until I'm finished. You will not want to believe what I have to say, but if you give me a chance, I can explain why the death of your daughter has really affected me." He stopped to gather his courage and hoped what he wanted to say would come out right. "Do you believe in angels?"

He could tell that the question had taken Griffin by surprise and he honestly couldn't blame him. Anticipating the worst, Riley gave him a moment to process the question. From the corner of his eye, he saw Maggie giving him a look of reassurance.

Griffin looked perplexed. "Yes, I know that they exist," he replied hesitantly.

Riley felt the load shift slowly off his shoulders as he continued. "Well, I hope that will make what I am about to say sound not quite so crazy. A little over a year ago, my wife and I were in a car accident that took her life. Afterward, a stranger came into my life. He told me his name was Jonathan, and that it meant 'Gift from God.' I honestly thought he was insane after our first encounter, but after listening to his story, I learned to trust and accept him for what he was. He said he had been my wife's guardian angel, but after her death, he decided to fall to Earth and become a fallen angel so that he could stay with me and look after me. He felt such guilt about not being able to save Allison. However, as a Fallen, he would have to give up some of his powers."

He looked at Griffin to gauge his reaction.

Griffin offered a reassuring smile. "Feel free to open up to me. I will listen to what you have to say."

Feeling the reassurance, Riley continued. "Jonathan is, indeed, an angel. I have witnessed everything he can do and has done for me." He looked over at Maggie and she nodded. "And Maggie has witnessed what Jonathan can do as well. You see, the accident happened on my wedding day because of an escaped rogue demon that wanted to cause a horrible accident and kill as many people as he could. But Allison was the only one who died. I know it sounds crazy, but I survived it." He paused to gather himself. "Griffin, can I ask you another question?"

"Yes, son," Griffin replied.

"Do you believe in the Devil—in evil?"

"Well, I don't know," he said cautiously. "Do you?"

"Well, I came to believe in all of that." Riley replied. "Jonathan told me that fallen angels are extremely rare. They are prized possessions to the Devil, if he can get his hands on one. He sends his demons to Earth to capture them, or kill them if they have to. Jonathan knew demons were coming for him, and because he had pledged himself to look after me for the rest of my days, I was in danger as well. I wouldn't have believed it if I hadn't experienced it myself, but evil found us.

"There were two demons that came after us. Jonathan put up a huge battle against them, but in the end, they bested him by inflicting a wound using a weapon that held poison. He barely survived it. We thought he was okay, but little by little I began to notice changes in him. He began to lose his temper. Before the incident, he wasn't even capable of such a thing. Eventually, it became so bad that we had to go back to Taupe City to try and find help from another Fallen he knew."

Riley had come to the part of the story that involved Griffin's daughter, the police officer. His eyes began to show signs of tears promising to come, as the weight on his shoulders actually began to subside. He wanted to be freed of this burden and hoped telling Griffin the truth was the right thing to do, for both of them. Fighting back the tears, he continued.

"We were stopped on the highway on our way to the hospital where we hoped to find the other Fallen. I know now that the officer who pulled us over was your daughter." Riley couldn't understand how Griffin remained so calm, in light of what he was telling him. Then again Riley chalked it up to shock as he plowed through with the rest of his narrative. "Jonathan was behind the wheel but didn't have a driver's license. I could feel his anxiety building, but then he tried to send out what I think of as peace. He has done it to me several times. But this time, instead of sending out a sense of peace, it was pain, extreme pain. I believe it came from the poison he was infected with. He was very sick, and even though he had good intentions, he ended up hurting so many that day. Your daughter was hurt because of how close she was to him when he sent out that energy. He didn't mean to hurt anyone. He couldn't control what it did."

Riley's vision was blurred by tears as he bumbled through the next part. "I will never be able to tell you how truly sorry I am because I just don't have the words. I don't expect you to forgive me. I should have known how sick Jonathan was but I just . . ." Riley trailed off, no longer able to continue.

Griffin stared back at Riley. "Is this why you asked me to call you that night after we met at the hospital?" he asked.

Riley reached out to take Griffin's hands, only for him to pull away.

"Why would God allow one of his servants to rip my daughter from me? I thought he was supposed to be all merciful?"

"Griffin, I am so sorry," Riley said, "but I don't know the answer to that question. I have prayed for understanding, but I can't understand why this was allowed to happen."

"I'm sorry, but I need to be alone for a while," Griffin said, excusing himself. Riley watched as Griffin first headed towards the house, then seemed to change his mind and veer off towards the dock. Riley expected Griffin to have asked more questions after learning that a fallen angel had killed his daughter. What was even more strange, as Riley wiped his eyes with the back of his hands, was that Griffin hadn't shed one single tear.

CHAPTER 35

Standing in the parking lot of a biker club hangout, Lucifer noticed that everyone who walked in and out wore leather vests all sporting the same logo. "Diablos," Lucifer said with a smirk as a grizzled, heavy-set man walked by, his arm draped around a woman. There was a faded green tattoo of an upside-down cross on the woman's neck. Lucifer was utterly pleased.

The heavy-set man noticed him looking at them. "What's your problem?" he demanded.

Lucifer, still staring at the woman's neck tattoo, realized they were expecting a response as they glared at him. "Well, actually, I am glad you asked because I do have a very large problem. It's really a pain in my ass. I can't seem to get a handle on the situation and it has been driving me crazy. You see, I sent a lackey to fix this problem. I should have known better. So then I sent one of my regional leaders to assist, but now I have a good hunch that he is going to need all the help he can get."

"What the hell is wrong with you?" the big guy snarled. "You think I wanna listen to your nonsense?"

"Well, you did ask," Lucifer replied innocently.

"Let me tell you something, bud. This hangout is biker territory. I don't see no diablo patch, so why don't you take your fancy ass somewhere else before you find yourself in a situation you can't walk away from."

"You think I am a bit overdressed?" Lucifer feigned surprise. "This suit is tailor-made by an Italian man I employ. I won't bore you with the details, but he does seem to enjoy cranking them out at the snap of a finger."

The woman of the profane tattoo was giving Lucifer a once over. *At least she thinks I look good, despite how simple minded she must be to go for such an idiotic poet*, Lucifer mused. "Anyway, let's go inside and I will buy everyone a drink and then I can see which of you wants to earn some easy money."

The big man's face softened as he began to laugh aloud. "Well, then it would be my privilege to welcome you into this fine establishment. I think the boys would be extremely happy to hear your proposal!"

The woman snorted, then spoke, revealing yellow teeth. "Yeah, I think they would be thrilled."

"Splendid," Lucifer replied, then clapped his hands together. He rushed past them to grab the door and pull it open. "After you two fine individuals." They both laughed in unison, then proceeded past him. As the woman walked by, he whispered to her, "I absolutely love your ink."

She grinned at him, showing her pearly yellows.

The music, which reminded Lucifer of wild animals screaming at the top of their lungs, was at ear-piercing decibels. His only thought was how anyone communicated in these kinds of establishments. The couple from the parking lot headed over to a corner of the bar. Lucifer watched as the man seemed to be screaming something into what he assumed was the leader's ear. Not caring what was transpiring between the fools, he made his way up the bar, receiving maddening glares from everyone as he passed.

"I would like to purchase drinks for everyone in here," Lucifer yelled to a bartender.

The music abruptly stopped, causing Lucifer to rub at his temples. "Thank the gods for whoever turned that off."

A large hand landed on his shoulder and spun him around. "Well, well, boys. Looks like this sharp-dressed turd has a proposition to ask us!"

"Oh, thank goodness you have a name tag," Lucifer cooed.

A patch over the left side of the man's chest read Buck, and underneath it was, President. He scowled. "What the hell did you just say to me?"

Lucifer shrugged, feigning ignorance. "I thought I was going to have to call you Bubba or Tiny. Oh, just listen to me ramble. Tell you what, Mr. President, I'm buying."

"No, you are not buying," Buck spat back. "It was a mistake, you walking in here, even though you were warned."

Lucifer eyed the man for a moment, then blew out an exasperated breath. "Well, hell, I thought we could at least be friends. In fact, I'd like to hire a few of you idiots for a job that I need help with."

Buck actually smiled at being called an idiot, which Lucifer found odd. Could it be they all had third grade vocabulary and couldn't understand when they were being insulted? That was just a waste of a good education.

"You know," Buck said. "I believe it's customary for a man to be given a last meal before he dies. Or in your case, a last drink. So, go on and order what you'd like. This one is on me."

"Underneath all that ink, leather, and body hair, you truly are a fine gentleman," Lucifer said. "Mamma raised her boy right," he crowed, mimicking Buck's southern drawl. "However, I hope you won't make me drink alone; it's downright rude, don't you agree?"

"Crazy fuck," Buck replied. "Jim!" he hollered over to the bartender. "Set us up."

The shot glasses immediately appeared as Jim walked down the bar, filling them, with several glasses only getting a splash.

Lucifer lifted his shot in a toast. "To new beginnings with fine gentlemen. Oh, excuse me, and ladies." He then looked down to the far end of the bar and raised his glass to them.

"Bottoms up, you soon-to-be-dead son of a bitch!" Buck said. Lucifer wanted to rip the man's head off his shoulders, but since he was the guest of honor he followed through with his drink and began his pitch.

"Tell you what, Buck—or do I call you Mr. President? If that was really my last drink, well, let's just say it was a bit of a disappointment. You don't have anything better to offer a man on his way out?"

"No," Buck replied, invading Lucifer's personal space. He nodded at a man who grabbed both of Lucifer's arms and pinned them behind him.

"Come on Buck," Jim the bartender yelled. "I don't need this place being shut down because of some damned murder investigation. Take him somewhere else."

Buck gave the bar owner a hard glare, not bothering with a reply. Reaching behind his back, he pulled out a pistol.

"Don't fire that damn thing in here!" the guy holding Lucifer yelled. "It'll cut me in half."

"He's got a point," Lucifer said. "Don't need one of your own getting shot by accident. Are you sure you are the President? If so, how dumb are the rest of you?"

Buck cocked the hammer and leveled the gun at Lucifer's head.

"Tell you what," Lucifer said. "If your colleague lets me go, I will kneel down so you don't have to worry about hitting any innocent bystanders."

"Shut the hell up," Buck hissed through clenched teeth.

"Just to be sure, was that directed at me or your friend gently holding me?"

Buck fumed. "Move it, Landry. Mr. Three Piece Suit is about to have an accident."

"No, wait a moment," Lucifer interjected. "I told you I would kneel first." Landry released him and moved out of the way. Wanting to be a man of his word, Lucifer fell to both knees and stretched out his arms to either side, maintaining eye contact with Buck. The tension of the crowd turned to amusement, so Lucifer obliged, giving them his best smile. The talk of death was his favorite subject, since it meant that one lucky individual would be coming to permanently stay with him. His senses overtook him as he felt himself losing control now that a gun was being pointed at his head. However, for some odd reason, several of them stepped back quickly.

"What in the hell?" a voice said.

Even Buck dropped the gun he had been aiming at Lucifer's head and stepped back.

"Well, what's going on?" Lucifer asked. "Are we going to have an execution or not?" Appearing to be dumbfounded, he stood up, turned around, and saw his image in the mirror that hung behind the bar. "Oh, that. Well, that's just this thing I have with my eyes." He turned back around to face his audience, his eyes now completely black.

Everyone turned to run for the exit, pushing several to the ground in the process.

"The doors are locked, my friends," Lucifer called out. "So there will be no escaping."

A few men pulled at the doors. Others grabbed stools and hurled them at the windows, but they only bounced off. Casually walking behind the bar, Lucifer noticed a bottle that he was quite fond of. Pulling it down, he located a glass, blew in it several times to rid it of any dust, then filled it to the brim. Toasting himself, he said, "'I looked, and behold, an ashen horse; and he who sat on it had the name Death; and Hades was following him.' It's truly one of my favorite scriptures. Well, that and the part where Jesus wept."

Holding his glass high, he brought it to his lips and drank it down in one large swallow.

The chaos had finally settled once Buck held both arms in the air in submission. All eyes now looked at him in terror.

"Now that is one hell of a good drink! You were holding out on me, Buck, you silly man. Shame, shame," Lucifer teased, wagging his finger back and forth. "Okay, well, now that you have all calmed down, I need you to come back to the bar and hear my proposition." When no one moved, Lucifer found himself becoming annoyed. "If I have to ask again, there will be more than one execution tonight."

The crowd cautiously eased forward, stopping a good ten feet away from him. "Closer, my loves, much, much closer," Lucifer said softly. Still hesitant, the crowd reluctantly took a few more steps forward. "Do you really think that a few feet between us could stop me from doing anything I wanted to any of you? Now, come sit at the bar and I will pour—while you drink."

A man at the end of the bar began to speak a choppy version of the Lord's prayer, until Lucifer held up a hand. The man began to smoke as though he had a fire burning inside of him. Others looked on in shock, some even whimpering.

"I hate to do this, but that really—and I mean *really*—pisses me off," Lucifer said. Snapping his fingers, the man burned into a statue of ash, and then crumbled to the floor. "Okay now, let's all take a seat, unless you want to join Mr. Ash Heap over there." Some of the crowd hesitantly found bar stools as others fainted where they stood.

"Not you!" Lucifer shouted in disgust, pointing a finger at a woman who was wearing a cross necklace. "Your kind is not welcomed here. Leave now, you disgusting maggot." The woman appeared to be no older than twenty. She took several quick steps back, confused about what she was being told to do. "*Leave now,*" Lucifer screamed, causing the floor to shake. She now understood and ran toward the door, which swung open for her, then slammed and locked again behind her.

"Disgusting," he hissed. "I can't stand to be in the same room as those maniacs." I mean, you call yourself Diablos, but you can't tell a believer from a non-believer? What does it take to join this pathetic group anyhow? A goofy handshake? Ass grabbing?"

A man tried to remain calm as a stream of urine ran down his pants leg and onto the floor. Lucifer immediately hurled a towel at him. "If we were in my world, I would have you lick that up. You are pathetic." He looked around at the rest of the crowd and continued his rant. "Pathetic. Each and every damn one of you."

Afraid to break eye contact with Lucifer, they willed themselves to look at him. The fear was so strong that Lucifer sniffed at the air several times. "That smell is by far the best fragrance ever created. Fear! I wish it could be bottled up and sold worldwide. Anyway, let's get down to the matter at hand." He scanned the room. "I will select four of you to accompany two of my minions on a little mission. Now, let me see a show of hands. Who wants in on this?"

Not a soul raised their hand. Lucifer shook his head. "Buck, you are definitely going, since you were so quick to want to execute me. Besides, wouldn't it make you appear weak if the President didn't go? What kind of example would that be to everyone?"

Buck started to protest but Lucifer held up a hand for silence. "Okay, so that's one. Mr. Third Grader, I think you're next. After all, it doesn't look like you've made much of your life, so here's your chance. Oh, and let's not forget your beautiful woman. For the record, I really am fond of that ink on your neck. Nothing like a whole-hearted believer, if you ask me. Okay, so that is three. I just need one more. Just one more of you," he said, walking along the length of the bar, contemplating his last choice.

Everyone looked down and held their breath as Lucifer walked by. He stopped in front of an older woman who was glaring at him. She appeared to be completely unafraid. Lucifer was impressed by her defiant nature.

"You want to volunteer, don't you?" he asked her.

She gave him a tentative nod of her head.

Lucifer placed both elbows on top of the bar and leaned close to her. "Well, my love, you are just too damned old. Despite all that caked-on makeup, you still appear to have one foot in the grave. I bet your joints crack as you crawl out of bed in the morning wondering where the time has gone. But don't be alarmed, soon I will feed upon you. After all, what did you expect smoking three packs a day? The cancer has already metastasized and is now in your lungs and lymph nodes. Won't be long until I welcome you with open arms. You're such a beautiful little doll and I admire you for putting up a strong front." He reached across the bar and placed a hand on the side of her wrinkled cheek. "Promise me you will keep fighting the good fight and continue puffing away for as long as you can."

He continued to walk along the bar, leaving the woman to sob at this revelation.

Next, he stopped in front of a strikingly beautiful young woman. The stitching on her vest read Ginger which, surprisingly, did not match her hair color, which had been dyed black. "Ginger, my love, I don't know how you got mixed up with these idiots, being a preacher's daughter, but you will be my number four." Her right hand went to her mouth, as she received the good news. Her legs then gave out as two onlookers steadied her, before positioning her atop a barstool. "Okay, the selection process is over," Lucifer announced. "The rest of you can leave. But be quick, as I just may decide that I need a few more."

The crowd ran out as fast as they could, leaving the four chosen behind.

"All right, my loves, now that we are alone, here are your instructions." He grabbed a pen off the counter and wrote on the back of a damp receipt. "Here is the address you will go to. There you will meet up with one of my associates, Tristan. Take whatever weapons you want. I don't care nor do I believe they will keep you alive, but take what you need to feel like you have a chance. When you meet Tristan, you are to do whatever he says. Understood? Any questions?" Hearing none, he pointed at Mr. Third Grader. "You can drive, correct?" The man nodded. "So, everyone is clear on what to do. You will meet Tristan and follow his instructions. Then, perhaps we will see each another again one day very soon."

Lucifer disappeared, leaving the four shell-shocked as they looked at one another with horror. They had danced in the fire for too long. Now it was time to burn.

CHAPTER 36

"**W**hat was I thinking inviting him here?" Riley said to Maggie. "You were right. I didn't think this through. I was selfish and only wanted to make myself feel better. And now I am a damned fool."

Maggie remained quiet as Riley continued.

"You were right," Riley said again. "Completely 100 percent right. If only I would have listened to you this wouldn't have happened. I am the absolute biggest, self-centered, bull-headed—"

"Riley," Maggie interrupted his self-flogging. "Stop berating yourself."

Riley closed his eyes and tried to figure out why he had opened himself up to this man, Griffin, an absolute stranger. Now it was time to figure out how to fix things—if it wasn't too late. Strangely, a calming sense of peace flowed over him. It was the same kind of peace he felt when Jonathan touched him.

Be still, my child.

The voice was so real that Riley almost opened his eyes, yet for some reason they remained closed.

Be still and know that I am God.

Nothing of the outside world existed in the moment. It was just Riley and his Father.

I know the plans I have for you. Plans to prosper you and not to harm you, plans to give you hope and a future.

"Jeremiah 29:11," Riley said. His Allison had loved that one. *Be guarded and be careful.*

Riley opened his eyes to find Maggie kneeling next to him, holding his hand. She pulled away, her eyes wide as if she had just seen a ghost.

"Riley, what just happened?"

Confused by her question. Riley was unsure if she had been a part of what he just experienced. "Did you just hear what I did?"

"Why did the voice tell us to be careful?" she responded.

If he wasn't sure before, her question had just confirmed it. "I honestly don't know. You heard exactly what I did."

"Yes, I heard everything," Maggie said. "One minute you were ridiculing your actions and the next you seemed unresponsive, as if you had a stroke. Whose voice was that?"

Despite the seriousness of the situation, Riley smiled at her. "That voice was our God, believe it or not. I mean, that is, if you are a believer. On second thought, even if you aren't a believer, it's the same because we are all—"

"Shut up and let me think," Maggie replied harshly. She stood and started to head back into the house but stopped and abruptly turned back. She sat down across from him and her eyes never wavered from his. "Has that ever happened to you before, Riley? Where God . . . actually spoke to you?"

Riley found that he couldn't hide his smile. However, from the look on Maggie's face he knew it was the wrong time to take her questions lightly. "Yes, after Jonathan battled those two demons and I believed that he was going to die from his wounds—that day God actually did speak to me."

"And?"

"He told me my trials were not over and to always trust Him."

Maggie leaned back in her chair and released a throaty

laugh. When she had settled down, she looked at him and began laughing again. "Thank you, thank you so much," she said.

"What is so funny?"

"I was not brought up in church. My mom thought it was ridiculous, and my dad was too focused on growing the business to care about much else. It wasn't until later on that I started to learn of God. I would see those massive churches and wonder what the point was of a church that looked like a shopping mall. When I actually decided to go into one to check it out, I saw that it had a restaurant, book store, even a coffee shop. Oh, and there was a game room for kids. I had no idea that a church could be so lucrative because people fear what happens to them when they die. Do they think if they give to the church, in return, God will look favorably upon them?"

She once more let out a loud laugh, except Riley could tell that this time it had been forced.

"I also found it odd that the pastor didn't actually have time to meet with people. Once, I emailed the pastor of a church because I was interested in learning about how this all-knowing God stuff worked. And do you know what I received back?"

Riley knew where she was heading with the narration. He even knew of these churches that ran religion as if it were a business. He didn't agree with their structure and even believed that they preyed upon people, which he found pathetic. But he let her continue.

"An administrative assistant replied using the pastor's personal email! What the hell is the point if you can't access the one person who is supposed to be a spiritual leader, or counselor, or guide? Well, anyway, I was informed that the pastor's schedule was too busy and he wouldn't be able to meet with me. Then she said she could direct me to someone else."

"I can see why you were frustrated," Riley said. "I agree that it's a poor design when the pastor who preaches to you has no other kind of interaction with you. But consider the other side of things for these megachurches—if that pastor is doing his job, and doing it well, the church is going to grow. Even though you weren't able to speak directly with the person you wanted, why not give that administrative assistant some credit for offering an alternative? You weren't turned away." He paused and looked at Maggie and leaned toward her a bit. "So, let me ask you this, and don't think I am making light of your frustration, but were you really interested in learning about God?"

Maggie's expression lightened a bit, providing Riley with a window of opportunity to continue.

"Listen, I am not saying it is right nor am I saying that the way megachurches go about the business of God is wrong," Riley continued. "But let me bring this into perspective. How many of your employees would like to have just a moment of your time to discuss their futures but are turned away because of your schedule?"

Maggie looked at Riley, frustrated. Riley knew there was no way that she could spend a few minutes with every employee that worked for her if she expected her company to continue to grow. "Point made, Riley."

"Let me ask one more thing, and please don't think I'm not on your side, but did you ever have the chance to learn about God?"

She went quiet, then looked down before she replied. "Well, one year, Stuart gave me a Bible for Christmas. I thought it was strange for him to give me such a gift. I mean, we grew up together and he knew my parents weren't keen on the subject of religion of any kind. But the Bible looked nice so I kept it on a bookshelf in my office. But honestly, it's just sitting there collecting dust." Riley could tell she was embarrassed by this admittance.

"Did you ever go to church?" Riley asked.

Maggie nodded. "A few years ago, I asked Stuart if maybe I could accompany him to whatever church he attended. I started going with him and his family to a very small church that they were members of. It was mostly older people, but they were genuine and sincere. Everyone there said good morning and actually meant it. Then they would ask how my week was going or how I was doing and actually listened to my response. They actually wanted to get to know me without having their own agenda. It was the first time that I wasn't treated like an outsider or someone that was scrutinized in the news and on social media."

Now Riley was getting a small glimpse into the world she occupied. "What was the name of this church?"

"Saginaw Park Baptist Church," she replied, not missing a beat. "There couldn't have been more than a hundred people in the congregation on its best Sunday. But I loved them for their generosity and how they became like family to me. During the work week I found that I couldn't wait to see the people of the church and find out how their own week had been." Then she stopped as tears welled in her eyes. "Eventually, I had to stop going because the media found out I was going there. In the end, I just couldn't put those innocent people in that kind of spotlight. It wouldn't have been fair to them having to answer questions about me and then having their own lives become subject to criticism."

Riley hurt for Maggie. Her social status had gotten in the way of finding what she needed spiritually. Now he picked up on the fact that she needed him to change the subject. "What do you think I should do now about Griffin?"

She gave him a small smile, thanking him for understanding. "Well, in my opinion, maybe you should go and talk with him a little more. I know he asked to be left alone, but a little nudge could go a long way. Besides, what could it hurt now that you have completely opened up to him? You have come this far, Riley, so go ask what more you can do for him. I think maybe God led him to you. Remember the scripture? 'I know the plans I have for you'?"

"Jeremiah 29:11," Riley replied.

Maggie gave him a small, encouraging smile. "Go."

CHAPTER 37

Walking down to the dock, Riley worked out how he hoped the conversation would go with Griffin. Since no one appeared to be left on the lake, the water was calm as the sun's last rays of the day danced across it before giving way to night. Drawing closer to the dock, it seemed to Riley that Griffin was nowhere in sight. Could he have left without telling them? He couldn't blame him. Turning to walk back up the path, Riley heard his name called from the top level of the deck.

"I'm up here, Riley. Please come up. I would like to continue our talk."

He looked up to find Griffin standing at the railing. Despite the fact that he had just torn the man's world apart, Riley felt a a strange connection with Griffin even though they were basically strangers.

He walked back and made his way up the stairs to the top section of the deck. Every step seemed a little more worrisome, not knowing what Griffin would say to him. As he reached the top step, Griffin was leaned back in one of the patio chairs, looking out at the water. Coming up next to him, Riley rested his arms on the side railing, his back to Griffin as he took in the view of the lake. The conversation he had played out in his head left him. Now he found that just being this close to Griffin made him uncomfortable.

"Would you like to sit down?" Griffin asked.

Might as well face my demons, Riley thought. He went and took a seat next to Griffin. Neither spoke. They just stared out across the lake as the sun descended for the day.

"Thank you, Riley."

Believing he had heard wrong, Riley looked over at Griffin.

"I know the burden you have been carrying has somewhat lifted now. I also know you are wondering why you asked me to come, believing it was a mistake."

He was right on both accounts, Riley thought.

"I don't believe in God. Never have, never will. Nothing you can say will ever change my mind."

Riley thought that was a strange comment. When they spoke the other day, Griffin had said that his pastor had stopped by.

"Yes, I know I spoke of my pastor when we talked over the phone. But to be honest, the woman has been trying to reach me for a long time. I enjoy our talks, but after what I have seen and lived through, I just don't believe that if God existed, he would have allowed something so terrible to have happened to me."

Riley looked straight at the man. "I don't understand. Are you—?"

"Reading your mind? No, but judging by the conversation we had earlier, I believe I know what you are thinking. Because if I were in your shoes, I would be having the same thoughts."

"Wow, you could have fooled me. I was getting paranoid," Riley said.

"Don't be. I promise I am not that talented."

Riley smiled at the comment, feeling a little more relieved now that his paranoia had been put to bed.

"Well, I am not here to convert you, but I almost feel I should ask why," Riley said. "I mean, I just thought God would be someone who you would want to talk to during this time."

"It's not that I wouldn't enjoy having a real heart-to-heart with God. But he gave up on me years ago."

Riley could relate. Not long ago he, too, believed God had given up on him.

"But let us stay on the topic that brought us here. Riley, earlier when I said I know angels exist, I was telling you the truth. I even think God exists, but I will not submit myself to following any kind of religion, of any form."

"Then how do you believe in angels and God, but not enough to follow God?" Riley asked.

"I never said the word 'believed.' I said I know they exist."

The strange feeling Riley experienced earlier had returned. He could hear Jonathan's warning telling him to always be prepared for the unknown. Apparently, he had not learned his lesson.

"Riley, the reason I know that they exist is because I remember the day my daughter was born. When I held her in my arms for the first time, I saw the very existence of an angel."

Riley's uneasy feeling left him and was replaced with sympathy.

Griffin issued a polite chuckle, then made eye contact with Riley. "This is strange for me to admit, but when you have kids of your own, you will understand. You will make outlandish promises knowing there is no way you could ever live up to them. For instance, can you believe I actually promised my daughter that I would always protect her, and that no harm would ever find her?"

Riley attempted to offer a polite smile but it never found his face. To hide his discomfort, he leaned forward in his chair and rubbed the bridge of his nose with his fingers.

"Listen to me, Riley. I made that promise knowing it was a fool's hope. We all want the best for our children. We want them to stay safe and to give us grandchildren who we can spoil one day. A parent's biggest fear is having to bury their own child. I had to do that and am having to come to terms with it. Alone, I might add."

Riley thought he would be free from the guilt after telling Griffin the truth, knowing now that he had been a fool for thinking that way. A simple apology wouldn't make up for stolen memories that would never come to pass.

"I do not, and never will, blame you, Riley. I actually thank you for opening up to me. That night in the hospital when we met was not by accident. We were destined to cross paths for a reason, and I am thankful you are helping me through this time."

"Griffin, you don't have to thank me. It is the least I can do to tell you what actually happened and try to comfort you, since we are the reason for the death of your daughter."

"No!" Griffin said harshly. "You are not at fault. If what you say is true, then it was Jonathan who should be apologizing, not you. If he really is an angel, then you have no control over him. I won't debate with you whether he is or isn't. If you say he is then he is. But I want you to understand you were never at fault."

Riley could actually see Griffin's point. True, he didn't have any control over Jonathan's powers. The only reason he felt guilty was because Jonathan had said they had to go back to the city. He was simply a passenger. So why was he apologizing? He was about to agree with him, but then he thought he saw a small glimmer of red in Griffin's eyes. Gooseflesh ran down Riley's arms, making him question if he had actually seen the eerie color, or maybe this was just the effects of that dream still lingering in him.

"Let's go inside," Griffin said hastily. "The wind off the lake is causing you to get a chill, and I am afraid my old bones won't be able to muster getting me up much longer."

Riley felt reassured that he had just imagined the red glimmer in Griffin's eyes. "Let me help you up."

"I can manage," Griffin said, standing with ease. "Why don't you go down ahead of me so that if I stumble you can catch me and I won't end up in the hospital with a broken hip."

Leading him down the stairs, Riley was happy when they made it to the bottom without an incident.

"Hello, you two," Maggie called out. She was walking around from the front porch. Joining them, Maggie took hold of Riley's arm to allow Griffin to walk ahead of them. With questioning eyes, she asked if everything was okay.

"I believe so," Riley whispered.

Once inside, Griffin sat in a recliner with Maggie and Riley, taking seats on the couch opposite.

"Would you like to call it a night?" Maggie asked.

"I don't think I can sleep right now," Griffin responded. "I've taken in quite a bit today and it's given me a lot to think about."

"Good, because lately we haven't been sleeping much here. Almost afraid to rest my head on a pillow," Riley joked.

"I wake up more tired than if I would have just stayed awake. Thank God for coffee!" Maggie added.

"My dream began a few days before Jonathan and I made the trip back to Taupe City," Riley said.

"Mine began the day before my path crossed Jonathan and Riley's," Maggie added.

Maggie and Riley were about explain what was happening until Griffin held up a hand letting them know they didn't need to. "It is not uncommon to have night terrors after a horrible event. I used to have them as well when I came back from Vietnam."

Riley knew firsthand what PTSD could do to someone. He had lived through it with Jonathan, watching his friend suffer as he became a former shell of himself and as his mind waged a daily war that he would always lose.

"What helped you overcome yours?" Maggie said, looking at Griffin. She hoped she wasn't intruding too far.

"Well, it wasn't any kind of religion or crazy belief system. It also wasn't a psychiatrist prescribing me pills. Not even my family helped, although they tried to help with my manic suicidal thoughts. You see, I question why I had survived when all but thirteen of my platoons were wiped out.

"I found that meditation was my refuge. It wasn't easy at first, and back then I am sure my own wife thought I was insane. I would put a cloth over my eyes and would sit for as long as I could, trying to focus on my breathing. I would try to block out as much of the outside world as possible. When my daughter arrived, I continued to do it so that hopefully she would never have to meet the monster. To be honest, I don't even know how I discovered meditation. Didn't even know it was called that at the time. I was just trying to escape my own mind. The more I meditated, the more I noticed that my mood would improve."

He paused and looked at them. "My drinking slowly came to an end, and for once I could control my own actions. Even my night terrors that left me drenched in sweat subsided. My wife was convinced what I was doing was helping and urged me to make sure I did my meditation every day. However, I never taught it to anyone else."

"Why not?" Riley asked.

"It was such a different time. People talked about you if they knew you were seeing a psychiatrist. Most saw it as weakness. If I had tried to tell other veterans to just close their eyes, relax their muscles, and just focus on their breathing—well, let's just say I would have been ostracized, and maybe even fitted for a straitjacket!"

"Would you teach us?"

"Well, it really isn't that hard. It's just like I said, block out the outside world, try to relax, and focus on your breathing. Tell you what. While I am here this weekend, we will do a few sessions. How about we start tonight so that, hopefully, you can both sleep a little better. Just be ready to encounter things that will seem very real to you. Your past, or something that you have never come to terms with, will surface."

Riley was uncertain, since he had just opened up to Griffin. However, Maggie jumped at the opportunity.

"How do we begin? Should I turn off the lights?"

"Actually, do you happen to have those sleep masks, or perhaps a cloth you can put across your eyes?"

"I will be right back," Riley said and then got up and walked down the hall.

Griffin smiled politely at Maggie as Riley returned a moment later with two eye masks.

"You sleep with one of these?" Maggie asked condescendingly.

Riley handed one to her and then took his seat, ignoring the question. Slipping the mask over his eyes, Riley leaned back in the couch recliner. Maggie almost laughed but followed suit as if curious to see if this would actually make a difference.

Once they had settled in, Griffin began. "What I need is for both of you to focus only on your breathing, nothing else. Let your muscles relax and allow the outside world to slip away with each breath. Inhale slowly, hold for a moment, and then exhale slowly."

As he continued to talk them through the process, Riley found that Griffin's voice faded faster than he had expected. The first thought that came to him was when God had spoken to him earlier. Then he thought about Maggie and how stunned she had been to hear the voice. A smile tugged at his lips. He reached for her hand, only to find that she was no longer beside him. Reaching up to remove his mask, he felt strong hands force them back down. He would have cried out, but his last lucid thought was what God had told him earlier. He hadn't known what to do with it at the time. Now it resounded inside his head.

Be careful!

CHAPTER 38

Maggie felt at peace, lying back in the recliner, as Griffin's voice gradually faded away. She felt as if she were dreaming, yet somehow awake at the same time. *Wow, Griffin should start teaching this as a course. He could make an absolute fortune.* Not even the sound of her own breathing interrupted the silence. Only her thoughts seemed to exist in this sanctity. *Strange, shouldn't I at least be able to feel myself breathing?* She exhaled with great force, but nothing happened, she couldn't even feel her breath. She attempted to draw in a large amount of air, only to realize that she couldn't even accomplish that.

Panic slipped into her thoughts, as she remembered Griffin told them specifically to focus on their breathing. This had to be death. Was she dead? She tried to reach up for the eye mask only to find that she was unable to lift her arms. She tried to call out for Riley, hoping that he would grab her hand and talk her through the breathing. *Why can't I move? Why can't I move!* Maggie tried to scream.

Griffin had said something before that didn't bother her at the time, since her only goal was to get some decent sleep. But now his words haunted her as she replayed them in her head. "Be ready to encounter things that will seem very real to you. Your past, or something that you have never come to terms with, will surface."

Why hadn't I asked how to make this stop if it became too much?

Maggie thought. *Please, someone help me!* she once more tried to scream.

"Mary Allison Gregory, why didn't you try harder to help me?" a voice said, bringing more fear with it.

Maggie knew the voice. It was the voice of her mother. She had cried so many times after her mother had passed, begging to be able to see her or hear her voice again. Now those tears were replaced with the desperate hope that she wouldn't have to see her mother ever again. *Please don't come to me,* Maggie begged. *Let me wake. God, please hear me and let me just wake from this nightmare.*

"Maaarrry, ohhh Maaarrry," it was her mother's voice, taunting her. "When I was sick, you didn't want to come see me. Even after they put my hospital bed in my room just down the hallway from yours. I called for you when I wasn't coughing so violently that I pissed and shit myself."

You aren't real, go away, just go away, Maggie pleaded. *I want to wake up now. Griffin, I want to wake up now!*

"Why did you never at least look in on me? I just wanted to see your face one last time to let you know that I still thought of you as Mommy's little girl!"

Maggie tried to scream, begging for God to rescue her.

"Oh, I am so sorry, daughter of mine. God isn't heard down here. I called his name when I passed from your world until, finally, someone told me of my ignorance. Then they bit into my shoulder and pulled away a large chunk of my fatty, diseased meat! You see, Mary, we are all food down here. Not just for the other damned, or even the flames of Hell. Oh no, it's the worms that never stop with their ferocious feeding. They are what drive us all insane. You feel them crawling under your skin as you scratch and slap at them violently. Let me show you the spot that I can't scratch at enough!"

Her mother's face appeared in front of her. It looked just as it had when she was a child. She was beautiful, with her large hazel eyes, long brown hair that fell to her shoulders, and smile lines that deepened from all the laughter that was shared in their home. Her mother then turned her face to the side and screamed, "Right here!" She revealed a rotten, gooey cheek that she began scratching until her fingers broke through.

The last thing Maggie heard as she escaped back into consciousness was her mother saying, "One day, not long from now, I will share one final meal with you!"

Riley once again heard the warning from earlier telling him to be careful. *Why am I so blind that I do the same things over and over?* he thought. *I am a fool. Jonathan tells me to always be prepared and I do the complete opposite.*

He hoped Griffin would wake him but knew it was a foolish thought. The hands that had restrained him earlier were now gone. He considered reaching for the eye mask, but what would be the point? He had been told to be careful. Now he would just wait for it to end.

"Wake up!" a voice yelled, striking him on the side of the face. A cold floor seemed to be his new resting place. His tongue located the metallic taste of iron in his mouth. Giving his head a shake to clear his thoughts, Riley hoped it was Griffin who had hit him to bring him back around. But that was wishful thinking.

"Wake, or I will give you a kick so hard that your insides will burst like water balloons!"

Riley opened his eyes to see the Devil dressed in a white suite, standing directly in front of him. Riley pushed himself up off the floor and spat out a wad of blood in defiance. He looked around and saw amidst the dark he was surrounded by the shapes of four black beasts that looked like some rare breed of dog. They were easily over two hundred pounds with cold red eyes locked on him.

"Yes, these are my hounds. Adorable, aren't they?"

Riley's fear amplified at the way their lifeless eyes bore into him.

"Would you like to pet one of my babies? They really are quite friendly, I assure you."

One of the hounds standing closest to Riley now bared its teeth. Its mouth looked like a shark's, with row after row of sharp fangs. Dark red blood drooled from the hound's mouth onto the floor next to Riley.

"Pardon their manners, they just finished feeding. How about we take a seat? I don't want these little rascals feeling intimidated."

The one standing next to the Devil barked so loudly that Riley put both hands to his ears, trying to muffle the sound.

"Calm yourself, my beauty." He rubbed the hound behind its ears, not taking his eyes from Riley's. "I don't know what gets into them sometimes. It's almost as if they have a mind of their own. You'd better sit. I don't know what they will do if they feel threatened."

Riley quickly did as he was told since there was no point in resisting. He was stuck here until something pulled him out of this nightmare.

"That is what I truly love about you. You will do whatever is asked. I have come to think of you as a puppet. Pull the strings this way and away you go, pull them another way and, once again, you follow without a care in the world."

Looking back at his adversary, Riley knew he could do nothing but let him have his fun.

"So, I'm guessing you are wondering why you have been brought to me?"

"No, I actually figured that much out for myself," Riley replied with an edge to his voice. "I now know Griffin is one of your own."

"Oh, you're a silly man," the Devil mocked. "Griffin isn't mine, but soon enough he will be. First his wife, now his daughter, and soon him. He isn't a believer, but soon he will be. One day he will enjoy the fruit of his labors and relish in this afterlife. When he does arrive, there are several of his old platoons from Vietnam who would like to have a word with him."

"You're disgusting." Riley said. But it was pointless to allow his anger to get the best of him. One of the hounds lunged at him.

Riley held up his hands to defend himself.

"Be gone!" the Devil commanded the hounds.

Opening his eyes, Riley saw that he was now alone with the Devil.

"If I didn't have control of them then this conversation would sadly be over," said the enemy. "They like to bite at the throat first. Drives me crazy since I have tried to teach them to go for the limbs. It's not as much fun if you can't hear the person screaming. I have tried time and time again, yet for some reason they are unteachable. Always the throat. Damn things. But I do enjoy having them around. They will never threaten me and will always offer protection. And it doesn't hurt to have them around for intimidation purposes."

You are intimidating enough, Riley thought but let it pass.

Lucifer's smile broadened. "Thank you, Riley. I know that I am very intimidating. But I still like to show off those babies. Besides, it's not every day that I have visitors."

Understanding that his thoughts were not his own, Riley looked around. The room was filled with huge, silver picture frames with a different person inside each one.

"You like my artwork?"

Riley didn't answer.

"These are displayed throughout my entire house. Literally millions upon millions of them. I created each of them myself. Come with me. I want to show you one I am most fond of." He stood and walked over to one of the walls. When Riley made no movement, a voice inside his head said, "I will not ask again." Fearing the hounds could return any moment, Riley stood and walked over to where the Devil stood, making sure not to get too close.

Lucifer noticed the large gap between them and grinned. "No, you are too far away to see the exquisite beauty in the frame." He yanked Riley by the arm to his side. "This is a mother and daughter. You can see the mother is welcoming the daughter to her final resting place. Look a little bit closer to see the flow of the lines."

Riley resisted moving any closer.

Lucifer shook his head. "If you do not look closer, I will push your head through the wall."

Riley stood his ground, not moving, until the back of his head was grabbed and placed just inches from the painting. He could see that the two women were actually moving inside the frame. *This can't be happening.*

"Just wait, it gets more interesting, because my art actually comes to life."

Riley couldn't help himself from staring more intently at the movements of each woman. When he was able to make out the faces, he leaned in even closer, believing that he could hear sounds coming from inside the frame. The closer he drew near, the more intense the sounds became. A woman was screaming for help. It was Maggie. The other woman resembled her—it must have been her mother. Riley pushed away from the Devil's grasp, unable to watch any longer.

"What did you do!" Riley finally managed to scream.

"Nothing. What could I do?" Lucifer said with a mocking grin.

"You are—"

"Finish that thought and the hounds will return."

Filled with rage, Riley stopped himself from continuing, as he trembled, wanting desperately to lash out.

"That's better. Now, let's sit once more and I will tell you what I want."

Reluctantly, Riley did as he was told. He had a feeling he would soon need to make a choice. An awful choice.

A year ago, shortly after he met Jonathan, the Devil had appeared to him and offered him the chance to have his old life back with his wife, Allison. All he had to do was turn Jonathan over. The choice was different now. He now knew that Jonathan was alive and that he was going to have to make the choice of which one tasted Hell, Maggie or Jonathan. There was no other way around it. Trying to reason with the Devil was incomprehensible. Dropping his head to his chest, Riley asked for forgiveness for what he was about to do.

"Riley, you are wiser than the puppet I thought you were," Lucifer sneered. "Yes, your Jonathan is very much alive and well, thanks to the sacrifice of that fool, Granny. How much longer, though, is up to you. So, which will it be? Your new friend Maggie, or Jonathan?"

Riley's head pounded as the questions and consequences of his actions began to pile up. Was Lucifer telling him the truth about Granny sacrificing herself to save Jonathan? If so, then why hadn't Jonathan returned yet? Furthermore, why had he not listened? Jonathan had tried to drill into him over and over about always being prepared. Even God had told him to be careful. And yet here he sat, asking for another chance. One more do-over and he would get it right this time.

With eyes still closed, Riley offered up a silent prayer. "God, let this cup pass from my lips. Please show me mercy." Riley knew that giving up Jonathan to the Devil would be a mortal sin. But giving up an innocent, like Maggie, was also a mortal sin. He couldn't bear the idea of either of them tasting the fires of Hell. "I can't offer either of them. So, take me. I will sacrifice myself for them. They don't need to suffer for my ignorance. I know this is wrong of me to ask, but I am begging you to take me and spare my friends."

Lucifer gave him a knowing smile, letting Riley in on the secret that he already suspected this request. "No, Riley. That is not an option. If you don't decide then I will make the decision for you and will take Maggie. Then you can live the rest of your life knowing that she is stuck in a frame on my wall being eaten by her mother."

"She is a believer!" Riley hissed back in defiance.

Lucifer shook his head slowly and smiled at him. Riley felt the world crash once more upon his shoulders.

"I'm curious now, but did she ever say that she believes in a so-called god?"

Riley remembered Maggie talking about a small church and how she had felt welcomed there. However, she never had expressed her beliefs to him.

"I hate to be the bearer of bad news, but she hasn't converted to your side. It's unfortunate for the predicament that you find yourself in. I am enjoying every moment of watching you wrestle with this decision."

Riley began to question why God was allowing this to happen

to him. "Why do I have to decide between two fates? Please wake up, please wake up," he began, whispering over and over. After several minutes passed, Riley opened his eyes, finding that the Devil was still sitting across from him.

"Boo!" Lucifer said, then cackled. "Time's up! I need your decision. Otherwise, Maggie is mine."

Riley looked down as tears fell from his face and onto the floor, "God forgive me." He looked up as Lucifer smiled at him.

"Wake up, my fool, wake up!"

CHAPTER 39

R iley pulled his eye mask off and pitched it onto the floor. Tears rolled down his cheeks, but he made no movement to wipe at them. Next to him, he heard Maggie sobbing, crying out something, but he couldn't make out the words. He wasn't sure he wanted to. A coldness enveloped him as he slowly stood, avoiding meeting Griffin or Maggie's eyes. All he desired was to be alone and to never again invite someone else into his life.

As he moved past Maggie, she reached out, taking his hand in hers. "Riley, what did you see? Please tell me. I am so afraid of what my future holds."

Locking eyes with her, he pushed her hand from his. Once more he started to pass by her, but she grabbed at him.

"No, Riley, you tell me," Maggie demanded. "You have to talk to me. Do you have any idea what just happened?"

Riley pulled her to her feet and squeezed both of her shoulders. "Yes, you fool, yes, I know what just happened!" he yelled at her. "I told you not to get involved and you, being the entitled rich girl, wouldn't listen to reason. I was an idiot for letting you come out here. I should have left you outside that hospital!"

"Riley, stop!" Maggie cried. "What the hell do you think you're doing? I'm losing my mind and I'm more afraid than I ever have been. Do you not understand how scared I am? And now you think you can just treat me—"

"*Shut up, you stupid bitch!*" Riley screamed at her. "I told you that a broken finger would be the least of your problems, but you played it off and thought I was kidding, but this isn't a silly game. When we lose, we don't go back to board meetings and hash it out like you do up there in your precious ivory tower. In this reality, we bury the dead and thank God that it wasn't our turn!"

Riley shoved her back down on the couch, glaring at her in disgust. Tears once more broke the surface and poured down his face. "Come morning, I want you out of my house."

Before Maggie could reply, Riley left the living room and a moment later slammed his bedroom door so hard that the glass in the patio door rattled.

Maggie was in too much shock to cry, wondering what Riley must have seen to cause that much rage. Then a thought came to her as she looked at Griffin, who just sat there innocently with his mouth open.

In a voice not her own, Maggie growled, "What did you do to Riley?"

Griffin's mouth remained open, clearly stunned by the events unfolding.

"This isn't my home but if it were, I would throw you out on your crippled ass!" She lunged at him, getting directly into Griffin's face.

"I—I don't know what happened," Griffin clamored.

"You know damn well what you just put us through," Maggie seethed at him.

Still, he acted confused as Maggie leaned in to one side of his face and whispered, "I just saw death, and it broke me in more ways than I will ever be able to describe. But Riley must have tasted it because when I looked into his eyes everything behind them was gone." She leaned back, staring directly into Griffin's confused face. "You disgust me." She stood upright and spoke evenly, "Tomorrow morning, you will leave at first light. I don't ever want to see your pathetic face again." She looked at him, waiting for a response.

"Okay," he agreed softly.

Minutes passed as Maggie stood looking down at him. Finally, she walked out of the room, flipping off the light as she went.

Legionaries watched as Maggie stormed out of the room, followed by a door slammed closed a moment later. "Good thing you didn't turn around," Legionaries whispered after her. "I would have shown you what death really looks like." Then he chuckled softly to himself. It wasn't ideal that he had to leave so soon, but this couldn't have gone better. However, Legionaries was frustrated that he couldn't control exactly what happened to Maggie or Riley once he put them under his trance. He knew that he would bring Maggie's mother into the fray. Riley, however, never got to meet the experience he had conjured up for him, which added to his growing frustration, since he wasn't as powerful as he thought he would be.

A soft prick went off inside his head. It was Lucifer reaching out to him. Keeping his voice low, he answered, "Yes, Master."

"I don't give praise, and to be honest I never have," Lucifer said. "This will be the only time that I do, so relish it."

Lucifer's voice was so overly enthused and out of character that Legionaries wondered if he were speaking to someone else. He hadn't a clue what Lucifer was rambling on about but sat patiently waiting for him to get to the point.

"Riley has just served up the Fallen. He should arrive to your location in no more than a day. When he does, there won't be a fight. Sorry to disappoint, but you won't get to test your skills. He will come willingly. Riley offered him up in an exchange."

Legionaries fumed upon hearing this news. The whole reason he had come was to fight a Fallen. Now the opportunity had been ripped away from him. The Fallen wouldn't fight back. Controlling his temper, Legionaries asked, "And as for Riley and Maggie?"

"When Tristan arrives—with some idiot biker gang—make use of them however you see fit. After everything is completed I want you to make certain that it is just you and him left standing. I don't want loose ends. And when I say all. I mean all!" With that, Lucifer disappeared from his mind.

Legionaries could taste the hatred building up inside of him. He couldn't care less about Riley, Maggie, or the ignorant humans in leather that Lucifer had recruited. Their deaths didn't make a damned bit of difference to him. However, since his hand had been forced, he would perform one more act of defiance. Lucifer needed to learn that he no longer had any control over him.

The next morning, Legionaries wasn't surprised when neither Maggie nor Riley saw him out. Just as well, he would be seeing them very soon. He just needed a few more pieces to fall into place and his job would be complete. He waited until he was back on the road to change back to his own body. His new destination wasn't far as it was the fallback plan if anything changed. He would meet up with Tristan, hear the new idiotic plan, and pretend to go along with it until he decided to reveal his true intentions.

———

Maggie had been up all night sitting on the edge of her bed—not because she feared sleep, but because she didn't know what would happen next after Riley's outburst. She heard Griffin leave and was thankful that the creep had gone. She hoped she wouldn't be following in the same footsteps. Leaving her room and knocking at Riley's door was something she may eventually have to do. But even the thought of having to face him after last night frightened her. Something he had encountered brought back a different friend than the one she knew. As she had told Griffin, she had seen death, but Riley somehow had gone beyond just seeing to actually touching it.

A soft knock came at her door, startling her. She leapt to her feet knowing it was Riley. She had what she wanted to say all worked out; however, it all went out the window when the knob turned and the door opened. Riley entered, avoiding eye contact, stopping just inside the doorway. Maggie felt as though she was looking at a stranger.

"I should have never put my hands on you."

Maggie thought of telling him not to give it another thought and asking what was going on, but she knew it was not the time.

"I need you to leave and to never come back into my life," he said quietly, but firmly.

He still had that dead, hundred-yard stare in his eyes from last night. She remained silent, wanting so badly to beg for more time with him so that she could actually speak with Jonathan for more than just a few minutes—that is, if he ever came back. She wanted to explain one more time that her whole search couldn't end like this.

"Here is my truck key," Riley said, holding it out for her to take. "I am sorry that I won't be able to drive you myself."

Accepting the key, Maggie tried to embrace him, but he stepped back, confirming that she was no longer welcome in his home or his life.

"You will be safe and won't have to worry about repercussions, but you have to leave now. Nothing else will come for you. I have been promised."

Before Maggie had a chance to ask what he had experienced, Riley left the room, pulling the door closed behind him.

CHAPTER 40

As nightfall came, the stars in the sky seemed to go on forever, each flickering their soft glow back and forth to one another as if having their own private conversation. Anyone who had this view, away from all the light pollution, would be overwhelmed with how many one could actually see. Jonathan's focus fell back to his leg. He massaged it where the blade from the cat-of-nine-tails had broken off inside him and released its poison. It should have killed him, but he'd been given a second chance. He knew God had heard his prayer during his weakest hour. He just didn't know the sacrifice it would take.

It appeared as though the blessing had a curse attached to it. Jonathan knew that he wouldn't have lasted another twenty-four hours. The poison had almost eaten up the last remaining part of his sanity. Not only did he want to inflict pain on those around him, but he began to have thoughts of taking his own life. His trial had eventually poured over into Riley as he tried to help him. Granny had died in a selfless act to heal him. Her final sacrifice proved there was no greater love than laying down one's life for another. Jonathan wanted to prove that he was worthy of yet another chance. However, he couldn't seem to stay focused on the one task St. Peter had told him he must do. Every time he closed his eyes to concentrate and try to hear God, his thoughts would drift. Sometimes it was the wind, a stray animal that called out in the night, or these blessed stars with their constant beauty. The one thought that stood out among all the others, though, was his beloved friend Riley and, of course, Granny.

He desperately wanted to apologize for what he had put Riley through. At the end of their time together it had been Riley taking care of him instead of the other way around. When they had left each other in front of the hospital, Jonathan couldn't even bear to look back, knowing that it would be the last time they were together. He hoped, somehow, that Maggie would pick up where he had been forced to leave off. But now that he was no longer sick and was thinking clearly, he couldn't understand his logic behind asking her to put her life in jeopardy.

"Which is why I need to get back to them!" Jonathan cried out, scaring off an owl perched above him. He closed his eyes once more, starting the process of inhaling slowly, holding it, and then blowing it back out. He continued the exercise, hoping to calm his nerves. Just as he was about to give up, the outside world slipped out from underneath him. The wind moving over the grass, the animals with their night calls, even the ground on which he sat was no longer present. The calm that Jonathan had been reaching for had now found him, as a whisper penetrated the silence.

Be still.

Jonathan did as he was told and anticipated the next instruction. When it didn't come, he grew frustrated despite knowing that everything was in God's time, not his. He resumed the breathing exercises once more. He felt his body relax, allowing him to slip even further into the serenity that he had so desperately waited for. It felt amazing to be able to channel himself into one specific thought and to remain still.

Once more God spoke, giving him the same instruction as

before. *Just be still, my child, and feel the breath come in and out of your new body.*

It was now easy to do what was asked of him. He could feel his patience return and didn't worry about what would happen next, knowing that his Father's plan was a perfect design. Then a vision came to him. It was Allison. Once again, he saw how she had looked when she was born. He had been there to welcome her into the world. He knew that he was spoken into existence to protect her and nothing else. "Perfect," Jonathan whispered, not breaking the peace that still surrounded him.

Then a vision of Riley came to him. He had first entered into Allison's life by tripping on his way to the front of the biology class. This was followed by further humiliation as he attempted to give a presentation in class. Somehow Allison had found Riley not only amusing, but intriguing. Then he saw their wedding day and how beautiful it had been when they were united as one. Jonathan tensed up with what would surely follow, only to be surprised by the vision of he and Riley meeting face-to-face for the first time. He once again saw the worried look on Riley's face as Jonathan towered over him.

The visions passed so quickly in front of him that they were jumbled together. He saw Riley learning to trust him, the battle of the demons that almost took his life, his and Riley's trip back to Taupe City, and then their last goodbye in front of the hospital. Then, finally, he saw Granny and how confidently she carried herself, even though death would soon take her. She never complained as she fought for each breath. When she passed, Jonathan knew that one day he would share a similar fate. At the time, he rejected the realization of where his road would end and the cruelty of it. But now he understood that despite how his life ended, it was a privilege to have been a part of Allison's, and Riley's, and Granny's.

Jonathan, open your eyes, my beloved.

Opening his eyes, Jonathan now looked upon the shadow of God.

Now, my child, you have glimpsed what I experience as each of my beloveds face their mortal death. I may never hold them again if they have chosen not to follow me. The gift of free will, Jonathan, is so precious that it was never a thought not to share it with the world despite knowing the outcome could be heartbreaking. I asked you to be still and you listened. You, Jonathan, have always been a blessing.

Jonathan could no longer suppress his tears as they ran down his face.

I know why you chose to fall and it was, indeed, an honorable act. Believe when I say that you are a selfless angel, not as the Fallen you think of yourself to be. You are my child. My beloved.

Jonathan prostrated himself before God, wishing that he could do more to show his trust and obedience.

Love is patient, love is kind. It does not envy, it does not boast, it is not proud. It is not rude, it is not self-seeking, it is not easily angered, it keeps no record of wrongs. Love does not delight in evil but rejoices with the truth. It always protects . . .

Jonathan joined in for the remaining verse. "Always trusts, always hopes, always perseveres. Love never fails." And then he added, "First Corinthians 13:4-8." Then, looking up, he saw that the shadow of God was no longer there.

Sounds of the outside world brought him back to Granny's meadow. The grass continued to flow with the movements of the wind, each flower dancing without worry. Oddly, Jonathan felt no urge to rush back to Riley's side. For now, he only wanted to be still and remain in this place for a bit longer. He would never again think of himself as a Fallen. He no longer had the worrisome thought of having to taste a mortal death. It had been replaced by a sense of peace that it was an honor to walk in mortal shoes. He hoped he would embrace death with the same selflessness that not only Granny had, but that Jesus had. It was a small price to pay to be able to spend the rest of eternity with his Father.

Hours passed as Jonathan watched the sunrise push away the night. Strangely, while he knew this would be the last sunrise he may ever look upon, there was peace. He also knew Riley had been forced into making a choice, one that he found impossible to make. The repercussions of his choice were starting to pull Jonathan in a direction that he had never wanted to go.

"I will come willingly," he said. "However, I must see my friend one last time." He knew time could be cruel. It brought things to an end without a welcome. Free will was the greatest gift, but time was the curse to all living things. Now the sun was nearly awake as the few remaining stars twinkled their final thoughts.

"I am thankful for you, Father." Jonathan stepped from the meadow and onto the cool green grass in front of Riley's lake house.

CHAPTER 41

Tristan sat on a worn-out mattress in the hotel room, unable to comprehend why Master had sent these four pathetic humans to help him. What could they possibly contribute? They would simply be in the way. Besides, a few more to throw on the fires of Hell didn't make a bit of difference to him. However, if any of these idiots managed to get in his way, he would personally send them to the afterlife.

He looked them over again. All four carried various handguns and the one Lucifer referred to as "Mr. Third Grader" sported a large knife that hung halfway down the outside of his pant leg. Tristan pointed at each one, calling out their names as if he were taking roll call.

"Buck. Ginger. Mr. Third Grader—"

"My name is Guthrie," the man interrupted him.

"Guthrie?" Tristan said.

The man nodded.

And who are you?" he said, pointing at the woman next to Guthrie.

"Missy. I am his old lady!" she declared.

Tristan then pointed to the one named Ginger. "Well, how about you? Do you have a specific title that I should be made aware of?"

"Sweet butts. It's what the female groupies of the "MC"—I mean motorcycle club—are called since we haven't been claimed

by a member. Then our title changes to old lady, like Missy's."
Her shoulders drooped, clearly embarrassed by the admittance
of her nickname.

Tristan cracked a smile, and was about to ask a follow up
question till Buck interrupted.

"Listen, we're not here by our own free will. Tell us your plan
so we can begin. We don't need to listen to you degrade us."

"Buck, you have a point," Tristan replied. "It is wrong of me
to take away from the matter at hand. However, when we get to
Hell, I will ask you all the questions I want. That is, of course, after
Master is done with his thorough review of each of you." Then
he chuckled to himself. "Who knows? Maybe he will assign you
to my region." Then he glared at each of them. "And if you ever
talk back to me, I will eat your tongue. Once it grows back, we
will proceed with the questions and you will tell me everything I
want to know."

Beads of sweat formed on Buck's forehead.

The door swung open, banging against the wall, as Legionaries
entered.

Buck and Guthrie pulled their guns out and began yelling
obscenities, until Legionaries drew a finger across his throat,
silencing them. Both began violently coughing, dropped their
guns, and fell to the floor followed by Missy, who attempted to
assist them.

Tristan immediately got off the bed and knelt before
Legionaries, but Legionaries backhanded him. "There will be
none of that!" Legionaries said. "We are here to finish a job, so
don't act like we are brothers or whatever the hell you think of
me as. Damn lackey!"

Buck's and Guthrie's faces had turned a reddish purple now
that the coughing had stopped. They thought they had almost
swallowed their tongues.

"Forgive me," Tristan said to Legionaries. "Yes, I understand. My role is to only assist and stay completely out of your way. As I said before, you will have all the glory when you bring the Fallen in."

"Well," Legionaries replied. "I should let you know it has come to my attention that you won't be receiving too much of a pat on the back after all."

"What?" Tristan said, getting to his feet.

Stepping over the two leather-clad idiots on the floor, Legionaries took a seat in the only chair in the room. Crossing one leg over the other, then fussing over a mark on his loafer, he took notice of a young woman in the corner, who went by the name Ginger, after listening in on her thoughts.

"Is she stupid?" he asked of Tristan, as he nodded in her direction.

Tristan, ignoring the question, had a question of his own. "Why will I not be receiving any kind of praise for a job that I helped to accomplish?"

"No, seriously," Legionaries repeated. "Is she stupid? Here are her friends suffering on the floor, but instead of trying to help, she is hiding in the corner."

"Stop ignoring me and tell me why I am not going to receive the praise that I am entitled to!" Tristan demanded.

"Well, from how it was told to me, the Fallen was offered up in some kind of trade," Legionaries said, smiling. "So, there will be no fight. He will simply go with you without struggle."

The men now lay lifeless on the floor, as Missy began begging. "Do something, please! They're sorry, okay? Just stop and give me my Guthrie back."

Legionaries took his eyes off Tristan and looked at the woman. Then he laughed aloud. "Seriously, his name is actually Guthrie?" He laughed again.

"Please show mercy," Missy cried. "I will do anything, just show them mercy!"

Legionaries, still amused, snapped his fingers. Then one of the two men began gasping for air. When he could finally breathe normally, he began to sob. The other man remained motionless, staring lifelessly at the ceiling. Legionaries nudged him with his foot, but there was no movement. "And then there were three," he said dryly. "Sweetie," he said, motioning to Missy. "Would you mind checking him for a pulse? I think Mr. Guthrie will live to fight another day, but I believe your other friend here has crossed over."

Missy could only stare back in terror.

"When I speak, you simply do as I ask. So, unless you want Guthrie to accompany Buck to the afterlife, you will move your fat ass when I tell you to. Is that clear enough for you?" Legionaries. asked.

Stepping over to where Buck lay and placing her head on his chest, she began chest compressions. "Not yet, Buck, it's not your time yet. You have a lot more to offer this world."

"Are you serious?" Tristan asked again. Legionaries turned his attention back to Tristan. "Sorry to be the bearer of bad news, but Riley gave up the Fallen. However, I do have some cheerful news. That lackey, Lucifer, still wants Riley and Maggie dead despite the trade—you know—loose ends and all. So, you still have one last job to do."

Tristan glared at Legionaries, who was now focused on watching with amusement as the idiot woman, Missy, continued pumping away on the dead man's chest. She was drenched in sweat. "I'll hand it to her, I admire her effort!" Legionaries chuckled. Then he turned toward her. "Sweetie, I am afraid your friend is gone; but don't worry, you will see him again soon."

Missy sobbed and then rested her face on Buck's chest. "I am so sorry that you had to go out this way. It was an honor to have worn your patch."

Guthrie made his way over to Missy, offering soothing words. "He's gone, baby. You did what you could. We have to let him go and honor what he meant to us. He is gone but never forgotten. So, come on now, you can't do anything else for him." He helped her to her feet and held her, whispering softly to her as she buried her head in his chest.

Ginger, who remained in the corner, began to sob as she fell to the floor and curled into a ball.

"I don't think you are going to be able to do much with these three," Legionaries said to Tristan. "Do you ever wonder inside that dull head of yours why your fearless leader would send you these idiots?"

Ignoring the question, Tristan spoke to the remaining three and motioned them over. "I want to go over what I expect from each of you."

Guthrie and Missy, still trying to compose themselves, stepped over Buck's body and took seats on the opposite bed from Tristan's.

"Ginger, get your ass over here. I won't ask again!"

Ginger remained curled up, unresponsive. Missy went over and helped her to the bed, placing her in between Guthrie and herself. She stroked her hair and whispered encouraging words.

"You never answered me earlier," Legionaries said, looking at Tristan. "Are you sure she isn't stupid?"

Tristan once again ignored Legionaries and turned back to the trio sitting on the bed. "We are going to a lake house not far from here. I will drop you three off a couple hundred yards away. Legionaries and I will then drive the rest of the way alone. When you arrive at the house, don't go inside, just put as many rounds into it as possible. Got it?"

When none of them answered, Legionaries stepped in. "For such a simple plan, that really isn't a bad idea."

Tristan looked at Legionaries, waiting for the mockery.

"I am serious. If a bullet doesn't hit Riley and Maggie, then they only have two options. Since the shots will be coming from the back of the house they will either run out the front door where you and I will be waiting, or the patio door that leads down to the lake. I am assuming it will be the front door since that's where the truck is parked."

"All right then," Tristan said. "Let's move!"

"Well, there is one thing I will offer," Legionaries spoke up. "I assume the Fallen will want to tell Riley and Maggie goodbye. He knows that it will be their last time to see each other, so tell these three not to begin shooting until after the Fallen is gone. We don't know what he will do. Then again—" he paused. "I do want to find out what he will do—so go ahead and shoot up the house as soon as the Fallen is in your sight."

Tristan rolled this over in his mind as he, too, wanted to test himself against a Fallen. He couldn't care less about Riley and Maggie. However, as Legionaries had informed him, he could accompany the Fallen back to Lucifer and not worry about what Legionaries did. Who cared if he screwed up as long as he had the Fallen?

"I heard that," Legionaries chimed in.

Tristan found that he was so caught up in his own glory, he had forgotten that his thoughts were not his own.

"As I said before," said Legionaries, "I am all for letting you have your so-called glory. I won't stand in your way. So yes, I will agree to that plan. No sense in both of us being preoccupied with taking out two insignificant humans. I mean, just look at how frail these three are!"

Ginger, still sobbing, was unable to look at the two strange men that, for the foreseeable future, now had control over her life. However, Guthrie and Missy were used to this kind of life, they just weren't familiar with being used as pawns.

"Very well." Tristan stood and headed toward the door.

At the last second, Legionaries stepped around him and pulled the door open for him. "After you, fearless leader!"

Taking his cue and walking out into the sunshine, Tristan turned and looked at the three on the bed. He was about to tell them to get moving, but Legionaries beat him to it.

"We will not ask a second time," Legionaries said in an annoyed tone.

Reluctantly, Guthrie helped Missy and Ginger to their feet, then escorted them outside. Instead of feeling relief from the warmth of the sun, it only reminded them of the gloom of things to come. Guthrie looked up at the sky as if he believed it was his last time to see the blueness of it. Tristan got behind the wheel of a small SUV as Legionaries slid into the passenger seat. Guthrie helped the two women inside what felt like a hearse.

Legionaries cried out like a drill sergeant. "Troops! I won't lie to you. Only a few will make it back alive. And when I say few, I mean just Tristan and me. But remember that we are here for the greater good and will triumph!"

Tristan cackled as he put the SUV in drive.

CHAPTER 42

The day had fully stretched itself awake as Maggie put the last of her things in the back seat of Riley's truck. She walked inside the house for one last time, hoping that he would at least see her off given everything they had been through. She was disappointed to find an empty living room and kitchen awaiting her. She considered going down the hallway and knocking on his bedroom door but decided not to risk making him angry again. She took one last look around the place that she had begun to think of as a safe haven, only to find that now the walls seemed to ask in unison for her departure.

As she opened the front door to leave, she was shocked by what stood before her. Was she seeing an apparition of Jonathan?

"I promise I am real," Jonathan said.

Maggie couldn't quite comprehend what was happening and wasn't sure she could trust her senses. She stood there, dumbfounded by the giant before her. Suddenly, she was knocked aside as Riley came running up behind her and jumped into Jonathan's arms.

As Jonathan placed Riley back down on the floor, he wiped tears away from Riley's face. Then he kissed the end of Riley's nose and rubbed both sides of it with his index fingers. Jonathan looked at Riley with a seriousness on his face. "Follow this, my brother," he said, tapping Riley's nose. "And you will find me."

Riley offered no reply as he threw his arms once more around

Jonathan. After a few moments, Jonathan let go of Riley and stepped inside, making the house feel much smaller than it really was. Jonathan put both of his massive arms around Maggie, sending immediate peace into her. After he put her down, Maggie felt dizzy and had to place a hand on a nearby table to balance herself.

"There is little time," Jonathan said somberly, looking at both of them. "Sit with me. I need to tell you what is about to happen."

Maggie, still dizzy, allowed Jonathan to help her take a seat on the couch. Jonathan was about to sit in the recliner then stopped, bent down, and blew out a breath far longer than humanly possible. Then he took a seat in the recliner where he had sat so many times before.

Riley started to speak, but Jonathan held up his hand to stop him. "Allow me to enjoy this moment," he said softly, looking at both of them. "I just want to take this image with me. I am looking at the closest thing to perfection that this world has to offer. I love you both so much." Although his eyes were a piercing blue, they shone with love as well as a fierceness that he would protect them always. "Riley, the answer to the question you were about to ask is yes, I am healed. Sometimes I think I can still feel the ache in my leg, but it is only a figment of my imagination. Granny gave her life to heal me. I was too sick to realize what she had done until it was too late for me to argue with her. She gave her life for me so that I could continue what we started. I won't go into detail about how she passed. Just know that she was perfect, selfless, and faced death without fear."

At this, Riley dropped his head and sobbed.

"Riley, I know you wish you could have had more time with Granny. Just remember that death is only the beginning. We will see her again one day. That, I can promise you."

Although Maggie had accepted the fact that Jonathan was

truly a guardian angel, she needed to know more about the paranormal so that she could try to understand why a god would allow this to happen. Just as she began to speak, Jonathan held up a hand once more, asking for silence.

"Your next question is 'why didn't God just heal me?'" The answer is simple but complex at the same time. Simple because He put Granny in our life for a reason. I believe it was to show us that there is no greater love than for one to lay down their life for their fellow brother. Complex because I believe the reason why this happened can only be answered within ourselves. To add to the complexity of our situation, I will only be by your side for a short time. Things are in motion that I have no control of. One day we will see each other again, but until then know that I love you both and always will."

Turning his attention on his friend, he took on a scolding tone. "Riley, you made the right choice. Now make me a promise that you will not allow that decision to consume your life."

Confused, Maggie looked over at Riley, who was staring at the floor.

Jonathan knelt down next to Riley. "My friend, my brother, my family. I will never stop loving you. You made the only decision you could. I look forward to the day that we are united once again. Now, I only have a few moments more, but I want to address something that I know has been a large burden on you. Griffin's daughter is alive and well. God would never allow one of his angels to harm one of his children. Although my powers were manipulated, I still must always abide by my Father. Not even poison conjured up from Hell can cause me to cross the lines drawn long ago. His design and His plan are always perfect."

Once again, he kissed the tip of Riley's nose, then touched both sides with his index fingers. Riley closed his eyes and lowered his head. Then Jonathan reached over and took both of

Maggie's hands in one of his. She wanted to hold his hand, give it a gentle squeeze, make him aware of how much she cherished him. However, the size of Jonathan's hand enveloped both of hers like a grown man holding a newborn. She, too, closed her eyes and lowered her head, just wanting to soak in this moment.

"Protect one another," Jonathan told them, "for there will be new trials that will push you both to the point of madness."

When they both looked up, he was gone. Now it was just the two of them.

CHAPTER 43

Pulling off to the side of the road, Tristan turned around to face the remaining three leather-clad idiots. "Stay close together, and when you come upon the house, shoot every last round into it once you hear Legionaries whistle."

"Do not stop firing until you are empty. Do you understand me?"

Guthrie gave a nod of his head, then exited the SUV, helping Missy and Ginger out. He closed the door behind them and then hurriedly walked both women away into the trees.

Rolling down his window, Tristan called out: "You have five minutes to locate the house. If Legionaries doesn't hear a gunshot after he whistles, he will find you and give you your first taste of real pain."

Guthrie waved to let Tristan know they understood. As the SUV drove away, Ginger asked quietly, "This is our death march, isn't it?"

Guthrie was going to reassure her, but then wondered what the point was. It wouldn't be true. "Seems that way," was his response.

Missy reached out and took Guthrie's hand, then Ginger's. "I don't know a thing about religion, but do you think we could ask for this to not happen?"

"We can always pray," Ginger said. "I just don't know if God is listening anymore. We have walked on the other side for so long that it would be a blind prayer at best."

"Well, Guthrie," Missy said. "I'm afraid this is it for us. After our lives are taken from this world, I doubt we will ever be remembered."

Guthrie's life had taken a road that he had never intended. He always believed he would eventually move on from the gang, begin a new life with Missy, and hopefully one day raise a family. But that life never happened since there was always another large score to be made, which led to another and another. Being part of the gang, money came so easily that he blew it quickly because he knew there would always be more. "I played the part of a fool," he said, "and was glad to have done it until now."

Missy gave his hand a squeeze. "I did too, Daddy. I always said that one day I would walk away, but I strongly believed if I did that, I would be walking away from a family who loved me."

"I am a preacher's daughter whose parents were more than good to me," Ginger said. "I was an only child so it was difficult for me to fit in. The club accepted me and I was thankful for the new friends, but I always wanted to just return home to my real family. So many nights I called home, only to hang up once I heard my mom or dad answer. I knew they were worried and would accept me regardless of what I had done. But I also knew that there would be judgment from the congregation of my dad's church. I wholeheartedly believe that Christians do the most damage with their limited views and how quick they are to judge."

"I am sorry you feel that way," came a voice from behind them.

All three turned around to find the largest man they had ever seen. Guthrie's first thought was to lift his gun, but instead he dropped it to the ground and spread his arms wide in surrender.

He closed his eyes, hoping that death would be quick. However, he found himself wrapped in the stranger's massive arms.

"You are loved, Guthrie."

The giant released him and then proceeded to gently hug Missy and then Ginger, telling them the same thing. After he finished, he stepped back and smiled at them. "All of your lives matter. Go from here, ask for forgiveness of your sins, and turn from your evil ways." The smile fell from his face as he spoke in a soft voice. "If you continue with the task that was forced upon you then you will meet a side of me that is not so kind. I have sworn to protect the two people who reside in that house. I will not fail them, but I also do not wish to cause any of you harm. If you take one step further, pray that God will show you mercy, for I will not."

The three of them looked down, no longer able to look at the stranger in front of them. Guthrie slowly pulled the large knife from its sheath and pitched it as far away as he could. Ginger and Missy followed suit, gently tossing their pistols down at the giant's feet.

"My friends," he said, "please embrace me as your brother. I take no pride in threatening you." He knelt, opening his arms to them. "My name is Jonathan. It means 'Gift from God.'"

Ginger launched herself into Jonathan's massive arms. Missy and Guthrie followed, thankful that they would live to see another day. This time they would make their lives count.

"Friends, you should know that death has come to this place, but not for the three of you. Hurry back to the road and follow it south. Don't look back, no matter what you hear. Now, please leave at once. I will keep watch until you are out of sight. You have nothing to fear from the two who brought you here, or the one who forced you into this situation. You will be safe."

CHAPTER 44

After pulling up a short distance from the lake house, Tristan was about to remind Legionaries of his promise, only to turn and see the passenger door closing. He got out and went around to the passenger side, joining Legionaries, annoyed at how he had been dismissed. He was about to tell him as much, but Legionaries held a finger to his lips, silencing him.

Tristan believed that even though they were no longer responsible for bringing the Fallen in, it was going to happen on their watch and they should receive praise for their vital roles. Legionaries would take care of Riley and Maggie, and he alone would bring the Fallen to Lucifer. Who cared if it was because of a trade? He was going to personally escort the damned thing into Hell, something those idiotic sons of Lucifer's couldn't accomplish. *I will be the greatest leader of all my master's regions. I will be worshipped and praised by all other leaders. That bitch, Esperanza, will now bow at my feet as I pass by, telling me how perfect and wise—*

Suddenly, Jonathan appeared out of nowhere and pulled Tristan out of his dream state, causing him to fall back against the passenger-side door of the SUV. Legionaries looked down at him in amusement. He had heard all the ridiculous pronouncements he had been making inside his head. He then turned to face Jonathan. "I have always wanted to test myself against an angel. Unfortunately for me, you are only a Fallen and already promised a quick trip to Hell. However, just think of how much fun it could have been beating the living shit out of each other in the process!"

Jonathan stared down at the larger of the two demons, with a look of stoic resignation.

As Tristan made his way back to his feet, he was unable to hide his eagerness to bring the Fallen in now that it stood no more than a few feet away from him. "You will be coming with me," he said as he reached up and grabbed one of Jonathan's shoulders.

Jonathan looked at the hand attempting to grab hold of him, then turned his attention to Legionaries and glared down at him. "Neither of mine will be harmed, is that clear?"

Legionaries turned toward Tristan. "You are far too easy to manipulate. I have no clue how you ever became a regional leader."

Confused by the shift in the conversation, Tristan was at a loss for words and loosened his grip on Jonathan's shoulder. As he did so, Legionaries plunged a hand inside his chest and grabbed his dark and dirty soul. With his eyes wide, Tristan grabbed furiously at Legionaries and begged. "Stop! We can negotiate. I promise to yield to you!"

Amused by Tristan's weakness, Legionaries leaned in closer. "Now you know what it is like to beg for mercy!" he whispered. "See you in Hell. Brother!" He gave a hard jerk and pulled out Tristan's cursed soul, letting his body crumple to the ground where it dematerialized.

Legionaries felt the outside world disappear all around him, as not even the Fallen now stood in front of him, knowing that what he had just accomplished had never been done by any demon before. This outlandish transgression would be forever frozen in time, marking the exact moment that he declared his independence from his maker, paving the way for other demons to attempt the same.

It would be one of many defiant acts that he would perform as he made his way into this new world. This one just so happened to begin with a monumental act, by taking the soul of the largest region leader, and making him his slave. As Legionaries's surroundings came back into focus, he noticed that the Fallen wore a confused expression, too stupid to comprehend what he had just witnessed.

"Trust me, Fallen, that demon was a tiresome, overzealous idiot that I am happy to be rid of." Holding the soul in his hand, Legionaries marveled at how it twitched beneath his grasp. Opening his mouth, Legionaries sucked in the black soul, consuming it all at once. Seconds passed before he dry heaved for a moment then spat on the ground. Gaining his composure, he looked back up at Jonathan. "Your size means nothing to me," he said coolly. "I am not what I appear either. As I said before, I would love to find out just how good you really are—that is, if you are up for the challenge."

Jonathan simply stared down at him and didn't bother with a reply.

"So be it," Legionaries scoffed. "Anyway, your fate has been sealed, so I guess it wouldn't do either of us any good. However, I do have one question."

Allowing the demon to have its fun, Jonathan remained quiet.

"Are you a little bit afraid of what is coming next?"

A small trace of fear crossed over Jonathan's stellar blue eyes, giving Legionaries his answer.

"I concluded as much, I just didn't know if the Fallen had that kind of emotion. As for your earlier demand, I have no interest in the two you protect. They will not be harmed unless they come for me." Legionaries turned away and made his way to the driver's side of the SUV.

Before climbing behind the wheel, Legionaries stopped and gave Jonathan a large smile. "Can you believe that I was once called a lackey!"

"And now?" asked Jonathan.

"Well, some knew me as Legionaries. However, as of late I have learned what my true name is." Legionaries watched as Jonathan's face took on a look of apprehension and concern at what he might hear next.

"My name is Legion. And yes, I met your god a long time ago in a small village in the country Gadarenes." Grinning back at Jonathan, Legion climbed behind the wheel and drove back down the driveway.

"Oh God," Jonathan said aloud.

CHAPTER 45

Jonathan began to say something, but his words were cut off as several arms reached out of the ground and pulled him under. Riley was off the porch and diving head first toward the ground just as the arms, and Jonathan, disappeared. He began clawing at the ground with great ferocity, believing that if he dug hard enough, he could find Jonathan and pull him back to the surface. "Help me, Maggie!" he screamed as he furiously threw huge clumps of grass and dirt to either side of him.

Stunned and confused by what she had just witnessed, Maggie knew that Jonathan was gone, no matter what they did.

"Maggie! Help me!" Riley pleaded. "It's not too late. Grab a shovel from the garage. Hurry!"

Maggie fell to her knees next to Riley and broke under the strain of seeing her friend so desperate. Tears streaked Riley's face. "Jonathan is just on the other side," he cried out in ragged breaths. "We just need to dig a little deeper. Just a little more and we will find him. We are almost there, just a little bit more."

Reaching out a tentative hand, Maggie touched his shoulder, but Riley slapped it away and continued throwing dirt with more ferocity. He had gone mad and Maggie couldn't help the deep sorrow she felt, not just from the loss of Jonathan but seeing Riley's agony grow with each pull at the ground. His shirt was drenched with sweat and dirt as he continued to pull with more force, causing his fingers to become raw and bloodied.

"Help me!" Riley cried. "I will never ask anything from you again, just please help me!"

Unable to watch the madness, Maggie threw both arms around him and clutched him with everything she had.

Riley made a weak attempt to push her away, yelling for her to get off him. Finally, he gave in, defeated, and sobbed loudly on her shoulder. He wrapped both of his arms around her as he shook with each gasp of air. "God, what have I done? Oh God, what have I done? Please forgive me, Father, please show me mercy."

Maggie held on, refusing to let him go as she spoke through her own sobs. "Riley, I am here, just be here with me. I will not let you go. I will always be here."

They continued to cling to one another in search of refuge as the sun then covered itself in darkness—not to give the moon its chance to control the sky, but rather as if choosing to give shadow instead of light.

Riley released his hold of Maggie. Although her face was just inches from his, he couldn't see her. "Maggie?"

"I am here."

Grabbing at her hand for comfort, Riley peered into the darkness, praying the light would return.

"What is happening?" Maggie asked.

He was on the cusp of telling her. They were cursed because of what he had done. But before he could speak, the sun broke through so powerfully that they let go of one another to shield their eyes. At first they were blinded and could only see dark spots, but then everything settled back into place. Maggie looked at Riley and desperately grabbed him, pulled him into her, and kissed him. He kissed Maggie back, an expression of gratitude for one another and what they had gone through.

"Thank you for sticking it out with me," Riley said quietly.

Maggie took in heavy breaths, unable to respond. Then a dark shadow raced toward them. They both sprang to their feet, still holding on to each other.

"Run!" Maggie screamed.

They took off as fast as they could for the house. They heard a deep growl coming from behind them and the sound of heavy feet hitting the ground. Just as they reached the porch, Riley turned to see a massive dog staring back at him. It growled at him, revealing rows of razor-sharp teeth, like those of a shark. Its red eyes looked right through him.

Cornered, Riley pushed Maggie behind him. The dog was no longer growling. It stood there motionless and silent as if waiting for a command. Riley finally realized where he had seen a dog like this before. It was one of the Devil's hounds that had scared him into submission during the dream he'd had the day Griffin was there.

"What do we do now?" Maggie whispered.

Just as she spoke, the hound came forward, sniffed them, then sat back on its haunches.

Barely able to control his breathing, Riley whispered back, "That is one of the hounds of Hell that serves only the Devil. I haven't a clue how it got here." He carefully reached behind Maggie and twisted the front doorknob. As the door started to open, he threw his body against hers, pushing them both in. Landing with a thud, Riley kicked the door closed and pressed his boot against it to make sure it didn't swing back open. He leapt to his feet and locked the door. He cautiously looked out the half-moon window and saw that the hound had turned its back to them and appeared to be on guard duty. Although its eyes looked out at the yard, Riley felt certain the damned beast knew everything that was going on behind it.

"You said it's a hound from Hell?" Maggie asked, still in shock.

"Yes," Riley said, still looking out the window. "That is most certainly one of the Devil's hounds."

Seeming to know that it was being watched, the hound looked over its shoulder and locked eyes with Riley. Stepping back from the window, Riley blew out a shaken breath.

"We're trapped here, aren't we?" said Maggie.

"Yes, until we can come up with a plan. Right now, that hound is just looking out at the property as if it's standing guard. It's there to keep us in. If it wanted to, that beast would come through the door like it was made out of cardboard."

"Trapped," Maggie said.

"Trapped," Riley replied. "There will be no help coming for us this time. Jonathan is gone, Granny is dead, we are on our own."

"Trapped," Maggie said again.

EPILOGUE

He knew it would be his resting place. Until God came for him, he would remain here. Jonathan stopped resisting and allowed himself to be dragged under. At last, whatever was pulling him stopped and let go of him. Looking around to see where he now resided, Jonathan felt teeth tear into his throat. Grabbing at it and jerking it effortlessly away, he found that he was holding a large beast-like dog that stared at him with a piece of his flesh hanging out of its mouth.

Jonathan pulled the hound toward him so he was facing it. "Go and protect my beloveds!" he commanded it. He released the hound and watched it stagger back, confused. Then it placed its cold, dead eyes on him once more and vanished into a cloud of smoke.

"Jonathan, I have literally waited centuries for this day," a voice said from behind him. Jonathan knew whom the voice belonged to as Lucifer came into view, wearing an all-white suit with the shirt buttoned all the way to the top. He had taken on the appearance of a man in his fifties, but with a trim build. His black hair had patches of silver scattered throughout it and had a large, perfect, bleached-white smile. "I am thrilled to welcome you into my kingdom." He leaned down and slapped Jonathan so hard that he felt his neck snap. As Jonathan's eyes began to close, a hand grabbed his face, forcing him to focus on Lucifer. "Not yet, my friend, oh, not yet. I have so many great things planned for us! Stay awake for me just a bit longer, for I want you to feel me suck everything out of you. When I am done and you have nothing else to give, only then will I cast you into the fires of Hell. That way, the doomed can have their first taste of an actual fallen angel. But before we begin, I want you to do one small simple thing for me."

Nose to nose with the Devil, Jonathan could see that Lucifer's eyes had changed to black, dead mirrors. Then a black tear slid down Lucifer's cheek and fell onto Jonathan's neck. It felt ice cold and stayed exactly where it had landed. Lucifer gave him a half grin and said one word.

"Burn!"

Jonathan's skin heated underneath where the tear had landed, causing that one spot on his neck to melt. Feeling as if he had swallowed a teaspoon of lava, Jonathan's esophagus spasmed, not wanting it to proceed any further. A fire began in the bottom of his stomach, came roaring back up his esophagus through his throat, and exited the hole where the tear had landed. The fire was so intense inside him that Jonathan tried to scream but was silenced from the pain.

Leaning back in pure ecstasy, Lucifer began chanting as Jonathan writhed on the floor, slapping at the side of his neck, unaware that the flames were no longer alive anywhere on or inside of him.

"You truly are everything I hoped you would turn out to be," Lucifer murmured. He leaned down once more and placed the Judas kiss on Jonathan's forehead. "Soon you will call me Master. I am not only going to hurt you physically, but I am going to toy with your emotions until you finally give me what I want. Just hand over your powers and I will send you back to Riley. I promise that will be the end of our arrangement and you can live out the rest of your days . . . as a mortal.

Jonathan ignored every lie that Lucifer said as he lay his head on the floor. The pain in his neck subsided as his breathing returned to normal. He wished that he could fight back, but he was in Hell, and it was ruled by a psychopath. His powers were useless here. All he could do was suffer and hope that death would reach him, or that God the Father would rescue him.

ABOUT THE AUTHOR

Kelly Hollingshead is an avid reader who prefers books over music. He found entertainment in books as a child due to growing up in a large family where money was always tight. However, the library was always free and entertainment was endless, simply waiting between book covers.

Kelly has been married for ten years to his wife, Melissa, and they have a one-year-old daughter whose nickname is Ms. Brynn.

From an early age, Kelly has approached writing as an enjoyable pastime until his wife convinced him to try to publish at least one story.

When not working on the *Riley* series, Kelly enjoys extreme workouts, cookouts on the grill with his friends and family, and late nights of watching UFC fight pass.

VOLUME 1 IN
THE RILEY SERIES

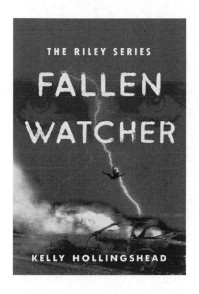

A paranormal suspense that brings good and evil into different perspectives.

Riley's world is torn apart on his wedding day when he and his wife, Allison, are involved in a hit-and-run accident and Allison doesn't survive. When Jonathan, Allison's guardian angel, chooses to fall to Earth to remain by Riley's side, the evils of Hell are unleashed to destroy both Jonathan and Riley. A ferocious battle of good and evil surrounds Riley as Jonathan tries to save him and the ugliness of Hell tries to consume him.